IRONIC

PAMELA LEIGH STARR

Genesis Press, Inc.

Indigo Love Spectrum

An imprint of Genesis Press, Inc.
Publishing Company

Genesis Press, Inc.
P.O. Box 101
Columbus, MS 39703

ISBN-13: 978-1-58571-404-9
ISBN-10: 1-58571-404-6
Manufactured in the United States of America

First Edition 2006
Second Edition 2009

Visit us at www.genesis-press.com or call at 1-888-Indigo-1

DEDICATION

This novel, written long before Hurricane Katrina
darkened our door, is dedicated to every New
Orleanian,
…those who evacuated
…those who rode out the storm
…those who were lost
…those who survived the horrors of the Superdome and
Convention Center
…and especially to those who stayed to protect and
secure what was left of our unique city in Hurricane
Katrina's wake.
WE SHALL RISE AGAIN!
Isn't it IRONIC that in times of crisis, the basic need
for survival is the same for all people, regardless of
economic, racial or social differences?

PROLOGUE

"It's not going to happen," Travis Labranch Jr. growled as he flew out of the trailer he had called home for the last year. Crisp, freezing wind lashed his face and bare arms as he stormed across the compound. The cold surrounded him, seeped deep inside without his consciously feeling it. Much more important matters were occupying his mind. Thrusting anger and frustration throbbed through every cell of his body.

"General!" Travis heard the call as it blew past his ear. He had no intention of answering. Whoever it was did not need his help or counsel as desperately as his fool cousin did.

"What's wrong with Cassie?" he screamed at the wind. Instead of being carried away by the violent blast of air as it should have, the question exploded inside his brain over and over again as he entered the airplane hangar. "Where's her common sense? Her dignity?" He muttered as he removed the blocks that kept the single engine plane in place.

He threw himself into the cockpit without making the necessary checks, without clearance from anyone.

He didn't have time for it.

He was on a mission, one that would save his cousin from the biggest mistake of her life.

The hangar doors cracked opened just as he knew they would. The shadow of whoever it was who had called out to him appeared a second later. Travis couldn't tell which one of his followers it was. It didn't matter. With two quick swipes of his hand, he motioned for the figure to open the hangar doors.

The man automatically moved to obey, but a second later yelled over the engine Travis had just fired up. "General, the commander wants to speak to you."

Because of the amount of money he had pumped into the cause, Travis had to answer to no one except the commander. But *not* now, *not* this time.

As a concession to the man who had shown him the only true path for his race, Travis stuck his head out of the cockpit. "I can't talk right now. The purity of our race and of my immediate family is at stake. I'll return when my mission is done."

"But—"

That was all Travis heard before returning to the cockpit. He immediately moved the plane forward. Ascending into the night sky, Travis knew that he had to succeed in his mission. He had to set everything right. Cassie could not be tied to a black man for the rest of her life. She could not defile her race. He chanted those imperatives over and over again.

They were all that was in his mind when the engine suddenly spluttered and died.

CHAPTER 1

"We're explosive, it's fate," she whispered.
He traced her outer ear, "Yes, it's fate."
Teresa Lewis closed the book.

"What a sweet ending," a soft voice declared with a sigh.

"You picked a good one, Teresa." A smile poured over the words.

"I knew they'd get together!" The thump of a cane on the hardwood floor was a resounding amen.

"Phooey! It's a romance. They all end the same. The middle's the only difference! And that one wasn't steamy enough!"

"Jude Stevens!" All four ladies turned to him with varying degrees of disapproval. He was the only man to sit in on their weekly reading sessions, and he always said the same thing about the books they loved. And as usual, the women had responded in the same way, leaving Teresa to grin as she said the only thing she could.

"He does have a right to an opinion, ladies."

"True, but romance—," Miss Mary began.

"—is not measured by heat," her twin sister Marie ended.

There were instant nods of agreement from the other women. Teresa made no other comment. She had learned two years ago that playing observer was her best bet.

Teresa leaned back into the soft, cushioned chair to listen to the discussion of her favorite group. Every Saturday she volunteered to drive the bookmobile to community centers and nursing homes in the New Orleans metro area. Being a part of this specially-funded program satisfied Teresa's need to honor the elderly and give encouragement to the young, who she also visited in the projects every Saturday during her bookmobile run. More importantly, this was her opportunity to give a little joy to men and women whose lives were winding down.

And by winding down, she did not mean ending.

As a hospice nurse, she had seen more life in some of her bedridden, dying patients than she'd seen in healthy, upright people. Providing comfort and care to those during their last days of life had led to her volunteering her time for the bookmobile in order to provide similar comfort and joy to senior citizens in care facilities. And perhaps, Teresa took in the scene before her, the discussion becoming steamier than the book she had just finished reading, more excitement.

Darryl, one of the workers at the home, poked his head inside. "They're just warming up, right?"

"You bet, but I'll bring them back down before I leave. I don't want to incite a riot."

"You can calm any storm, Teresa," Darryl assured her before leaving to see to other duties.

The debate went on. Teresa loved to see her elderly friends excited about something. She remembered her dilemma in adding this nursing home to her schedule of stops. Since it was privately run, Teresa had thought that the residents would most likely be less needy, something she'd found was not true. Then there was the fact that it extended her day, easily adding an extra two hours. But it had been worth it. Seeing Miss Marie's and Miss Mary's brown, wrinkled faces reflect elation rather than depression was quite gratifying. Lady D's formerly listless demeanor was now charged with energy from the enjoyment she found in life again. As for Mama Lee, now she stayed awake for Teresa's entire visit, even participating in the discussion, waiting excitingly for her next treasure, a book to hold and keep until Teresa returned the next week. She suspected that Mama Lee never stayed awake long enough to actually read the large print books she gave her. Teresa wondered if she even knew how to read. Either way, Mama Lee was always thrilled to get her book.

"I still say a love scene needs a bit more oomph to it!"

Teresa laughed out loud. "Mr. Stevens, ladies, shall we agree to disagree?"

"Like always," he grumped.

Mr. Stevens, her favorite grumpy old man, wasn't really grumpy at all. Teresa had figured him out a long time ago. It was simple. Here was a man with strength and intelligence and nothing to do. His body was weak, but his mind was active and sharp, and every week, no matter what book they were reading, Mr. Stevens took an opposing opinion, sparking the fire that led to their weekly debate.

Teresa was going to miss them all. She took a quick breath and closed her eyes tight to keep them from tearing. "I've got something special for all of you today."

"I knew that cart looked fuller than normal," Lady D announced to everyone.

"Yes, it is." Teresa turned to the cart of books she had rolled into the community room when she arrived. "It's fuller because I have gifts for you." She lifted the canvas bags she had filled with everyday items she knew they would appreciate. Visits, not to mention receiving necessities from family members, rarely happened. She'd also included copies of the last book she had read to them. Teresa handed a bag to each of her friends.

"With lots of love, Teresa," Mama Lee read on the card in the bag Teresa had just handed her, clearing up the mystery of whether or not she could read.

"What does this mean?" Miss Mary and Miss Marie asked, their voices tinged with dismay.

"It means she's leaving us! Pulling out!" Mr. Stevens told everyone in a loud voice. "*Adios, amigos!*"

"Is that true?" Lady D asked, her bag sliding to the floor.

This *was* going to be harder than Teresa had thought. It wasn't easy saying goodbye to her other groups, but these people sitting before her were special. She had seen the difference she made in their lives. "Yes, it's true."

"Told you!" Mr. Stevens yelled, rolling his wheelchair straight to Teresa with a strength and speed she had never seen before.

"All right, out with it. Tell us what kind of reason you have for deserting us. Are we taking up too much of your time?"

He was ready for another debate. Teresa wasn't. "Not at all, I love being here with you, but there have been some changes that will force me to stay away."

"Like what?"

"The funding for the bookmobile program hasn't been renewed."

"Government!" Mr. Stevens growled, rolling away, his will to argue deflating with the news.

"But why didn't you tell us sooner?" Lady D wanted to know.

"I didn't want to spoil our time together."

"It's spoiled now," the sisters moaned.

"But it doesn't have to be. A friend of mine has promised to come by and read with you every Saturday, like always."

"Why not you?"

Teresa looked at the faces surrounding her. She could barely keep her eyes on each for more than a few seconds, and not even that long when she got to

Mr. Stevens's back. She suddenly felt very selfish. Now that she was finally getting the chance to do something she really loved, it just happened to coincide with the end of the bookmobile program. It was the bookmobile idea that had led her to it. The bookmobile, funded by her first grant, had led to another grant geared toward writing historical literature. One grant cancelled; another approved. She knew it wasn't her fault, but still, she felt guilty.

"Well, Mama Lee, everyone," Teresa finally answered. "I've been awarded a grant to write a book about the history of black Americans in aviation."

"History? Black history?" Mr. Stevens turned to face her.

"Two books," Teresa nodded. "One for small kids and one for adolescents."

Mr. Stevens stared at her a good long time. "We'll give you up then. But only because it's a good cause." With a rigid expression, he scanned the room. "Right, ladies?"

They all slowly nodded in agreement.

"But that still doesn't explain why you can't come see us every Saturday. Can't you take a break from writing to visit?"

"I'll be away. I'm going to the mountains to write, but when I get back, I'll bring pictures and tell you all about it."

"My son has a place in the mountains," Lady D said.

"I know he does. That's where I'm going. He's letting me use the cabin so that I can have peace and quiet."

"He's a good boy."

Teresa nodded and patted the sweet woman's soft, brown hand. Teresa had come to know Dr. Ramsey through Lady D. The doctor was one relative who was a frequent visitor. About a year ago, he had visited during one of their reading sessions, saying that he had to meet the woman who had brought about such a miraculous change in his mother. They became friends. The offer of his cabin was a thank you for bringing back his mother's spirit.

"When I'm done, I'll be back to visit," Teresa promised, bending to wrap her arms around each of them once more. "You'll be the first to read my books."

"We're holding you to that!" Mr. Stevens grumped as she walked out the door.

CHAPTER 2

Teresa had never done this before. She was doing a lot of things she had never done before. Driving up a mountain in the middle of winter was one of them. Her hands gripped the steering wheel like a vise as she rounded the next curve and spied a small wooden sign ahead. Teresa slowed her already snail-dragging-through-molasses pace to read it. Gray's Outpost. That was the name of the family outpost Dr. Ramsey had told her about.

Teresa followed the rocky road, creeping even higher into the Smoky Mountains. She soon stopped to read another sign. The last one, though weather-beaten, hadn't been difficult to read. This one was impossible to decipher from the Jeep. She got out of the warm comfort of the vehicle, glad, despite the cold wind, to stretch her legs. She'd traveled nonstop for the last three hours.

Giving in to a sudden urge, Teresa spun around on her heels, spread her arms wide and laughed out loud. Having so much of God's creation surrounding her filled her spirit with joy. She skipped, actually skipped, to the sign and read it.

Almost there

Veer to the right
But not too hard
Then you'd be a sight

"Mountain humor," Teresa smirked, noting the wisps of vapor blowing past her lips. She then laughed so hard her back ached, surprising herself and any wildlife that happened to be around.

Wondering if mountain air affected the brain, Teresa hopped back into the Jeep and drove further down the road that soon narrowed into a rocky path. Rounding another bend, she came to a fork in the road, and just as the sign said, veered slowly to the right. Stopping to peer out of the passenger window, Teresa could see that the message had been there for more than humor. Her amazed eyes viewed a straight drop that went so far down she couldn't see bottom. She continued on the path that narrowed even more before opening into a clearing where a huge plank shed and mid-size log cabin stood.

This was the place. It looked just the way Dr. Ramsey had described it. Excitement pumped through her blood. Teresa opened the car door only to slam it shut again.

Two huge dogs, one black and one brown, stood not ten feet from the Jeep. Teresa shook inside. Not with surprise or even a tinge of healthy caution. She was knee-shaking, I-think-I'll-spend-the-next hour-in-the-Jeep afraid. The dogs came closer, settling on their hunches right beside her door, staring at her.

Now she was terrified.

In the calm, rational part of her brain, she realized that the dogs had shown not one bit of aggression. They hadn't so much as bared a tooth. The animals appeared completely calm, friendly even, but that observation didn't help to calm *her* nerves.

A heavy voice reached her ears. "Hello." A tall, brawny, middle-aged man with a thick mustache and long dark hair stood at the front of her Jeep. "Need something, ma'am?"

Teresa rolled her window down no further than necessary as her mind filled with visions of huge paws viciously clamoring to reach the small space and somehow invading the Jeep to maul her. A ridiculous fear, she knew, especially since she would be surrounded by every manner of wildlife imaginable during her stay in the mountains. But wild animals would be just as afraid of her as she was of them. Dogs had proven otherwise, turning on their owners. She'd seen the shows on TV.

"Yes," Teresa finally said through the crack in the window. The man remained in the same spot. One of the dogs walked up to him, his colossal tail wagging. The man absently rubbed behind the animal's ears as he continued to stare at her. The other dog stayed put, tongue lolling as it quietly—patiently waited for Teresa to come out of the Jeep.

"Well, ma'am?" The man paused, impatience in his tone and his body language. What if that impatience transferred to his dogs? Would they then attack her as soon as she got out?

Stop it, girl! Enough of wasting this man's time on a silly fear. *These dogs are not going to harm you, Teresa Lewis. Get out and greet your closest neighbor for the next year.* If she could drive a bookmobile through the projects of New Orleans for two years without harm, then facing two friendly, gigantic-looking dogs should be a simple matter. Hadn't she just acknowledged that she was doing things she had never done before?

This was just another one.

"When you get up the nerve to get outta that Jeep and walk past these two fruitcakes, I'll be inside," he said loudly *and* clearly. "City woman," he mumbled as he went back into the shed.

Embarrassed and tossing her fears aside, Teresa opened the Jeep door without giving her mind a second to reconsider. The two dogs moved in, tails wagging and panting, their faces tilted up, begging for her attention.

Her body was sandwiched between the open door and the front seat of the Jeep. Teresa took a good look at the dogs. The word *harmless* came to mind. "Nice dogs," Teresa said as a reminder for them to remain that way. "Good little fruitcakes." Teresa sang as she eased herself completely out of the Jeep, closing the door with her hip. Little, of course, was entirely inappropriate. The dogs were standing on each side of her, reaching to her hips. "Fruitcake Number One and Fruitcake Number Two, if I give you both a pat on the head, will you leave me alone?" Teresa reached out and tapped one dog on the head. The pat lasted no longer than a second. She gave the same attention to the other giant dog.

"A rub or two more, lady, and they'll be your friends for life."

"Oh, really?"

"Can't you tell? They like you. Do they have to open their mouths and tell you with words?"

The impatient man went back into the building. Teresa assumed that he was Mr. Gray, the owner of the property she had to pass through in order to get to Dr. Ramsey's cabin. Mr. Gray was also the caretaker of Dr. Ramsey's place and in possession of the keys she needed to get inside the cabin that would be her home for the next year.

The dogs were still beside her, not only panting and wagging their tails, but now moving around her in a circle. A rub and they were her friends for life, huh? Friends were better than enemies. Closing her eyes, Teresa reached down and rubbed behind the ears of one dog, exactly the way the big man had done. She could have sworn she heard the dog sigh as he sat down on his haunches. The other giant, obviously feeling left out, nudged her other hand with its head. Teresa found herself rubbing the heads of both dogs who happily sat before her, reveling in the attention she was dishing out.

Teresa laughed out loud as she continued to give the dogs the rubs they longed for. They hadn't turned on her. They hadn't suddenly attacked and mauled her. The last bit of nervousness she felt dissolved into nothing. That nothing grew into an enjoyable experience. They were her friends, wanting nothing more than someone to show them love. Not so different from any one of the of kids in the projects who would run to her when they saw the bookmobile or the senior citizens whose faces would brighten when she'd visit them. Teresa's heart went out to the huge fruitcakes.

"You can stop now, Miss Lewis. You about rubbed the fur off them dogs."

"Oh, sorry."

"Nothing to be sorry for. Here are the keys to Doc Ramsey's place."

"How did you know who I was?"

"Doc told me how you looked. And you act like you never been in the mountains. Doc told me that too."

"Oh," was all Teresa could think to say to that.

"If you need anything, I'll be right here. We've only had snow a couple times this winter. Most people think it's about over, but we got a big one coming soon. Be ready for it."

"I will be. Thanks." Teresa caught the keys he tossed and gave the dogs one last rub before getting back into her Jeep.

Her new friends whimpered as she started the engine. "See you around, neighbor," she mumbled. "Bye, Fruitcakes," she called, rolling the window down to wave as they ran beside the Jeep.

Teresa's arms ached. Carrying boxes and boxes of supplies and clothes into the cabin was another some-thing she didn't normally do, having lived in the same home all her life. Not to mention taking up residence in a cabin that was bigger than the two story house she'd grown up in.

Teresa had been expecting something more on the line of what she'd seen at Gray's Outpost, not this luxurious version of a log cabin. It was log all right. Solid wood through and through, and it was beautiful. The walls, the high-vaulted ceilings, loft, and floors were all constructed with a natural wood finish. But to apply the word *cabin* to this building was a bit of a stretch.

Teresa could spend a day in each room without occupying the same space twice in a week's time. And they weren't small rooms. The same openness and freedom outside had been extended to the interior of the cabin. Teresa would have no problem getting used to this. Her parents would enjoy spending some time here, she thought, wanting to call her mom and describe every detail to her, but she couldn't. Her parents were off on a twenty-one day vacation, which included a week in Jamaica, before sailing back to New Orleans. They would be unreachable by cell phone, but she would have plenty of time later to share the details with them. Picking up her cell phone, she called her cousin Monica. Ness was there with her. Teresa excitedly described the layout of the cabin, knowing they would appreciate what she had to share. Their husbands were business partners and had built and restored homes all across the country. After chatting with them a few minutes and delivering an open invitation for them to come visit, she heard the cries of babies and the three-way conversation ended. Both

Monica and Ness were new moms. She'd definitely invite them up here for a visit.

Teresa raised her arms high, stretched and flexed them in an attempt to get the kinks out. She laid some logs on the grate, adding a bit of kindling to build a fire. A novice, Teresa was proud to succeed in actually getting a fire started.

Easing into the soft leather of the recliner, she sighed. A moment later, she reached for the book she had planned to finish reading. An end to a perfect day filled with giant dogs, grumpy neighbors, strenuous exercise, and pure mountain air. Her hand lazily hit the side table with a soft thump and glided across the smooth surface, only to fail in its mission.

No book.

It wasn't there.

She must have left it in the Jeep. Teresa distinctly remembered thinking about putting the book on the table. She had even pictured herself in the chair, in this exact same position, but with the book in her hand. Her aching muscles didn't want her to move, but the characters in the book were yelling for her to find them. Zain had finally found out Asa's secret, only to think the worse. Teresa had to get up. Zain and Asa would have it no other way.

When she slipped on her shoes and dashed out the front door, the cold hit her. What a drop in temperature! Moonlight shone softly through the treetops. Instead of going back for her coat, Teresa stood where she was. The cold wind blowing through her sweater didn't matter. The gentle sway of the treetops had caught her attention. The long, thin needles of the evergreens, and the broad leaves of another tree she couldn't name moved together, gently bobbing in the wind, to and fro as if they had some secret to share.

A secret for her?

Did the trees know what the mountains would bring her?

Peace, solitude, and the inspiration to write two wonderful books, she hoped.

The trees stopped their swaying motion as an eerie stillness filled the air. "So, there *won't* be any sharing of secrets tonight," Teresa whispered as a chill, from the cold, or perhaps the sudden stillness around her, shook her from inside out.

She darted to the Jeep and got the book. Needing the warmth of the fire after that dose of cold air, she opted to lie before the hearth on top of a soft rug, trying to melt away the strange moment she'd just experienced outside.

She rested her head on a huge, stuffed pillow and pulled an Indian blanket off the leather sofa to use as a cover. Teresa read until the embers of the fire died out, and her eyes drooped.

~~~

The next morning, feeling as if she had just dropped off to sleep, Teresa sleepily rolled over. An instant later, she was wide awake. Always a light sleeper, she knew that some noise from somewhere had awakened her. Teresa waited. A scratching at her front door had her scrambling to her feet.

A wild animal?

Maybe it was a raccoon or worse, a bear. But it was winter. Wouldn't bears still be in hibernation? The scratching came again. There was only one way to find out. Tying a knot in the blanket to keep it around her shoulders Teresa hopped up to the window with a view of the porch, moving way too fast, her sore, achy muscles told her. Stiff as a robot, Teresa moved to the window and laughed at the sight. Her two fruitcake friends were making every effort to get inside.

Not wanting the dogs to even consider stepping a paw indoors, Teresa slowly pulled the door open, stepping out through the smallest crack possible. Pushing back the bit of apprehension that had begun to creep through her, Teresa reached out to rub behind each dog's ear. Her movements were quick and jerky at first, then more natural as the dogs wagged their tails in approval.

As she continued to rub, Teresa scanned the mountains surrounding her, the smoky haze in the early morning light clinging to them, a mystery within itself. She shivered in the cold that was even more biting and harsh than last night's. Still, she stood, her hands absently rubbing the dogs' pleasure points as she appreciated the beauty and greatness around her.

"When my dogs become bald, you'll be the one to put some of that fancy hair-growing tonic on their heads so they don't freeze the rest of the winter."

Teresa's hands stilled. The dogs whined, their heads nudging at her. "And good morning to you too, Mr. Gray. I guess I got carried away."

"Morning. Hope that won't happen again."

"Excuse me?"

"Get carried away. By the storm." When she didn't respond, he let out an exasperated grunt. "The one I told you was headed this way. I came to make sure you were ready for it."

"A storm? I guess I'm ready for it. I was hoping that we'd get some snow."

"More snow than you want. Been knowing that for some time now. The weather man's just gotten 'round to lettin' everyone else in on it. One of those bomb cyclones looks like to me."

"A bomb cyclone?"

"Winds like a hurricane, snow like a blizzard, and fast."

"Sound ominous. I noticed the change in the weather. When will the storm be here?"

"Sometime today. We got a couple of hours. At least past noon, I'd say. If you want to spend any time outside, you better do it now, Miss Lewis."

Teresa nodded.

"It's gonna be a big one. The winds will be strong so the power's sure to go out. Come with me. You need to know a few things about the generator Doc's got set up here."

Barely having enough time to slip on her tennis shoes, Teresa followed the big man around as he showed her the attached shed where the generators were stored. The shed had both an outdoor and inside entrance. There were also two portable models still in boxes but he ignored those, going straight to a huge, rectangular, metal contraption that took up one corner of the shade.

"This is the Generac Guardian."

"Guardian of?" Teresa asked, still eyeing the generators in the shed.

"Electricity. It's an automatic standby generator. Doc had it set up and wired to keep electricity flowing even if the lines are blown down."

"Standby? That means it kicks in if the power goes off."

"*When* the power goes out and with only a 30 second delay. You'll barely notice a difference."

"Good. What do I have to do?"

"Nothing. Doc paid to have a gas line connected to it, costing more than I'd care to sneeze at. I'd have used propane myself, but being a city fella…" He trailed off, running an appreciative hand across the generator despite his disagreement over the source of fuel. "You'll have nothing to worry about. A gentle hum is all you'll hear to know it's working. It fires up once a week to keep itself in working order."

Teresa nodded, listening to the terse instructions concerning the other generators to be used as backups if, God forbid, anything should stop the Generac Guardian from doing its job. As she followed Mr. Gray around, the dogs became her pals. She nearly tripped over them more than once. It seemed as if the last bit of apprehension she'd had about the dogs had vanished as completely as the sun, which was now obscured by heavy, dark clouds.

Mr. Gray mumbled something about wood, and Teresa went inside, leaving the dogs behind. They weren't too crazy about that, but no matter how much she'd come to like them, they were not entering this plush cabin to ruin anything with those colossal paws.

Teresa made hot chocolate for herself and Mr. Gray. She liked the older man, though he wouldn't win any awards for being friendly. But he was straightforward and helpful. Teresa sensed that he really cared about her safety. He reminded her of Mr. Stevens from the nursing home.

She poured the chocolate into two mugs. The heavenly smell wafted up to her nostrils. This was the real thing, made from rich cocoa powder and evaporated milk. She dropped a few marshmallows into hers and brought both mugs to the porch.

"Cocoa?" she offered.

Mr. Gray dropped an armload of logs on top of an already huge pile stacked on the porch.

"Thanks," he said, accepting the mug and drinking the hot liquid straight down.

"How'd you do that?" Teresa asked, wide-eyed.

"It's a gift," he said, his eyes actually twinkling. He peered into her mug. "Who said I didn't want marshmallows?"

"You can have my mug. I haven't touched it yet. There's plenty more."

"I'll accept the offer." It was gone in one big gulp. "Warms a man inside and out." He smacked his lips, licking the white goo with his tongue.

"Cocoa will do it every time."

"And you."

And me? Was he hitting on her? Naw, the man was old enough to be her father, was married if she remembered correctly, and white. But none of that really made a difference to some people, Teresa realized, as he handed the empty mug back to her. She took it, the apprehension she'd had about the dogs now directed to him.

"You may be a city girl, but you're a nice one," he went on, his tone in no way lecherous. It held a fatherly note that relaxed her instantly. "I probably won't see you for a while. Don't be nervous. You got enough wood to last a couple of months. I'll be by to check on you sometime after the storm, whenever I can get through, that is," he said as he started down the road.

Teresa waved goodbye. The dogs bounded after him, but came back for a final farewell rub before leaping down the mountain with their master.

Teresa went back inside to pour another mug of cocoa for herself, smiling as she added marshmallows. It was nice to discover that her new neighbor had a touch of sweetness in him. She sat on the porch bundled up in the heavy down coat she had bought before coming to the Smokies. There was no way she was going to miss the experience of what it felt like before a snowstorm. She was certain that the feel of the air would be different from what she had ever experienced before. The mountains were dominated by trees that held a smoky mist which seemed to blend with the clouds, forming a layer, a blanket of protection for the mountains. These mountains held so much power, so much mystery…

She had come here to write in peace and solitude, but there was much more to experience. Teresa could feel it. These mountains would give her more than she expected. She was looking forward to it.

And what would be her first gift from the mountains? Snow and tons of it, if she were to believe Mr. Gray. Teresa swallowed the last of her cocoa and went back into the house in search of her hiking boots. Before the storm actually got here, she intended to explore some of these beautiful mountains.

Her city girl toes securely tucked into her boots, a hiking stick kindly left by her neighbor, and a warm cap on her head, Teresa hopped off the porch and followed the path that took her higher up the mountain. The upward climb, Teresa figured, would be no problem. She was in great shape.

Great shape, ha! the wind whispered in her ear with a laugh.

Teresa had to laugh right back because laughing was better than crying. The climb was a brutal awakening to her already sore muscles. Her legs were heavy and slow after only ten minutes of hiking, but she didn't stop. Not even when she began to lose her breath, each step forward forcing a heaving puff of air from her lungs.

Teresa didn't stop until the trail narrowed into a much smaller path. She sat on a rock, forcing herself to take long, deep breaths, pulling the heavy scent of precipitation into her lungs.

Spinning on the rock, Teresa made a 360-degree turn. Her eyes lifted skyward. The clouds had darkened even more, promising that this storm was a sure thing. She stood, the view of the large cabin a perfect postcard photograph.

The cabin.

Now that was where she needed to be. There would be another day for explorations.

With the aid of gravity, the hike down was much easier. The cabin was in sight in no time. Leaning on the rail of the porch, Teresa took one last deep breath before going inside. Yep, something was in the air, and it was coming just for her. She could feel it.

CHAPTER 3

Teresa's eyes blinked open. The sound of a sputtering engine coming from somewhere outside drew her to the window. Peering out, she saw only the whirlwind of snow.

Snow!

Real snow!

Seeing the snow momentarily distracted her from the reason she had gotten up to begin with. That noise. She heard it again. It was coming from outside, and it didn't sound good. Something was definitely wrong.

Teresa flew around the room, grabbing her boots and jacket. She laced and tied her boots with anxious hands and slipped on her jacket as she went out onto the porch. That's when she saw it.

Forgetting her first snowfall, ignoring the miracle, Teresa watched as a small plane sputtered across the gray sky. The unexpected sight mesmerized her. She watched in stunned silence as the plane skimmed the tops of the trees, decapitating many of them as it skittered lower and lower, tilting sideways before it finally crashed, shaking the ground so hard that snow was the last thing on her mind. It took a second for her to take in the fact that a plane had crashed in what she probably should consider her backyard. For the first few seconds, she could only stare in the direction where the plane had gone down.

"Survivors!" she muttered. "There might be survivors." God, she hoped there were survivors. If there were, she had to find them.

Putting her thoughts into action, she ran to the shed where the Generac Guardian and the other generators were stored. Hadn't she seen a sled there earlier? Not only did she find a sled but some heavy rope. A sense of urgency filled her as she pulled the items out of the shed. The feeling intensified as her two friends, the fruitcakes, bounded around the house barking frantically. They ran past her in the direction of the fallen plane only to come back, circle her a few times, then once again take off in the direction of the crash site.

"I know. I saw it too. I'm coming." Wrapping the rope around her shoulders and pulling the sled, Teresa followed, moving down the steep mountainside at a careful, steady pace. The dogs continued their barking and circling ritual, their one-track minds forcing her to focus only on the survivors, not the possibility that she might slide down the steep mountainside and gouge her leg on a tree limb or sharp stone; not the fact that the snow was falling even faster and heavier than before; not the fact that her fingers were now icicles because she wasn't wearing gloves.

No, Teresa would only think of survivors. She didn't want to even imagine someone dying in such a horrible way.

She smelled the fire first. The smell of the fuel-based inferno was repugnant to her, so different from the pleasant scent of the cozy fire she had been sleeping before not long ago. The large dogs deftly leapt over fallen treetops in her path. Teresa had to maneuver over each one, the sled constantly twisting and flipping behind her.

Suddenly, she had a picture to accompany the smell of burning fuel. The rear end of the small plane was engulfed in flames that were racing to the small cockpit.

Despite the fact that the snowfall was even heavier, it wasn't dousing the fire. Abandoning the sled, Teresa rushed forward, knowing that she was the only hope for any survivors. Her two fruitcakes suddenly bounded out of nowhere, blocking her path and barking frantically.

What a time for them to turn on her. Lives could be at stake.

"Hey Fruits, I thought you were on my side," she said as calmly as she could. They stopped barking at the sound of her voice. "It was your idea to come here, remember?"

As if the dogs understood, they whimpered, looked toward the burning plane and back at her. Realizing she had their consent, Teresa stepped forward just as a treetop came crashing down, landing near the top half of the plane and creating a barrier to the cockpit.

Teresa ran to the other side of the plane and climbed onto the nose. There was someone inside. A man's head lay against the window. Was he dead? Then she saw circles of condensation form as his breath touched the glass. A deep sigh blew past her lips and she attempted to lift the cover of the cockpit.

"A latch, there has to be a latch," Teresa mumbled to herself. "A button or something." Her finger traced the outline of the window and door to the cockpit without any luck. "How does this thing open?" Teresa yanked on the door and fell on her rear with the handle in her frozen fingers. It wasn't going to open the way it was supposed to, that much was obvious.

Getting back on her feet, she realized that the newly fallen treetop had become fuel for the fire. The heat reached toward her with an intensity she could barely stand. Smoke rose from the cockpit as Teresa stood on the nose of the plane. Using the handle from the door as a lever, she shoved it into a jagged spot where a small chunk of plane was missing and began to pry. The sound of tearing metal fueled her determination to save the man inside. Now able to fit both her hands into the opening, Teresa lifted with all her strength, her muscles protesting with pain.

It wasn't enough.

How else was she going to get him out?

She tried again. This time with a screech, the door of the cockpit gave an inch, then two.

"Don't give up now, we almost have him," came an unexpected voice. Teresa smiled into the face of Mr. Gray. "Those fruitcakes got me out of bed with a mess of barking. I saw the fire and smoke from my bedroom window. I figured somebody needed some help. You figured the same, I see."

Teresa nodded. Together they pulled, yanked, and strained, pushing their muscles to the limit. The satisfying groan of metal tearing away from metal was the sweetest sound she had heard that day.

"Step back," Mr. Gray ordered. "I'll pull him out."

"Careful, he may have injuries. We could be making them worse."

"Better than dying," he grunted as he lifted the tall man from the cockpit placing him across his shoulder. "He looks like the only one. Let's move before this plane explodes."

Pulling the sled behind her, Teresa followed Mr. Gray down the same path she'd taken to get to the man lying across her neighbor's back. Putting the man on it might cause further injury since it would have to be pulled over so many fallen treetops and stones on the path. So far, a huge gash across his forehead was his only visible injury. However, various other possible injuries ran through her mind, and she tried not to think of all the damage Mr. Gray could be doing to the unconscious man slung across his shoulder.

Before long, they reached the cabin and were stomping across the porch. She ditched the sled, opened the door, and led Mr. Gray to the downstairs bedroom she had claimed for herself.

She stripped the wet and bloodstained clothes from his body as she checked for injuries from the crash or the trip on Mr. Gray's shoulder. With knowing hands, she carefully felt for broken bones, her hands traveling over every part of the pilot's still form. More than once she checked to see if he was breathing, and each time she found his breath to be shallow but steady.

She felt a few cracked ribs, but no broken bones. His hands were badly burned from the fire that had begun in the cockpit. If she had been able to open the door, that wouldn't have happened.

"He's one lucky man," Mr. Gray said as she tucked a blanket around the still form in the middle of her bed. "Looks like you're keeping him here," he added as he handed her a mug of cocoa.

Teresa accepted the mug filled to the brim with marshmallows.

"I took the liberty. I figured you could use a boost."

"Thanks." She took a sip before going into the bathroom to get the first aid kit she had seen there.

"You look like you know what you're doing."

Teresa nodded. "I'm a nurse, you know."

"Didn't before; now I do."

Mr. Gray watched as she cleaned and bandaged the wounded man's head and wrapped his hands. "Head wounds tend to bleed a lot. He won't need stitches, thank goodness," Teresa said aloud, feeling the need for conversation. She had always thought that she talked to her patients to calm them, but perhaps she talked to calm herself.

"He's gonna wake up with an awful headache."

"More than that." Teresa stood gathering her supplies and putting them back into the first aid kit. She pulled off the latex gloves she had worn and then went to wash her hands. Coming back into the room, she found Mr. Gray staring at the stranger.

"You trust this guy? We don't know a thing about him."

"I trust you. And I don't know much about you."

"Yep, that's true, but we have a mutual friend."

"He's unconscious, Mr. Gray."

"For how long?"

"Not too long, I hope. We ought to call for an ambulance."

"That won't do no good. They couldn't make it up here in the snow."

"The snow wasn't too bad a little while ago."

"That was a little while ago. It's bad now. Don't know how long the phone lines will hold up at my place. And you don't have service up here. Doc Ramsey wanted it that way. I see you got one of those cell phones," he said, his head nodding at the dresser where she had laid it earlier. "But the storm could interfere with you using it."

"Guess I'll just wait and see."

"This is the storm winter's been waiting to bless us with."

"Some blessing."

"Humph. Look, I have a wife to take care of. I need to make it back down the path before I'm trapped. Are you sure you're okay taking care of this guy?"

"I don't see why not." There were many reasons why not. A five-minute peek at the news was all it took. Instead she told him, "We need to have more faith in our neighbors."

"I don't feel too good about this," he told her, his eyes never leaving the unconscious man on the bed. "You're way too trusting." He stared at her a good long minute before commanding, "Come here."

Mr. Gray led her to a little room next to the kitchen and pulled a rifle from a closet. "Use it if you have to." He handed it to her. "Here's a box of shells." He grabbed a rectangular white box from a high shelf and handed it to her. "There are more—same place where those came from."

He took the rifle from her saying, "This is how you load it." With quick, sure motions he loaded the chamber. "I'll be by to check on you after the storm. God's gonna watch out for you. If you're not one of those fools they say He takes care of, you got to be one of His angels." With that off-handed compliment, he walked out the door, the dogs following behind. Teresa watched the three figures disappear in the heavy snowfall, and suddenly she was afraid.

The push to find survivors and caring for the one now lying in her room had left no room for thoughts of her own safety.

Should she be afraid of someone whose life she had just saved?

Of course not.

This man would be grateful to have been spared from death. As grateful as she would be.

Unless…

Unless he was a psychopath or maybe a schizophrenic.

Teresa raced to the bedroom, the rifle and box of shells still in her hand. The possible psychopath/schizophrenic lay on his back in the exact position she had left him earlier. Ridiculously, Teresa found herself studying his features for hints of mental illness. He had sandy-colored hair cut short, military style, and he was white, too white for just skin tone. He was extra pale because of the strain on his system. He had a long straight nose and lips that were thinner than she preferred on a man, but nice. Teresa froze. *Back up your thinking now. A minute ago you were looking for evidence of mental illness. Now you're making comparisons to what you like in a man? And doing it in front of a helpless unconscious one at that?*

Teresa leaned the rifle against the door jamb and placed the shells in one of the dresser drawers. Before her lay a poor guy who'd had the misfortune of crashing during a snowstorm. Nothing more.

"So help the man and stop staring at his lips," she told herself, taking his wrist to check his pulse and noting the light-colored hairs on his arms. Their roughness against her fingertips was another distraction.

His pulse was slow, but steady. She lifted his eyelids to check the pupils. One was smaller than the other, which could mean a slight or serious concussion. Slight, she hoped, saying a prayer that there wasn't too much hemorrhaging in the brain. She hoped he didn't need more medical attention than she could provide.

Teresa put the rifle into the closet where she had hung her clothes and pulled on another pair of latex gloves. She gathered the wet, bloodstained clothes and began emptying the pockets of some change and a wallet. When she pulled out a damp slip of paper with a phone number, she recognized the area code as New Orleans. Teresa laid everything on the dresser and went to put the clothes in the washing machine. She came back into the room, checked his breathing and realizing that there was nothing more she could do for him, tucked the covers around him, and left the room. She took his possessions into the den, hoping to discover who her tall, sandy-haired stranger could be.

Teresa glanced at the slip of paper with the phone number again. If he was from New Orleans, maybe her cousin Randy, a police officer, could help her locate his family.

That idea gave her a direction as well as a feeling of protection. Hoping to find more, she dug into the stranger's wallet.

She discovered a few hundred dollars and the driver's license of one Travis Labranch Jr. Teresa studied the face in the picture. Here was one angry man. His face was stern, his eyes hard, his lips, the ones she had admired, a firm straight line of disapproval.

"Aw, this doesn't mean anything," Teresa said aloud. Most guys tried to put on the tough act when they took a picture for their license. She should be more concerned that she had a name and a hometown. Travis Labranch *was* from Louisiana. The address was a street she knew to be in uptown New Orleans.

Teresa went back into the bedroom and got her cell phone and dialed the number on the slip of paper. The phone rang and rang, ending mid-ring when someone finally answered.

"Hello," a little voice came across the line. Maybe he was married and this was his little girl.

"Can I speak with your mommy please?"

"Mommy!" Teresa heard the child yell.

"What are you doing on that dirty phone?" A highly upset woman's voice came through the line. "Hang that up right now and don't you ever pick up a nasty public pay phone again. That's why mommy has a cell phone. Now come here so I can wash—"

The phone went dead. "A pay phone." Teresa let out a laugh. So much for her first lead. She hit the end button and went to investigate the contents of Mr. Labranch's wallet. The only item left inside was a small, white card.

Teresa took it out, hoping it was a business card with a phone number that would help her find Travis Labranch's family, and flipped the card over. A cold chill went through her body, beginning with the fingertips that held the card, and spreading through her until it completely took over, causing her body to shake violently.

The card fell to the hardwood floor, landing face up. What had she gotten herself into?

Her eyes went to the card again. Had she read it wrong? The bold, italicized letters told her otherwise. Teresa read the words aloud, *"White power, the only power."*

CHAPTER 4

Self-preservation kicking in, Teresa quickly got herself under control and grabbed her phone again. She would call the police and then Mr. Gray, in case they took too long to come. Mr. Gray had been right to worry. Teresa marveled at her own naiveté as she punched the numbers 9 - 1 - 1.

As she held the phone to her ear, her other hand flew up into the air in protest of the static, then the beep. Looking at the phone, she saw the message *signal lost* flash on the screen. Unwilling to believe that the phone that had worked a matter of seconds ago could no longer get a signal, she tried again. Once again she heard static, followed by a beep. Slowly taking the phone from her ear, she read the same message, *signal lost*.

Stopping herself from throwing the useless phone across the room, Teresa eased onto the sofa and pushed the cell phone across the wooden coffee table. What was Doc Ramsey's excuse for not having phone service? Peace and solitude, she reminded herself. To remove all distractions. The distraction of a police car coming up the road right about now would be a wonderful sight, she thought.

Her cell phone had been her only connection to help. And she was going to need it. There was no way she was going to care for a bigoted white man who would not only be unappreciative of the fact that she had saved his life, but would probably resent her for doing it.

Oh, Teresa had heard enough about his kind. She had seen them on talk shows. Her fascination with the very idea that a whole group of people could hate others with such complete passion for no good reason had had her eyes glued to the television.

And now she had a representative of a white supremacy group lying in her bed.

Not if she could help it.

Teresa pulled on her jacket, remembered to grab her gloves and was out the front door, instantly discovering something else Mr. Gray had been right about. The snow *had* worsened. The Jeep was covered with it, and she could see that the road was now impassable. The wind screamed that fact into her ear. The trees whipped back and forth in a frantic movement, as if to warn her not to do anything crazy. Okay, she couldn't drive. She would walk. Teresa had seen snowshoes somewhere inside and went back to find them as well as a flashlight. She needed help. She would make her way down on foot if that was the only way. It wasn't impossible. Mr. Gray had left no more than a half hour ago.

Forging forward, Teresa turned to get a view of the cabin. She had been trudging through the snow for about ten minutes. Waving her flashlight in the direction she had come, Teresa could see that it wasn't all that far behind. The flashlight landed on the path behind her. Signs of her shuffling progress were being erased by the steady snowfall and insistent wind. One more thing to worry about, but not enough to turn back.

As she made progress down the mountain, Teresa's concern for getting to Gray's Outpost began to ease until a swirling gust of snow blew her way, almost blinding her. The wind had to be a sample of those hurricane force winds Mr. Gray had warned her about. Fat, white flakes swirled all around her. The freezing wind blew straight through her, forcing her to take refuge against a huge tree. Even before the wind subsided, Teresa knew she had no choice. She had to return to the cabin.

It was either die in the snow today or deal with a bigot tomorrow. He wasn't worth her life. With that thought, Teresa turned to head back to the warmth of the cabin.

Except…

… she had no idea of how to get back. Hugging the tree for shelter had completely turned her around. Walking around the perimeter of the tree with her eyes begging for signs of the direction she had come from brought nothing but despair. There were no tracks, no indication of the direction of the cabin. "Which way do I go?" Teresa asked the swirling wind, wishing for a giant map to suddenly appear with a red dot marked "you are here" and an arrow pointing to another dot marking the cabin.

Leaving the safety of the cabin to run away from an unconscious man who might or might not be a threat to her had not been a smart thing to do, the wind cutting through the layers of clothes told her. Teresa had to get back to the cabin. It was certainly closer than Gray's Outpost. She could be safe and warm within the hour if she could only figure out which way to go.

"Which way to go?" she asked the swirling wind once more. But the whirling snow ignored her.

Helpless to do otherwise, Teresa chose a direction and took two dragging steps before a huge creature threw itself against her, its paws landing on her shoulders. The hot and smelly breath of one of the fruitcakes was the warmest, happiest greeting she had ever had. The dog barked and licked her face. Instead of frantically scrubbing her face free of doggie germs, Teresa laughed and hugged the furry beast. God was looking out for her. According to the old saying, God looked out for fools and babies. She was the fool, and here before her was an angel sent to guide her. When the dog dropped to all fours, Teresa followed it and peered in the direction from which the animal had come. If the fruitcake had come bounding at her from that direction, then the cabin had to be in the other. Teresa had been going the wrong way.

"Thanks, Fruits," she told the dog, rubbing its neck once more. "Think you can help me find my way home?"

The dog began to circle her as she set off, making slow progress. The winds threw snow in every direction, but mostly straight into her face.

Soon the dog's barking was the only guide she had. For the first time in her life, Teresa truly understood what zero visibility meant. She was a blind woman dependent on her sense of sound and an angel of a dog to get her to safety. How the dog knew where to go, Teresa had no idea.

Instinct?

Maybe.

Whatever it was, she was going to give the animal a huge steak and a cozy spot inside the house, right in front of the fireplace.

After what seemed like an hour of dragging her frozen body forward in deep snow, the lights of the cabin came into view. Fruits circled Teresa until she made it onto the porch. She went inside, snowshoes and all, the dog right behind her.

The warmth of the cabin hit her all at once, but it wasn't enough. Teresa threw off her wet clothes on her way into her bedroom, not giving her patient a second thought as he lay on her bed while she stood naked hunting for the thick terry cloth robe and fleece-lined slippers she had brought with her.

When she was completely covered, Teresa glanced at her patient. He *was* still her patient. Not wanting to, but feeling obligated, she went to check his pulse. It was the same. If the touch of her frozen fingers wasn't enough to wake him, then he was still unconscious.

Good. The longer he stayed that way, the safer she felt. A stab of guilt went though her. That would mean he was more severely injured and would be in even greater need of medical help. That wasn't what she wanted.

Turning to find the dog beside her, Teresa saw that it was the brown one, the female of the pair, who had guided her. The poor animal was shivering and dripping all over the hardwood floor.

"Ignoring my angel is a horrible way to show my appreciation, isn't it?"

Grabbing a large, thirsty towel, Teresa led the dog to the fire, which she stoked to a flaming blaze, and gave the dog the best rubdown she had ever given as they both soaked in the warmth of the fire.

"How's that, angel?" Teresa asked, having gotten the dog as dry as possible.

The dog yawned and lay down on the rug Teresa had enjoyed sleeping on the night before.

"I thought you'd like that. Call it part one of my thank you for saving me from freezing to death. Go ahead and rest; you deserve it."

Teresa watched as the dog placed her head between her front paws and fell into slumber.

Placing the screen before the fire, Teresa went back into her bedroom. She stood in the doorway. She didn't even want to call it her room anymore. It was contaminated by a man who thought by right of birth that he was better than she. Not just Teresa, but most of the people in her life. There he was lying in her bed, surrounded by her things, everything from the clothes she wore to the pictures she had brought of her family. He lay right next to a picture of her entire extended family, taken at the wedding of one of her cousins this past January. Her parents, cousins, aunts, and uncles smiled at him from no more than a foot away.

Teresa hoped that picture was the first thing he saw. Let him have a good look at integration in action. Two of her cousins had married people outside their race. Not only that, they were some of the happiest married people she knew.

Feeling buoyed by that thought, Teresa eased into the room, heading straight to the closet to reclaim the rifle Mr. Gray had handed to her. She had no idea how to use it. Teresa wished she had asked him how. At the time, the idea of even needing a weapon had seemed ludicrous. Well, simply having it in her possession was going to have to be enough.

Exhausted, Teresa slid into a comfortable chair across the room. The cushions were soft and welcoming. Keeping her feet firmly on the ground, she laid the rifle alongside the chair. She stared at the still form on the bed until her eyelids refused to stay open. The last thought in her mind was exasperation at what the mountains had sent her way.

Loud barking followed by a retching sound brought Teresa to her feet. A furry obstacle crossed her path, tripping her as she moved toward her now gagging patient. Using both hands to catch herself, Teresa landed on the floor, the last bits of sleep literally falling away from her.

Realization came quickly. She was stuck in a snow-storm—

—with an injured bigot—

—a huge dog—

—and a rifle she didn't know how to use.

Seeing her patient choking on his own vomit, Teresa went into action. She grabbed a wastebasket and propped him up. The angel of a dog stopped barking and sat on her haunches to watch.

When it seemed as if he had completely emptied his stomach, Teresa adjusted the pillows to keep him in an upright position. Throwing up was an expected symptom of a concussion. She hoped it wouldn't be a continuous one. That would mean the injury to his head was more severe.

"Worry about it if and when it happens," she said aloud as she slipped on a pair of fresh rubber gloves and went about the business of cleaning him and the bed. As she gently moved him from one side of the huge bed to the other to change the sheet, Teresa didn't allow herself to think of him as anything other than her patient.

"I know he's sick," she said, launching into a one-sided conversation with her watchful assistant. "My concern is just how sick in the *head* he actually is. And I'm talking about before the accident."

The dog gave a whine in reply.

"You're saying he might not be sick in the head? That I should worry about the sickness I can see?" Teresa paused as she fluffed a freshly covered pillow. "I get you," she said, adding talking to dogs to the long list of things she had never done before.

The dog walked over to her, nuzzling her hand for a rub. "Something else I shouldn't worry about, it seems. If he becomes a threat I'll deal with the situation then, right?" Teresa scratched the dog behind the ears. "Makes sense to me." She took the rifle and stored it in the same closet Mr. Gray had taken it from, then settled back into her chair. This time as she stared at him from across the room, all she saw was another human being in need.

A sweet, soothing sound filled the air. It floated around him and softly eased into his eardrums, sending a vibrating warmth of comfort across his aching body. It lessened the pounding in his head, pushing it aside. He tried to turn toward the sound, but it hurt to move. He was sore all over. Every part of his body ached. Moving one small muscle seemed too huge a task to undertake. But then, he didn't have to.

That sound.

That voice stopped him from trying. It held him. It covered him with a blanket of peacefulness that lulled him back to sleep. But he didn't want to sleep. He wanted to open his eyes to see who belonged to this beautiful voice, but his eyes refused to open. Trying took too much energy, was too painful. It pushed the pounding back to the front of his head.

The voice stopped.

Or else the pounding in his head was so loud he couldn't hear it.

He strained toward it. He needed to hear it again. His heart raced with fear that he wouldn't hear it again.

Then it came.

Just as sweet, just as beautiful as before.

Finally, he slept.

Teresa woke up and glancing at the clock across the room, assumed it to be eight o'clock in the morning, though it was dark outside the bedroom window. The dog whined at her feet, darted to the front door and back again. The speed that she was moving had Teresa imagining lamps and pictures crashing to the floor. Getting the message that the dog needed to go out, Teresa wasted no time in opening the door. The wind forced its way into the cabin, pushing Teresa against the wall. The dog could not have gone too far to do her business because she was back by the time Teresa finally won the battle to close the door.

"I'm sure the phone lines are down," she told the dog. "I know that the electrical lines have bit the dust cause Doc's good ole Generac Guardian has kicked in." She headed back to the bedroom. "Thank goodness for powerful generators," she declared, appreciating the warmth and light provided by portable electricity.

Teresa walked over to her patient, immediately noticing the ease with which he was breathing. She checked his pulse and changed the bandages on his hands, applying the ointment she had found in the first aid kit. In the meantime, Angelfruit, the name she had unofficially given her new, best friend, stood by inspecting as usual. "I don't think we have enough bandages to take care of these burns, though they're not as severe as I first thought," she confided to the dog. "He's going to need at least one change every day, and first aid kits don't come with a huge supply. We may have to resort to using sheets as bandages." The dog tilted her head as if she agreed.

"He's looking a little better, don't you think, Angelfruit?" A bark was the only answer to that.

"I hope he's looking as good on the inside." Teresa didn't want him to die under her care. His death would be different from those of her hospice patients. She got to know them and their families. She bonded with her patients, all the while making them as comfortable as possible.

That hard-looking man named Travis Labranch on the license wasn't someone she cared to know. But the man lying in bed, in pain, in need, she could care for him. But she wouldn't be bonding with him.

Going into the kitchen, Teresa busied herself with mixing a batch of blueberry muffins and popping them into the oven. She went back into the bedroom armed with a cup of crushed ice and a glass of water with a spoon and a straw resting inside. Teresa gently eased the straw into his mouth, hoping that he would instinctively suck, pulling water through the straw. "Take a sip," she encouraged. "Go on, try it. It's good for you. Just water, nothing to hurt you."

Nothing happened.

Removing the straw and placing a hand on his jaw, Teresa gently opened his mouth. The warmth of his skin and the rough stubble on his chin caused an unwanted surge, a remembrance that she'd found him to be just a little bit attractive. But that was before she knew what she knew about him.

Ignoring the surge, Teresa went back to being his nurse. She spooned water into his mouth and massaged his throat to encourage him to swallow. He did. She spoon-fed him water and ice for the next five minutes. Satisfied that she had gotten some liquids inside him, she went back to the kitchen.

She fed the steak she had defrosted to Angelfruit. "Finally, part two of your reward for saving my life," she told her, settling down herself to a hot muffin and a steaming cup of coffee.

Sore and achy from sleeping in a chair all night, Teresa decided to take a shower, banning the dog from following her into the bathroom. "Keep an eye on our patient," she commanded before treating herself to the warm, pulsating blast. Drying herself, she realized that she hadn't brought any clothes inside the bathroom to change into.

"Well, girl, exactly who is going to see you?" she wondered out loud. "Not the unconscious 'him,' and Angelfruit *is* a girl."

Tossing the towel into the hamper, Teresa went into her bedroom, slipped on a pair of undies, and ignoring the need for a bra, found a comfortable terry cloth jogging suit, the softness and warmth of the fabric the exact layer of comfort she needed to feel right now.

"What now?" she asked the dog who looked up at her in question. "I guess I should finally begin to do what I came here to do."

Still feeling the need to be near her patient, Teresa settled in the same chair she had slept in last night and silently read through her notes, filling her head with the amazing details of black aviators and the struggles they'd undergone. Becoming excited by the facts before her, Teresa began to read them aloud, using the same expression and animation she would if she were reading for one of her groups.

She read on, delving into the facts, stopping only to lean over and pick up her mug of coffee resting on the floor, then sip. A movement from the bed distracted her. She stood, letting the papers, all of her notes slide to the floor. As usual, Angelfruit followed suit.

He was moving, turning his head toward her, clearly agitated. Not a good response. "He's restless," Teresa told the dog. "Let's hope he's not dreaming about blowing up a church." That bit of dry, inappropriate humor released some of the tension she was feeling. Unsure of how he would react to the sight of her and uncertain of how she would react to his reaction, she felt an unfamiliar nervousness spread through her, causing her to talk even more than usual. "Shhh, it's okay. You're safe and warm and smack in the middle of a king-sized bed. Angelfruit is here too. She's a dog. She helped us find you."

"Us?" she questioned, when his sudden stillness seemed to ask for more details. "Mr. Gray, my neighbor, is the other part of us. He carried you, and I followed along. Then he made some cocoa and—here you are…"

Teresa let her ridiculous rambling trail off. But as soon as she stopped talking, he began the same restless movements. "Calm down," she said and he did, but his head began moving toward her, his body following as a low moan trailed from his lips.

Teresa gently but firmly laid both hands on his shoulders, holding him still as her no-nonsense nursing instinct took over. "You've got to stop moving or you're going to hurt yourself."

He became still once more, but not until the side of his cheek rested against her fingers, trapping them between his face and shoulder. Before she could pry her hand away, he very slowly, almost deliberately it seemed, moved his face up, then down. The stubble of his beard created a friction that went beyond the physical abrasion of skin against stubble. An awareness of him as a man and herself as a woman ran through her. Her fingers experienced a heated charge that was unexpected, unwanted, yet exciting. She wanted to snatch her hand away and deny what she was feeling, but she had just got him to calm down. Just as she drew in the deep breath that she suddenly needed, his cheek once again pressed into her hand, moving in a widening circle that heated her fingers. Fingers that wanted to turn and cup his cheek within her palm.

Teresa shook her head. This wasn't right. The man was sick and delirious and definitely had no idea what he was doing or what that doing was doing to her. Not wanting to upset him, Teresa mentally tried to ignore what such a simple touch was doing to her. Physically, she needed to get away from it as quickly as she could. Carefully turning his face with the hand that was not the recipient of the most simple, most sensuous caress she had ever received, Teresa eased the hand away from him, not daring to give in to the urge to linger, to caress his stubbled face. She reminded herself of the card she'd found in his wallet and backed away from him.

A low moan rumbled from him. It was a weak, wanting sound that came again as she watched him. Teresa didn't know exactly what to do for him without touching him, which would probably start up those surges all over again.

"What do you want?" she asked.

As she spoke, a long sigh of intense relief seemed to flow from his lips.

"You want me to talk to you? I can do that. Yes, I can do that," she repeated, watching the way his breathing slowed, and his face became still and calm. "What do you want to talk about?"

Teresa glanced around the room, her eyes landing on her notes. "I know exactly what to talk about. The Tuskegee Airmen!" she shouted, pausing and wondering if it was wise to read about the accomplishments of black Americans to him. "Well, suppose he isn't what you think he is?" Teresa challenged herself. Another low moan from her patient decided it.

"The Tuskegee Airmen were the first African-Americans to qualify as military pilots in any branch of the armed forces. By the end of WWII, almost a thousand African-Americans had won their wings at Tuskegee Army Air field in Alabama. They destroyed over a thousand German aircraft and received hundreds of medals."

She read aloud until he lay still, and his breathing became even in sleep. The silence in the room was profound. Teresa knew that reading or simply talking to an unconscious person did wonders for bringing them around, but this was different. Reading was a calming effect, but she was surprised that the subject matter didn't disturb him. "Maybe he *isn't* what you think he is," Teresa told herself once more. That card could have been something he found or something that had been given to him as a distasteful joke, or even something that had been slipped to him without him paying too much attention.

"Innocent until proven guilty," Teresa decided, dragging the chair and positioning it next to the bed. She read, reread, and organized the facts before her, working until her stomach and Angelfruit told her it was lunchtime.

She fed herself and the dog and decided to try a bit of broth on her patient. He responded well to the liquid diet, but it took longer to read him back to sleep. She was almost finished with one book by the time he showed signs of sleeping. That was fine; she had a wealth of reading material. Teresa knew exactly what book she would use during their next reading session.

Finding it hard to believe that this was the fourth morning after the accident, Teresa stood and watched as the snow continued to fall. It had stopped now and then, the wind lessening, but the storm wasn't finished yet. Never before had she thought the sight of snow would leave her feeling so frustrated. Teresa went into the kitchen, which opened up as an extension of the spacious den. Having finally consumed the last of the batch of blueberry muffins she had made earlier in the week, she felt like a hearty breakfast. "Bacon, eggs, and grits hearty enough for you?" she asked the dog who lounged in front of the fire. The rug before the fireplace was her favorite place when she wasn't following Teresa all over the house. Teresa clanged pots and pans as she started breakfast, hoping Mr. Gray would forgive her for feeding his dog so much people food.

Angelfruit's head shot up and turned in the direction of the open bedroom.

"He's restless again, huh? He seems to be this time of morning. I'll go in to see him in a minute. I don't want my bacon to burn." A steady diet of African-American literature from a book of short stories and poetry had kept her patient calm over the last few days, but sometimes she'd just talk, her voice alone seeming to do the trick.

As she was taking the cooked bacon out of the pan, a scream filled the entire house, and Teresa nearly splattered hot grease all over herself. Angelfruit bounded into the bedroom, barking as she ran, with Teresa right behind her.

Her patient was sitting up in bed, his hands covering his eyes. What had made him scream? Pain?

The picture of her family? The dog? Had he glimpsed her cooking in the kitchen through the open bedroom door? It could have been any of those things, but Teresa hoped that it wasn't from seeing the picture or her. That would mean he was a bigot, and she didn't want him to be.

He hadn't moved from his position. Teresa hadn't either. She could see he was taking labored breaths. He seemed frightened. Hey, she was too. She was afraid to find out the truth about him.

Angelfruit barked, breaking the silence.

"Who's there?" he asked, keeping his hands over his eyes.

Was the sight of her so terrible that he couldn't look at her when he spoke?

"It's me, Teresa."

"Your voice. You're the beautiful voice." His hands fell away from his face, but his eyes remained closed. "I thought you were a dream."

Talk about voices, his was heavy, deep and definitely a New Orleans one. And of course, it sent one of those surges straight through her.

"Are you a dream?" he asked.

"No," she cleared her throat. "No," she repeated, "I'm Teresa. I'm your nurse."

"I'm in a hospital? This doesn't feel like a hospital bed."

"It isn't. Your plane crashed in the mountains."

"The mountains?"

"The Smoky Mountains."

"I piloted a plane?"

"I saw it crash with my own eyes."

"You saved me?" his head lifted toward her voice, though his eyes remained closed.

"With some help."

"You saved me in more ways than one," he said mysteriously, his eyes squeezing together tightly. "Maybe you can help me a bit more."

"I can try," she answered, feeling sorry for him one second, then leery the next. Why was he keeping his eyes closed? "It's just—"

"It's just what?" he asked.

"When I talk to people, I like to look into their eyes so that I can read their expression."

"I understand. I want that too." Before continuing, he pulled in a huge breath that lifted his entire upper body. It was a completely masculine action and directed her mind to surges, attractions, and other thoughts better left un-thought. It was also totally unexpected from someone who was so badly hurt. "That's exactly my problem," he was saying. "When I opened my eyes a few minutes ago, I saw nothing."

"Nothing?" Teresa was surprised but shouldn't have been. Hadn't she just yesterday discovered a medical journal and looked up concussions to refresh her memory of what to expect? Blindness could occur. It could be temporary or not. "Not even light?" she asked, hoping some vision had remained.

"The world was dark."

"Meaning you could see absolutely nothing?" she asked, needing to clarify.

"Which is why I screamed like a bear." A sad, lopsided smile twisted at the corner of his mouth. "It brought you to me, though. I feel a little better just having you here."

"That's good," was all Teresa could think to say, relieved that his aversion to opening his eyes didn't have a racial cause. Not that she was happy to hear that he couldn't see.

"What was your name again?"

"Teresa."

"Teresa, I'm not ashamed to say that I'm afraid to open my eyes again."

"It's understandable."

"And something I have to do."

"Yes."

"Will you help me?"

"How?"

"I'd ask you to hold my hands, but they seem to be bandaged."

"Yes, they are, neatly and completely. I did the job myself." Teresa tried to downplay that injury in order to distract him from thinking about it or the others he'd suffered. She could fill him in on them later. Right now, the loss of his sight was enough to deal with. He was quiet for so long Teresa wondered if he had worn himself out with talking. This *was* the first time he'd been awake.

"Just stand next to me. Talk to me. Sing. Anything. As long as I can hear your voice."

"Okay," she answered as he twisted so that his entire body was squarely facing her. He grunted in protest of the movement he had just made. After a minute's thought, Teresa broke out in song, hoping her voice wouldn't crack as she sang the Negro national anthem, 'Lift Every Voice and Sing.' She knew why she had picked this particular song. It was another test.

As the first stanza flowed from her lips with a full-bodied volume and tone that surprised her, his lids relaxed, no longer squeezing together like a vise. As the second stanza rolled from her lips, his eyes began to open. She stayed focused on his face, waiting for him to respond, hoping that he wouldn't suddenly tell her to shut up or scream again like an injured bear when he saw her face.

His eyes fully opened. They were wide, dark eyes, a deep blue color, that held an unfocused, vacant stare. He couldn't *see* her or anything else.

"You can stop now. I'm blind," he said almost matter-of-factly.

Teresa's heart went out to him, but she couldn't deny the truth. "You are, for now."

"What does that mean?"

"It could be temporary."

He sat up straighter, groaning at the sudden movement.

Teresa gently laid both hands on his shoulders. "Sit back. Try not to move too much." *Please try not to move too much*, she silently added as she pulled her hands away from his bare skin. It had happened again. This particular surge had been quick, intense, and mutual. He'd felt it too. Teresa was sure he'd felt it. That last sharp intake of breath that reached her ears had not been from pain. Then there was the way his brows raised as he twisted in her direction all over again. "You have to be still," she repeated.

"Of course."

Don't mention the surge. He's a sick man. Keep your focus on him, Teresa pleaded inside her head.

"But—"

"But what?" she asked, afraid of the but.

"Are you telling me the truth? About my sight? How do you know? Is there a doctor around here? Get the doctor so I can talk to him!" he threw at her.

"There's no doctor." Teresa paused, thankful that his focus was where it should be. She answered him slowly and calmly, for her benefit as well as his. "We're in a cabin in the Smoky Mountains outside of Chattanooga, Tennessee. We are in the middle of a snowstorm. An ambulance couldn't get through. I'm a nurse. I have been and will continue to take care of you until the storm ends."

He leaned back against the pillows. "I'm not in a hospital and can't get to one," he said, seeming to be digesting the words as he repeated what she had told him.

"That's right."

"There's no doctor."

"No."

"And you're a nurse?"

"Yes."

"And you're telling me that this blindness won't be permanent?"

"It may or may not be." Teresa paused, wondering just how much to tell him. Giving him information seemed to have a positive effect. "You hit your head pretty hard. Hemorrhaging inside the brain could cause pressure on the visual cortex. The result—"

"Blindness."

"Possibly temporary blindness."

"But possibly permanent?"

"Depending on the amount of pressure."

"In your opinion, is there much?" His sightless eyes turned toward her, demanding the truth.

"Without x-rays I can't say for sure, but looking at the short amount of time it took for you to become conscious, *most likely* not."

"Are you grasping at straws to make me feel better, Teresa?"

"No, just giving you facts." She could admit to a few facts. Her name on his lips? Perfect.

"Thank you, then. I think I need a minute or two to digest it all."

"I'll be in the kitchen if you need me."

"If you don't mind, I'd like a glass of water."

"I don't mind at all," Teresa told him, cataloguing the many clues that pointed toward his not being a bigot. He was frustrated and a bit down, but wouldn't anyone react similarly to discovering that they were blind? He was also polite and direct. If she went by first impressions, Teresa had to say she liked this man.

Then again he hasn't *seen* me yet, Teresa inwardly reminded herself. He just may be imagining me as a blond-headed, white woman. "Save judgment," she added in a whisper, bringing him a glass of water with a straw. "Here you go." Teresa put the straw to his lips.

He took a long draw, stopping a second later to say, "I hate using straws, they're for kids. Think you can help me drink this like a real man?"

Teresa laughed.

"What's so funny?"

"I now understand why I couldn't get you to drink from a straw before." She removed the offending object and placed the glass to his lips. Using one of his bandaged hands, he managed to tip the glass, surprising her, and drained it in two big gulps. His hand bumped into hers, almost knocking the glass out of her hand.

"Sorry about that. I was thirsty."

"I could see that," Teresa said, noting a few other things she was definitely keeping to herself. Like the fact that any physical contact with him caused a reaction. A bandaged hand touching her shoulder should not make her fingers tingle to touch him herself.

"I'm also starving. Is that bacon I smell?"

"Yes."

"You're not going to let a blind man go hungry, are you?"

Amazed at his ability to accept his disability so quickly and easily, Teresa unintentionally kept him waiting for an answer.

"Maybe you would," he answered for her.

"Would what?"

"Let a blind man go hungry."

"Of course not. I'll bring you some food." At the mention of food, Angelfruit barked to get her attention. "You'll get some too," she told the dog before turning back to her patient who she was coming to like much too much. "Angelfruit can keep you company while I get you some breakfast. She likes you." Teresa stopped at the door. "Do *you* like dogs?"

"I don't know," he told her, a strange look crossing his face.

Teresa scrambled some eggs to go with the bacon and the grits that she had left bubbling on the stove. She took out a tray for his breakfast and found herself humming the tune to "Lift Every Voice and Sing" as she moved about the kitchen.

She felt good.

She felt relieved. Teresa was certain that she was not harboring a bigot. He didn't fit the personality. She was almost positive.

He?

Teresa couldn't continue calling him 'this man,' 'him' or 'he'. She would have to use his name.

"Travis," she said out loud, spooning grits into a bowl.

The name didn't sound right. It didn't fit. Travis was that hard-looking man on the license she had found. He wasn't the man sitting in her bed. But in truth, he was. Despite the difference in expression, the basic facial features were the same. Which meant that if the man's name was Travis, then that's what she had to call him. Travis.

After fixing a plate for Angelfruit and leaving it in the kitchen, the only place she allowed the dog to eat, Teresa brought his tray of food into the bedroom.

"I like dogs," he told Teresa as soon as she walked into the room. "I didn't realize it until she jumped on the bed."

"She did what? That sneaky little something. Did she jump on top of you? Did she hurt you?"

"No, don't worry. I got her off without injury to either of us."

"Good, here's your breakfast, all nice and neat on a—"

"Who am I?" he asked in the middle of her sentence.

"—tray." she finished.

"Trey? My name is Trey?"

Trey, that was a nice name. She liked it. It fit better than Travis. He looked like a Trey.

"Teresa? Is Trey my name?" he asked again. For the first time, a grating frustration filled his voice.

"You don't know your name?"

"No." The frustration disappeared almost as quickly as it had come. "I can't seem to remember a thing about myself," he growled, then paused as if in deep thought. "I don't mean to take it out on you. I owe you a lot. I owe you everything. I just wish I knew one simple fact."

This was the time to tell him. Teresa looked at the handsome, confused man on her bed. He had lost both his sight and his memory. He had to be feeling lost. His name was one piece of information she could give him. It was one fact she knew about him, but he didn't look like Travis Labranch. One day he might remember that he was Travis Labranch, but she preferred to think of him as Trey. "Do you want to be called Trey?"

"If that's who I am, then, yes."

Teresa set the tray on the bed, knowing that she should tell him the truth. Hearing his real name might trigger something since it was obvious that he was also suffering from memory loss.

"You know what? It's not as important as the fact that I'm alive," he said saving her from having to decide. "Call me Trey."

"Trey it is," she agreed, relieved that the decision had been taken out of her hands.

"I can't do much with these wrapped paws. I hope you don't mind helping me." His sightless eyes seemed to stare at his bandaged hands a long moment before raising them to cover his face. Suddenly lifting his head and looking in her direction, his hand stretched until it connected with her arm. "Thank you," he said simply.

The contact sent more than a surge through her. A shared feeling, a mutual awareness had passed between them, simple and strong. Unvoiced, but obvious just the same.

CHAPTER 5

Trey was awake.

He knew he was awake due to the intense pain that made him feel anything but normal.

Normal?

What was normal?

He certainly didn't know. Having no inkling of who he was or where he came from, Trey could not begin to know what was normal. Even if he could see, he wouldn't know exactly *what* normal looked or even felt like.

"What do you think about that, Angelfruit?" Teresa asked the dog from somewhere in the house.

"Teresa." He whispered the name, a gentle a breeze across his lips. He strained his ears, hoping to hear Teresa's voice again. The sound of it had already began to ease the tension rising inside. Each time he awakened, Trey had to deal with the realization that he had lost both his memories and his sight, causing his entire body to stiffen with frustration until...

Until Teresa came near. Her presence would melt the tension, soothe and relax his muscles. Without saying a word, she made him appreciate being alive despite his injuries and the loss of his sight.

How?

Why?

Trey had no answers, just as he had none to the million other questions constantly running through his head.

Why had he been flying a plane in the middle of a blizzard?

Was it his plane or had he crashed someone else's?

Could he afford to replace it?

Why couldn't he remember anything before waking to the sound of Teresa's sweet voice and the startling blackness?

Why hadn't he died?

Was there a reason God sent Teresa to save him?

God?

Trey paused in thought.

God. Yes, he believed in God. Another small piece of who he was, his beliefs, fell into place beside the other tidbits of realization he had already uncovered about himself.

Lying flat on his back Trey listed the few facts he knew. He liked dogs, grits, and eggs. He knew how to fly a plane *and* how to crash one. He appreciated the care of a beautiful woman.

Beautiful? He chided himself. As if he could possibly know that Teresa was beautiful? Well, he didn't have to see her to know. "I know," he whispered to no one but himself. "I know—by her touch and her voice."

Trey slowly sat up, though various parts of his body protested with pinpoints of pain. He strained to hear Teresa speak again. What he got instead was a series of resounding barks and rapid doggie foot-steps. But not long after, exactly what he wanted.

"Trey? I was starting to worry about you. I was hoping you hadn't slipped back into Neverland."

"No," was all he could say as the softness of her voice reached him. It held a hint of a smile. Trey relaxed on the bed, letting all that was Teresa surround him.

"Are you in a lot of pain? Are you hungry?"

"No pain," he said again in answer to her first question, trying to convince himself that the pain he felt all over his body was minor. "But I'm starving." He surprised himself with his answer to her second question.

"Then I'll fix you—"

"No!" Trey interrupted, wincing as he jerked his body forward to answer. "Not for food!" he explained, not quite understanding what he was saying, especially since he actually *was* hungry.

"You're starving, and you don't want food? You *have* been asleep too long."

She placed a warm hand on his forehead, a quick, professional touch that left a very unprofessional desire in him. Trey wanted her hand to stay there. He wanted *her* to stay, not dash off to another room to get food.

"You don't understand."

"Okay then, make me understand."

Trey could hear, almost feel her arms folding, her stance patient but insistent as she waited for an answer.

The dog barked as if she were waiting for an explanation too.

"I *am* hungry. But right now I feel, I need—" Trey paused, finding it difficult to say exactly what he needed. Maybe it was because he couldn't find the words or didn't have the words.

Was he an educated man?

Uneducated?

More questions rose to the front of his head.

Teresa stood at the head of the bed watching as evidence of frustration appeared on his face. Her heart went out to him. Since he had awakened two days before, he had been calm and quiet, taking his injuries and disability in stride, it seemed. She had come to admire his strength. He never once complained, though Teresa knew he was in constant pain from the burns, cracked ribs, and various cuts and bruises all over his body. His only relief came from the over-the-counter medicine she had brought to the cabin herself.

"You need what?" she asked, coming closer to the bed.

Trey tucked the numerous questions crowding his brain into the back of his head. His brow furrowed, his eyebrows came together as he tried to find a way to express what he was feeling. Finally, he forged on. "This is going to sound strange."

Whatever it was he wanted, Teresa decided, her heart going out to him, she was going to make sure he got it.

"I've only known you for… how long?"

"A long time. For me six days, but for you, you've known me about two, give or take a few hours."

"No…It feels longer than two. The sound of your voice…" He had been addicted to it from the minute he heard it. That's what it was. That was the word. Addicted. "I remember your voice," he told her. "I remember the sound of it more than anything else."

"It's possible," Teresa told him, still unclear as to the direction this was heading. "Then I'll give you four days," she joked, trying to stay upbeat. "But no more, those first two days you were too far gone to notice anything."

"I'll take the four. Tell me, in four days is it possible for someone to become addicted?"

Surprised by the question, Teresa cautiously asked, "To what? I haven't given you any medicine that you could possibly become addicted to."

"No, you've given me something else, and I don't know if it's because my senses aren't what they should be or if I even have the right to say this."

"If you feel it, you should say it." Teresa grimaced at that advice. She had been feeling things she knew she wouldn't reveal.

"Okay then," he said, diving right into the opening she'd given him, "I'm addicted to you." Was he usually this straightforward with women, he wondered as soon as the words left his mouth. Was he a woman chaser? He couldn't answer those questions, but knew, somehow, that this confession was unique.

"To me?" Teresa squeaked, the possibility of being an addictive substance completely unexpected. This from the supposed white supremist.

"I know I sound crazy." He leaned toward her, pausing to draw a long breath between his teeth as his bruised body protested, before going on, "Or maybe I hit my head too hard. Though everything else in my life is an uncertainty, I *am* sure that I'm addicted to you. It's your voice, your presence, your spirit." He rambled on, afraid to stop to hear her reaction. "Having you near me makes me feel good all over."

There.

He'd said it.

He'd found the words.

He'd told Teresa what he felt. He didn't have to understand any of the whys. He just needed to say what he was feeling. Somehow, having the ability to control something, to at least say what he was thinking and feeling, had become extremely important.

Not quite knowing how to respond to such a direct declaration, Teresa stood next to the bed staring at the earnest expression on his face, which in a matter of seconds fell into a frown.

"Teresa? Don't just stand there." His voice remained calm. "I told you this was going to sound strange."

"It does."

"Say something. I can't read your expression. Are you upset? Horrified? Stupefied? Happy? Don't leave me hanging," he ended in a soft whisper, only to add in a factual tone, "remember, you're talking to a blind man."

"I don't mean to leave you hanging," Teresa slowly answered, needing time to make sense of it all. "It's just that this is so unexpected." Taking a long breath and using her best nurse's voice, she continued. "What do you mean by *addicted*? Is it that you've gotten used to having me around? That you like having me around? Is it that you appreciate the care I've given you? That would make sense." More sense than Trey actually being addicted to her. In all her years of nursing, Teresa had never experienced such a thing. What was it called? The Florence Nightingale Effect. It was either that or the possibility that he *had* hit his head harder than she thought.

"All of the above, I suppose." He paused before asking, "Am I making you nervous?"

"Yes," Teresa answered immediately. He was making her nervous, uncomfortable, uncertain, and a whole batch of other things she didn't want to admit.

"I don't mean to." He'd messed up. He'd stated this whole thing wrong. The pain in his head must have caused him to blunder. That or a natural ineptness in talking to a beautiful woman.

"I don't want to make you uncomfortable. I only want to spend some time with you, talk to you, listen to you read again." He heard a sigh of relief that seemed to echo within the room. Good. Maybe he had fixed things. "*Addicted* might have been too strong a word."

"*Might have?*" she asked.

"Okay, it was. What I meant to say, Teresa, is that I enjoy having you near me. I enjoy the sound of your voice."

A loud rumble interrupted his next words, causing them both to laugh.

"Even more than food?" she asked him.

"Even more than food," Trey admitted, "but I'll suffer the loss of your presence if the offer of something to eat is still open."

"Wide open," Teresa was relieved to say, leaving Trey's side to dish up a bowl of gumbo she had spent the morning cooking. She absently wondered if he even liked gumbo. For all she knew he was allergic to shellfish. "Or it could be that he's addicted to shellfish," she whispered to herself. Not her. Teresa shook her head in disbelief. "And after only two days?"

Angelfruit whined. "Okay four," Teresa corrected, not knowing if the whine was a protest for food or honesty. She fed the dog yesterday's leftovers of baked chicken and macaroni before getting out the wooden tray she had been using to serve her patient.

Addicted to me? she wondered, placing a glass of water on the tray. *My voice?* The bowl of gumbo came next. *My presence?* Next came the napkin and the spoon.Suddenly she decided, there was no addiction. Trey simply liked having her around and she enjoyed reading to him, and talking to him, and looking at him…

Talking. She forced her mind to go back. Yes, that was what she enjoyed best. After all, there was no one else to have a conversation with.

A loud, slurping noise drew Teresa's attention to Angelfruit, who looked up at her with big, brown doggie eyes. "Sorry, girl, you saved my life and are good company, but if you begin to have a conversation with me I'll know that I've come down with some serious cabin fever." If she took what Trey had said to heart, that would mean one or both of them had come down with some kind of fever. But talking was fine and safe. She had always talked to her patients. It was her way of calming them. And besides, her conversations with Trey had been interesting, relaxing, as free as if they'd known each other for a very long time. Not only that, Teresa had to admit that she looked forward to visiting with him when he was awake. Going into his room was the first thing she did every morning. Did that mean she was addicted to him?

No. Not addicted.

Neither one of them was addicted.

That conclusion firmly placed in her mind, Teresa brought Trey the meal his stomach had called out for.

"Gumbo?" he asked, sniffing the air.

"You bet." Teresa answered, seeing not a bit of revulsion on his face, which made it safe to assume that he probably didn't have a problem with the meal.

"What I can't see, I can certainly smell." Trey was trying hard not to let their earlier conversation put a strain between them.

"What you're smelling is the best gumbo in the world," she quickly responded, easing his worry.

"I don't know about that. It depends on the roux," he stated. That's the basic beginnings of any good gumbo. Dark or light?"

"Light."

"One star. Seafood or everything?"

"Everything from shrimp to andoullie sausage."

"Two more stars! Filé or okra?" Trey asked not exactly sure where he was digging these questions from, but knowing they were the right ones to ask.

"Filé all the way!"

"One more star, then." Trey felt himself smile in anticipation.

"Four stars so far, that's pretty good," Teresa said, placing the tray on the wide rustic dresser near the king-sized bed.

"The final test comes in the tasting, but of course I'll need your help with that." He raised his bandaged hands in an appeal for help.

"Gladly!" Teresa grabbed pillows to place behind his back, then laid the tray across his lap. "Final test coming up." She lifted the spoon from the bowl to his mouth, making sure he had a bit of everything on it. Her eyes stayed trained on his lips. The ones that were thin but strong. The ones that pressed against the spoon, then against each other as he emitted a pleasurable hum, a sound of complete male satisfaction. The sound teased a side of her that was far from being satisfied.

"The final star goes to the chef," he quietly announced, "Five star gumbo."

"Five star gumbo," she repeated, her eyes still taking in his lips.

"Five star gumbo," he repeated a little louder. Then, "Five star gumbo!" he shouted with a rush of excitement.

"That's what you said," Teresa said with a perplexed laugh.

"I like gumbo!" Trey realized.

"Yes, you do!"

"And not just any gumbo."

"No, not just any," Teresa agreed catching on to the reason for his sudden excitement.

"I love filé gumbo with a light roux and everything from seafood to andouille sausage! Oooooo yah!"

"Oooooo yah!" Teresa repeated, enjoying this side of Trey. His exuberant reaction to the simple things he was relearning about himself sucked her in.

"Why did I say 'ooooo yah'?"

"It's a Cajun expression."

"Cajun! Louisiana! Am I Cajun?"

"Who knows?"

"Oooooo yah! I don't care. Just dish me up some more of that gumbo."

Teresa did, finding that if anyone was at risk of becoming addicted to anything, it was she. She could easily become addicted to Trey's excitement. He made her smile. Most of her patients did, but in a different way and not as much as Trey. Then again, most of her patients were dying. Trey was getting better, healing, and his joy was reaching out to her. Which was normal and harmless, she told herself.

"Another bowl?" she asked when he had eaten every drop.

"Oooooo yah!"

Teresa laughed as she went to dish up another bowl, coming back almost immediately.

Between spoonfuls he said, "You know, it's a shame that you have to feed me."

"I don't mind."

"I do," he told her. His suddenly serious tone caused her to drop the spoon into the bowl and place it back on the tray.

"Between your bandaged hands and those cracked ribs, you can't raise your hands as far as your mouth," she gently explained. "I'd say, at least for now, you don't have much of a choice."

"Is that what you think?"

"That's what I know," Teresa stated firmly.

Without another word, Trey's bandaged hands reached for the bowl, tipping it on its side as he awkwardly grabbed hold. He lifted it up, aiming for his mouth.

Teresa jumped back as Trey knocked over the glass of water, spilling it into his lap. He ignored it as he loudly slurped at the last drops of gumbo in the bowl and clumsily dropped it back onto the tray. "What do you think now?" he asked.

"I think you've made your point as well as a mess. You've got a puddle of water in your lap."

He shivered before casually observing, "And it's freezing cold."

"You've got gumbo dripping down your chin and rice on your nose."

One bandaged hand waved at his nose flicking the grain across the room. "Don't you dare." She halted him before he could use his bandages as a napkin. She leaned forward to wipe his chin with a real napkin. The friction of the stubble against the thin material sent a few of those surges thrumming through her fingers. From the sudden stillness, Teresa knew he was aware of it too. Searching in her mind for some way to break this impossible-to-go-anywhere-too-wonderful-feeling of I've-got-to-kiss-his-lips thing, Teresa hoped that Angelfruit would come rescue her with one of her opinionated barks. But she didn't. So Teresa did the only sane, sensible thing she could thing of. She took a step back, waited a minute for her brain to remember what had happened before she found another reason to touch him, and asked into the charged silence, "Do you know what else I think?"

"No, what else?" he asked, wondering if she'd say what he wanted her to say. If she'd admit that something was happening between them. Something good. Something glorious.

"I think you need to get cleaned up."

"Do I look that bad?" he asked, his tone deep, serious.

Not at all, Teresa thought, noting once again the mixture of brown and blond hair that was the stubble on his chin and the lips that...

That she wasn't going to kiss.

"Not bad at all, just a mess," she managed to say.

"A mess. Overall, I guess that's the perfect word for me."

"I wouldn't say that," Teresa heard herself tell him. A raised eyebrow showed that he detected more in that statement than she had wanted to say. She wouldn't in a million years admit that she thought he was gorgeous. Not knock-out-super-fine gorgeous, but gorgeous all over, inside and out. White or not, she found him attractive. Then and there, Teresa was certain that he couldn't be what she suspected. Trey was too in-your-face, this-is-just-me kind of genuine. And she was attracted to him. Too attracted to him.

"I'm dying to know," Teresa heard him say as she removed the tray from his lap. "But I'm not going to ask what you *would* say."

"Good."

"But you must realize that being stuck in this cabin we're going to have to eventually do some sharing." There. He was getting bold again. Trey hated to think what the ease in which he fell into flirting meant about his general interaction with women.

"Perhaps."

"Per-definite," he answered, forcing away thoughts of who or what he was or might have been.

"Do you have a habit of making up words?"

Before he answered, a thoughtful expression crossed his face, replacing the determined, sensual one that had begun to make her nervous all over. "I don't know," she heard him say.

"You don't know," Teresa repeated, watching the various expressions run across his face, from passionate to thoughtful to direct. Being able to see his face somehow made her feel at a disadvantage. Just looking at him made her want to do things with a patient she had never considered doing before. Was this what Trey meant by addiction?

"What I do know is that I'm starting to freeze." He shivered again as proof.

"And it would serve you right for being so—"

"—determined to do something for myself," he finished before she could, not feeling a bit of regret for the throbbing pain in his hands and the razor sharp one in his ribs. "That little exertion didn't kill me," Trey found himself bragging. "Besides, I was getting a little tired of being a helpless bump on a log, not that I don't appreciate your attention. I look forward to it." He raised his bandaged hand to say, "It's just this healing thing is taking too long."

"I've got a feeling you're not use to being idle."

"I've got that feeling too, among others," he said, his head turned in her direction as if he were looking straight at her. Teresa felt as if he could see her, as if he knew she had some of those other feelings. "Bear with me and have mercy," he added, his entire body suddenly taken over with shivers.

Not wanting him to catch a cold, Teresa walked closer to the bed. "Only because you're my patient—"

"—and you like me," he finished for her. Trey hadn't meant to push the issue, but he needed to hear her admit to something.

"Of course." Teresa turned away even though she knew he couldn't see her face. She crossed the room to find a set of bed sheets in the closet. Coming back to the bed, she found him twisting from side to side under the covers, grunting, as he pulled at the pajama pants he wore.

He stopped, panting from the exertion "I know my limits," he called out. "I'd appreciate it if you could get rid of these ice pants. I pulled them down as far as I could but I don't think I can get them past my knees."

"Sure," Teresa answered, moving in slow motion across the room. Her plan had been to get him out of the bed, lead him into the bathroom, and hope and pray that he could take care of himself while she changed the sheets. Which was absolutely unrealistic. She was surprised that he had been able to do as much as he had already. No big deal, she told herself. He's a patient; you're a nurse.

Teresa went to the foot of the bed, leaving the damp sheet as cover as she reached beneath it, her fingers grazing the silky cloth covering his upper thighs. These were Doc Ramsey's pajama pants and she had put them on him, so she shouldn't have any trouble taking them off. Her fingers landed on the elastic band. The material was wet and cold, but the band itself held warmth from his body. She carefully stretched it, pulling the fabric away from him, desperately trying to avoid skin to skin contact.

As she began to pull the pants below his knee, he jerked, and her hand slipped and landed on his upper thigh—his firm, muscular upper thigh. She moved her hand immediately, using the mattress to steady herself.

"Sorry, I forgot to warn you about my knee. There must be a heck of a bruise there."

"There is; I should have remembered." Remembered? Teresa could barely think, let alone remember. That wasn't exactly true. She *was* thinking about the hair on his thigh that felt like tiny electrical wires sending multiple surges of heat straight through her. "Your knee must have slammed against something in the cockpit during the crash," she said, resuming the task at hand, finally removing the damp pants and throwing them on the other side of the room to deal with later. "It must still be pretty tender," she continued, before falling quiet. The rustling of cloth was the only sound for the next few moments. "I've got a towel open and ready for you," Teresa explained, tapping the side of the bed before gently guiding his legs in her direction. With an extremely professional hold on the towel, Teresa's gaze never once wavered from his face. A quick tuck of the towel around his waist and a gentle shifting had Trey safely seated on the wide, soft chair near the bed, the exact place she had sat to read to him. Though she was relieved that he was in some state of decency, her mind continued to tilt in the direction of indecency. She was finding it difficult to stop it from wandering in such directions. What else could she do?

Talk.

Teresa talked to Trey in detail about what happened the night of the crash. She helped him to the bathroom, paused as he used it, and continued her monologue as she helped him into the chair next to the bed once again, pretending that he was still wearing pajama pants instead of the towel that was loosely wrapped around his waist. She talked about Mr. Gray and his dogs as if they were the most important beings on the earth.

Instantly understanding Teresa's evasive technique, Trey indulged her by listening intently. Her ramblings were significant proof of the fact that she felt something for him. She couldn't deny it or ignore it any more than he could ignore that part of him that had instantly hardened when her hand had pressed against his thigh. If every muscle in his body didn't ache so much, if he was certain she wouldn't run screaming from the room, if he could see her face, her lips… If he could use his hands, he'd pull her down onto that huge bed, hold her against him, kiss her lips, allowing every part of her to melt into him.

"What is it?" She stood up from spreading a fresh, clean sheet across the bed.

"My knee; it's still tender."

"Oh, then we had better be more careful when we go to put a fresh pair of pants on you."

"Not pants. Shorts. Boxers if you have them."

"If boxers are what you want," her voice came from across the room, "then boxers are what you'll get," she finished, no more than a foot away from him. The towel never leaving his hips, with quick and quiet efficiency, Teresa discreetly helped him into a pair of Dr. Ramsey's boxers she'd found in one of the drawers and helped him back into bed.

"There you go," she announced, her voice so full of triumph and relief he wanted to laugh. Had he ever met anyone like her before? She'd risked her life to saved his, a stranger. She took care of him, changing his bandages, feeding him, but doing so much more.

Sore and exhausted from that bit of exercise, Trey lay back against the pillows patting a spot on the bed.

"Join me."

"That's not a good idea," Teresa told him, taking a step away from the bed. Moving him, touching him, trying to avoid touching him, noticing his arousal, which was impossible to hide, none of it was a good idea. "You need to rest," she added taking another step back.

"No, I don't need that," Trey said in a quiet, much too seductive voice.

"Are you trying to tell your nurse what you need?" Teresa countered, crossing her arms instead of falling under the spell of his voice.

"Of course, he answered in the same tone, then almost immediately asked, "You have your arms folded, don't you?"

"And what if I do?" Teresa asked, unconsciously moving closer.

"It's your nurse's stance, isn't it?" At the telling silence Trey added, "Admit it."

"I never thought about it, but I guess it is."

"Sit with me a second."

She stared at his handsome face, the stubble on his chin giving him a rugged quality. She wondered at the attraction she felt for this man, this stranger who was so different from her.

"I promise not to grab you or slurp you up, no matter how tempted I am."

Teresa let out a breathy laugh at the gumbo reference. Her legs already resting against the high mattress, Teresa conceded, easing herself to sit next to him.

"Thanks," he told her, stretching a bandaged hand to find one of hers. "I'm too exhausted and in too much pain to try anything anyway."

"You're also my patient."

"Oh no, Teresa," Trey said, his other hand eerily reaching for and finding her face. His wrapped hand skimmed her cheek, barely touching it. His warmth somehow seeped through as his hand moved to gently turn her face toward his. "You are so much more to me. I hope to be more to you."

"Trey." Teresa firmly said his name as she attempted to pull herself out from under the strange magnetism he exerted on her. "You don't know what you're saying," she gently told him. "You don't know me, you don't even know who you are. I helped to rescue you from a plane crash and have taken care of you. What you're feeling is gratitude."

"How about what you're feeling, Teresa?"

"What are you talking about?" Teresa pulled back a little, getting dizzy from this yo-yo motion. She wanted to be near him, but she should be doing her best to stay away from this kind of conversation. But how did you pull yourself away from something that automatically drew you back?

"No, don't go. I'm making you nervous again. I'm sorry. We don't have to talk about this anymore. Just sit with me until I fall asleep, okay? Help me make a memory so I can have something to think about."

"A memory," Teresa repeated, melting inside at the romantic idea of making a memory with him, for him. "Okay," she finally agreed, not fully comfortable with his questions, his so-on-the-mark observations, and the ease in which he got her to do exactly what he asked.

Trey relaxed, falling deeper into the pillows Teresa had placed behind him. He released a contented sigh, and his hand reached for and found a resting place on her leg. She was surprised when, not a moment later, Trey's breathing became low and even as if he were in a deep sleep.

How could he have fallen asleep so quickly and without the pain reliever she had intended to give him after lunch?

The pain reliever. How could she have neglected the needs of her patient?

How could she resist this attraction she felt toward him?

More importantly, should she? Teresa asked herself as she quietly slipped away.

CHAPTER 6

The snow had stopped falling, and a step onto the porch revealed a beautiful winter wonderland. The bushes were snow-covered, icicles hung down from the roof, and layers and layers of snow covered every path. So many layers that the road leading to Gray's Outpost, the trail she had climbed on her first days here, and the one they had made bringing Trey up the mountain were completely impassable. There was no way out. At this moment, she didn't want to find one.

Why? Teresa had asked herself that question the past three mornings. As she stood on the porch sipping a steaming cup of hot chocolate, she savored the quiet moment, knowing it would end soon. For now, Teresa drank in the sweet liquid and the beauty of the fallen snow that seemed to be in no hurry to melt and release them from the mountain. Not that there was any pressing need. Trey was in no danger and healing quite rapidly. So rapidly she was finding it hard to keep him still.

As the days passed, they had fallen into a routine. Just as her cocoa would turn into lukewarm chocolate milk, Angelfruit would sniff at the door exactly as she was doing now. Teresa opened it. Her companion bounded out, then inside once again. Teresa smiled into her mug as she heard Trey say, "Where's Teresa, girl? Go find her for me. Tell her I'm *dying* to say good morning."

Angelfruit came back to the porch with a loud, demanding bark.

Coming back into the house, Teresa asked, "Who's asking for me?" playing along as if she didn't know Trey was sending the dog to find her.

"Tell Teresa I'd love some of that cocoa she makes every morning," he told the dog.

"Tell Trey I drank it all." The excited dog ran off to bark out the message as she turned to pour the hot liquid into a mug.

"And one of those blueberry muffins she made yesterday. No, two, I'm starving."

And so it went on. This little game kept Teresa from dashing into the room the moment she heard Trey's voice, giving her a chance to get hold of herself, to calm the excitement she felt at seeing him every morning. She was very easily falling for him, something that felt so right, but then again, not quite right.

Angelfruit didn't stop her own personal brand of messenger service until Teresa had the tray in her hand and was walking toward the master bedroom. Issuing a final bark, she went to her own breakfast, leaving them so that she could nap in front of the fire for the rest of the morning.

Usually, Teresa would find Trey in the middle of the bed wearing a huge grin and patting an empty space in invitation. Not this morning.

"Trey," she called, placing his breakfast on the dresser before moving to the bathroom door, the only logical place he could be. "Where are you?"

"Right behind you."

Teresa jumped as she spun around to face him. "Where did you come from?"

"From the sky. The plane I happened to be flying crashed into your backyard. Don't you remember? And here I thought I was the one with the memory loss."

"No, I mean—I didn't see you there. Did I just walk past you?"

"Now you're really confused. I'm the one who can't see."

"No, you're the one who's going to be in a whole lot of trouble. What are you doing out of bed? And why were you hiding from me?"

"Hiding from you? Never," he said, taking two confident strides forward with an outstretched hand that found the side of her face, his newly exposed finger briefly caressing it before resting on her shoulder. "I was exploring."

Teresa didn't pull away from his touch, realizing that he needed to use that sense to balance what he had lost. "Exploring?" she asked, instead of concentrating on the imbalance his warm fingers threw her into.

"I was getting a feel for this place. Trying to find my way around. There's someone here, who shall remain nameless, who won't let me do any more than go to the bathroom and back."

"That someone has her reasons. You're still recovering. You need to rest. So let's get you back into bed." She gently laid a hand on his hip as she guided him back to the bed.

"Only because I know you're leading me exactly where I want to go."

"Is that right?"

"Absolutely."

"At least you know where you belong," Teresa grunted. "And I'm advising you to behave. If not, I might just leave you there."

"All alone? I'll lose my appetite if you don't join me. And that would be an extreme loss because I'm starving this morning." Trey forced his facial muscles to remain relaxed, hoping they wouldn't spring into the grin he felt growing inside. He loved teasing Teresa. Loved her hand around his waist. Loved knowing that she would soon be sitting next to him on that big, wide bed, laughing and talking with him before they settled into a day of reading. Well, for his part, listening.

"Can't let that mighty appetite of yours decrease," Teresa casually answered, watching him settle back into the bed with an ease that surprised her. He looked as if he had gotten in and out of the king-sized bed at least a hundred times. He even went so far as to reach behind himself to fluff the pillows. Looking much too pleased with himself, Trey wiggled his recently unbound fingers at her.

"I can smell them, so I know they're here."

"What's here?"

"Muffins," he sniffed. "Blueberry muffins."

Teresa laughed as she reached for the tray, placing it across his lap.

"Finger food!" he announced as his fingers searched for and found a muffin, peeled away the paper, and nearly bit it in half. Teresa watched as he gleefully chewed, swallowed, and repeated the process with little difficulty, his sense of smell more than enough to get him what he craved. He finished the first muffin and demolished the second, washing it all down with the mug of cocoa she had set in the middle of the tray. "Finger food!" he groaned. "I love it!"

"I can tell." Teresa said, sitting on the edge of the bed and taking in his genuine excitement.

"Miss feeding me?"

"Not at all," Teresa laughed. His mood was contagious, lifting the guard that usually kept those surges Trey inspired in check.

"No?" he asked in mock disbelief.

"Not one iota," she repeated, almost immediately realizing that she actually did miss feeding him. Not that she wanted Trey dependent on her. She was glad that he was excited about doing for himself. But, she had to admit, the act of watching him as he ate, the movement of his lips, the way he swallowed and savored his food, had been an intimate encounter. If anything, she should have felt a need to be more guarded, more careful around him.

"Can I feed *you*?" he asked.

Teresa shook her head, feeling much too comfortable, too warm, too wanting to answer verbally. Realizing too late that he couldn't see her response, Teresa let him continue as if she hadn't tried to answer his question.

"It only seems fair. I mean, I've got the use of my fingers. The burns there have healed, right?" His face turned down as if to look at his fingers. He turned his hands as if he were inspecting them.

Teresa nodded, remembering to add sound to the motion this time around. "Yes, your fingers weren't as bad off as your hands. And even your hands will be fine in a couple of days."

"So how about letting me return the favor?"

"By feeding me?" she asked.

"Yep!"

"I can do that all by myself."

"What's the fun in that?"

"The fun? I get food into my mouth and inside my stomach," Teresa felt free to joke.

"So you think I can't manage that?" He leaned forward, his face stopping two inches from her nose. His breath, as it blew across her lips like a warm caress, sent a few surges that instinctively caused her lips to part and pucker before she had the sense to pull them in and smack them closed.

"I accept the challenge," Teresa heard him say, obviously taking her silent battle of the surges as consent. Teresa watched as he leaned back against the pillows. What now? Should she play along with this little game of his, knowing full well that she was in dire need of a good surge protector? Lying there in the middle of the bed wearing that sexy, boyish grin, he seemed less of a patient and more like a man she wanted to know. That was only natural. He was getting better. Despite the blindness and memory loss, he was getting better. And Teresa was thrilled. But the better he got, the more he teased and flirted, and the more she surged with desire. If he kept getting better, she was sure to get into a situation with Trey where there was no turning back.

"No answer. I can only interpret that to mean that you're *not* up to the challenge." he said.

"Sounds like more of a challenge for you than me," she whispered, not permitting her bossy nursing instincts to take over. She had no desire to think of Trey as a patient. He didn't feel like a patient just now. He was a man she found attractive inside and out, despite his recent difficulties.

Difficulties? Teresa nearly laughed out loud. Memory loss and blindness were a bit more than *difficulties*. Still, he handled them quite well. Teresa recalled hearing somewhere that the true measure of a man was revealed by the way he handled life's hardships. If so, Trey was a strong man, able to handle life's punches with humor and dignity, which was one of the many reasons Teresa found herself drawn to him. She truly liked him, which was why she was allowing what she was feeling for him to simply *be*.

The next thing she knew, Trey had the last muffin in his hand. "We'll see," he uttered mysteriously, peeling the paper away from the large muffin. This time, his fingers took great care as the wrapper slowly came away from the muffin. It almost seemed as if Trey was undressing it, as silly as that sounded. The outer layer came away, exposing the golden-brown goodness. His fingers seemed in no hurry to reveal the tasty treasure within. He then carefully broke it in half, then fourths, then eighths.

"If you break that muffin apart any more, it's going to be nothing but crumbs."

He stopped and looked up at her in that way he did when he seemed to be looking straight into her. "Then you'll have to lick them from my fingertips," he whispered.

Teresa wanted to put him in his place, to tell him how ridiculous the suggestion was, but she couldn't. The idea sounded...appealing. So she didn't say a word. Instead, she watched as he lifted an eighth of a muffin toward her mouth. She was so intent on the vision of crumbs and fingertips that as it came closer, she forgot to open her mouth. The piece of muffin bumped against her lips. A few crumbs fell down the V-neck of the sweatshirt she was wearing to land between her breasts. She stared at the crumbs, idly wondering what Trey would do if he knew they were there. A sudden image of his face following the crumbs to their resting place and his tongue rescuing them flashed through her mind. The sweatshirt suddenly became much too warm.

Her thoughts had turned to the ridiculous. Trey couldn't possibly see what had happened to the crumbs. Teresa pulled at the sweatshirt, flicking the crumbs from their resting place, amazed at how sensitive her breasts were to that quick brush of her fingers.

"Was that your nose?" he asked, the flirtation gone from his voice.

"No, my mouth, I forgot to open it," she whispered, hoping her voice didn't sound too breathy.

"*You forgot*? Doesn't that mean that you cheated?"

"I don't cheat. I honestly forgot."

"How could you forget when the sole purpose of this challenge was for me to feed you, my fingers finding your mouth—" He suddenly stopped talking. "Oh."

"Oh what?"

"I think I might know why you forgot to open your mouth."

"Oh, so you can read minds now?" she asked, hoping that wasn't true.

"No, I can read feelings, Teresa, and there are a lot of them in this room."

"Really?"

"Really, real feelings that we've both been trying to ignore. Ones that could possibly make you forget."

"Really?" was all her brain could come up with.

"Really," he grinned at her. "Are you up to a new challenge?"

"We never finished the first one," Teresa said, hoping to somehow stay within the confines of the simpler task of a blind man feeding her.

"We'll get back to that one later. This one is a bit more exciting."

Certain that it would be, but not completely sure what this challenge entailed, and not actually sure she wanted to know, but unable to resist after days of holding in and holding back, Teresa heard herself say, "Sure."

"Close your eyes."

"Why?"

"To level the playing field."

"Okay," Teresa agreed.

"Are they closed?"

"Of course they are."

"Just checking. I wouldn't know, and I can't have you cheating again. I wouldn't have thought that you would take advantage of a blind man."

"But I—"

"Shah," Trey said, cutting off her reply, knowing full well she hadn't cheated. Knowing that what had started out as a game had revealed to him that Teresa had feelings for him beyond patient care. It thrummed between them and had made her forget. "I know," he whispered, moving the tray from his lap and pushing the cover away.

Teresa felt the bed move. A second later, his fingers found her face. They traced her eyebrows, lightly grazing her lids before cupping each side of her face between the tips of warm, gentle fingers that traced her bottom lip before whispering, "Don't move." He paused, then added, "And *this* time, open your mouth."

Knowing there was no food coming her way Teresa did exactly what he asked. When his lips landed lightly on her own parted ones, his tongue flickered inside, barely entering her mouth. He tasted like...

Teresa opened her mouth wider, reaching behind him to find his neck. She pulled him closer, to explore, to taste and feel the lips she had been dying to kiss. He tasted warm and fresh, Teresa decided as they pulled away from each other, like just-baked bread. Almost as if by mutual consent, they reconnected, their tongues issuing a final caress, their lips gradually parting.

"Really," Teresa said, still holding him close.

"Really sweet," Trey whispered, his fingers resting against her face.

Teresa opened her eyes to find him peering at her as if he could see, with an intensity that let her know exactly what that kiss meant to him. She wondered if her face looked the same.

"I wish I could see you now. What are you thinking, Teresa? Does it match what you're feeling? What we're both feeling?"

"Umm."

"Be honest." The backs of his fingers caressed her cheeks, trailing down to her arm until he found her fingers.

"Maybe."

"Thanks for telling me the semi-truth."

They both laughed.

"What now?" she asked.

"I feed you. You must be starving." Trey carefully moved back against the headboard, settling himself in place, fluffed pillows and all. He moved around the bed so easily Teresa wondered if he stayed up at night practicing. She wouldn't know. She had stopped her nightly vigils on the chair a few days ago. Grateful for the respite, Teresa shook her head in amazement at Trey and what he could do, and what he could do to her. She placed the tray between them.

Trey successfully fed her pieces of the muffin, finding her mouth each time with a little help from her. In between bites, Trey found ways to place a kiss on her lips, the corners of her mouth, or her nose. Teresa couldn't tell if his kisses were misplaced or precisely intended to land where they did. Either way, they had the desired effect. She wanted Trey to go right on kissing her. She should have felt silly, not throbbing with surges of excitement. He had pulled her feelings to the surface. There was no point in hiding. She couldn't go back to pretending, even to herself, that Trey was just her patient anymore.

What he was was a man quickly healing, one she wanted to know.

"Crumb number eight. Are you full?" he asked after the last bite and a kiss that had landed on her chin.

Full of blueberries, full of kisses, full of Trey, she thought before answering, "Yes."

He was full. He was chock-full of emotion beginning with the intense pull he had for Teresa and the relief that she felt something similar for him. He wanted to see her, to touch her without wondering if his hands were moving in the right direction. He wanted to see her reaction to his kisses. The feelings that lately kept him awake at night began to rise inside him: anger with his blindness, frustration with his loss of memory, impatience with his body. So many emotions were churning inside him, he was finding it hard to focus.

"Trey, I didn't expect this."

"But I'm glad we found it," he said, meaning every word.

"What is this 'it' that we found?"

"A bond, a closeness," he said aloud. To himself he added, *A joy that pushes away the negative feelings that sometimes overwhelm me late at night.* He felt all those emotions melt away as he focused on her. "Come sit with me," he said.

"I am sitting with you."

"No, closer, come here." He motioned, wanting her as close to him as she could get. He pushed himself back against the pillows, ignoring the small twinges of pain in his ribs, opened his legs wide, and patted the space between them, silently repeating the request, hoping that she was looking at him.

Teresa watched as he maneuvered himself without much difficulty. Sitting on the bed, talking and reading as they had done these last few days was one thing. Keeping him company and sharing a meal was similarly equal. Sitting between his legs, feeling the heat of his body and the heat of his…other parts pressing against her was a completely different thing altogether.

Trey waited, not saying another word. He hoped she joined him. If she did, Trey felt that they would take the next step, whatever it was. He wanted to take the next step with her.

"Do you normally ask women you've known for barely a week to sit so intimately with you?"

"Well—" he began.

"No, don't answer that. That was a stupid question."

"Not stupid. It was a normal question to ask under normal circumstances," he answered, glad that she was still here, that she hadn't found an excuse to leave. Which meant that she wanted to sit with him. "If I were to attempt to answer that question, I'd have to say no."

"Now how can you say that, Trey? You don't have any memories."

He looked at her with a touch of sadness in his face. "True." He laughed in a self-deprecating manner. "I don't remember much of anything."

"I didn't mean to say that, Trey. I don't want to hurt your feelings."

"I understand. You're trying to protect your own feelings. You don't have to protect them from me. I'm pretty sure they're the same as mine. I was just hoping to make a new memory. With you."

As Trey waited for her to respond, he silently cursed his blindness, but only for a few seconds. He could sense every emotion coming from her. The attraction, her apprehension. Was this how he normally acted with a woman? Was this how he normally felt about a woman, any woman? Was all of this normal for him? His reaction to Teresa somehow felt out of the ordinary. He didn't know how he knew; he just knew.

"I can't sit with you."

A tremendous weight of disappointment landed in his stomach, but she instantly lifted it with her next words.

"Not like that. I'll hurt your ribs."

Trey heard her moving around the room. He wanted to see her face, her shape. His head followed the sound of her movements. She had gotten out of the bed. She was standing beside it, near him.

"I'm going to move the pillows."

Trey didn't move a muscle as he heard a rustling sound beside him. Was she putting something on? No, no, she was most likely taking something off. Damn his eyes. But no, at this moment his sight didn't matter. Teresa was coming to him. They were taking the next step. A soft, firm hand rested on his shoulder. The pillows he had placed behind him disappeared. Cool air hit his back. Slowly, Trey felt her ease behind him. One leg grazed his back as her body moved into the bed. Her breast, lightly covered, pressed against his back for an instant as she centered her body. She did take something off. The thick sweatshirt she was wearing was gone. She was close. Not exactly close the way he wanted her, but she was close.

"Can I move now?" Trey asked.

"Of course, lie back against me."

"Are you sure I won't hurt your ribs?"

"Have you forgotten? You're the one with the broken ribs," she told him, her hands reaching for his shoulders. Teresa gently pulled him against her, lightly wrapping her arms around him, releasing a sigh as heat pressed against heat. A similar sound came from Trey. They both laughed. Never having held a man in her arms like this, Teresa quickly sobered. She was in no way a tiny woman, but there was so much of him, all hard, solid, warm male. "So this is the next step."

"Yes, being with you. Being close to you. I want us to just be."

"Until the snow melts, and you leave here."

"And where would I go?"

"Nowhere perhaps, until you remember who you are and that you have a family." The license with his real name and address flickered through her mind, along with a bit of guilt. What good would it do to tell him now? Her cell phone was still not working, and there was no way off the mountain, no way even to get to Mr. Gray to see if his phone was connected. For now, she should just let it be.

"I can't live today worrying about what I might remember in the future. I want to know you now."

"In the biblical sense? That's not what I do—"

"No, at least not yet," he interrupted her to say.

"Not yet, huh?"

"What I meant to say was not until..." His shoulders lifted and the silk pajama top he wore glided against her t-shirt, giving her breast a quick, gentle stroke.

"Finish that sentence for me," Teresa said, closing her eyes as her hands moved across his fingertips.

"Not until I'm well enough to make it wonderful for you."

"Not until we're both ready."

"Not until you're ready. I'm about there now."

"What does ready mean, Trey? When or if you gain your sight? When your memories return?"

"I don't know if I'll regain my sight or my memory for that matter. I'm living for today. I'm living in the here and now, and Teresa, you are my here and now. And I'm not feeling gratitude. *Ready* is when I feel, when we both feel it's right."

"Then you're talking marriage. That's when I feel it's right."

"So, I crashed into a woman of high moral background," Trey felt a grin split his face. Knowing that she held herself in such high regard and that she must be a virgin made him feel proud. "I could deal with that."

"Trey, we're not talking marriage. We barely know each other. You barely know yourself."

"I know what I feel, but I don't think you want to hear any of that yet."

"What I know is that I shouldn't be lying in this bed with you this way." She shifted, moving her long legs as if to get out.

Trey placed a hand on her leg. "Don't go. Stay. Make a sweet memory for me. Sing me that song that I like."

Teresa paused, looking down at his sandy brown hair, the pale skin resting against her own brown skin. She remembered the reason she had first chosen this song to sing to him. It had been a test to see if it would offend him. He had passed that test, and so many others she had unconsciously given him. The reasons for them all faded as the words to the black national anthem flowed past her lips. His breathing slowed, becoming even. As his lids began to droop, Teresa wondered if Trey had a dark past. Even if he did, he was definitely full of hope for the present. He was her gift from the mountains.

CHAPTER 7

Trey's eyes popped open, and his body jerked upright. The blackness he had become accustomed to greeted him. A thought—one he could almost *see*—lingered at the corners of his brain. He concentrated on it. It was a memory. Something about him. He sensed a feeling of pride, dedication, and discipline.

"Trey?"

He felt Teresa move behind him but couldn't answer. He was almost there, a revelation was just out of his reach. If he kept his focus, he would *know* it. Suddenly a piece of it became clear. "I'm a military man," he whispered.

Trey felt both of Teresa's hands on his shoulders. She didn't say a word as he tried to force his mind to dig deeper. There were more details, more facts trying to break through. Teresa's touch was a steady comfort, the drops of sweat from his brow falling into his eyes an annoyance. Both he was aware of. One he appreciated, the other he ignored. It was the sudden, intense pain in his head that pushed it all away, making it unreachable. The tension left as quickly as it had come. Feeling his body go as limp as a dishrag, Trey allowed Teresa to pull him back into her soft embrace.

"You remembered something," she whispered in his ear. "Congratulations."

Somehow those words were the best she could have said. She didn't dwell on the obvious effort it took or the disappointment he was definitely feeling. Teresa went straight to the positive. Teresa, his Resa, was wonderful.

"Thanks for the memory."

"I had nothing to do with pulling that out of you."

"Not the old one. The one we're making right now. You are special, Resa."

"So, it's Resa. I think I like that."

"Good."

"You're a military man," she said after a long pause.

"That's what my brain told me before it decided to shut down."

"Does it hurt?" Her fingers moved to his temples.

"Yes," Trey answered, appreciating the relief the slow, circular pressure was already giving him.

"I'll get you some medicine."

"No, for now, you're all the medicine I need."

"Really?"

"Truly, Resa. Stay."

Teresa continued to massage his temples, thinking about what this small breakthrough would mean for them. Not that there actually was a "them."

She could admit that a "them" was developing, but what was it, exactly? They lay on the bed in silence as Teresa massaged his temples. He made a few deep, groaning sighs of pleasure, causing her to wonder if this was what if felt like after making love. Would there be the same lingering feeling of accomplishment… satisfaction… relief…?

A few minutes later Trey's fingers landed on her own. "Thank you, my head feels much better." He sat up, turned, and placed a peck of a kiss half across her mouth and nose. He was out of the bed and across the room before Teresa realized it.

"You *have* been practicing getting around this room."

"Every night," he stopped and turned to say. "Why do you think I take a nap in the morning? I'm exhausted from my night time ramblings."

"If you've got that much energy, I officially release you from this bed."

"Good, because I intended to work my way out of here to explore this place."

"Something a military man might feel he needs to do."

"Exactly. Now this military man needs to use the bathroom."

"Go right ahead," Teresa laughed, getting out of the bed. If Trey came back and asked her to stay she probably… Who was she kidding? She would stay if he asked. Which was why she needed to work. The problem now was that she was out of material.

Through her daily readings with Trey, she had gone through the extensive research she had brought with her. She had no access to the Internet or the outside world to dig deeper into some key facts surrounding the brave Tuskegee Airmen. She needed the complete picture before actually settling down to write the books. Which meant she had nothing to do.

Couldn't she at least get started on the books, begin a general outline? Had she just created a convenient excuse to keep her from working? she asked herself as she straightened the sheets on the bed.

No.

No, it wasn't. She was the type of person who needed all the facts before diving right in. *Then how is it that you seem to be diving right into Trey/Travis Labranch, without having all the facts on him?* she asked herself.

"Resa," Trey called as he came from the bathroom.

Her heart jumped at the sound of his voice calling her by a name no one else ever used. A surge of awareness and anticipation went straight through her. Trey was much more to her than facts, she realized. He was heart-thumping, gut-wrenching feelings.

"How about inspecting my bandaging skills?" he asked, his hands held high for her to see. "These *are* bandages, right?"

Teresa walked to where he stood in the doorway of the bathroom. Fresh white gauze was wrapped around his hands somewhat loosely, but doing the job. "Not bad. Where did you find that? I thought I used the last roll on you yesterday."

"I remembered you saying that, so, during my latest nocturnal adventure I decided to make myself useful and scrounged around for supplies."

"How? I mean—"

"The sense of touch is a wondrous thing," he said, wiggling his fingers. "Especially when you've been denied the use of such amazing tools."

Trey had had the free use of his fingers for only a day, and Teresa was indeed amazed at their skill. They helped him to find his way around and had led him to a stash of bandages she could have sworn didn't exist. They fed her and touched her with a simple gentleness that took her breath away. "I suppose it is," she told him, redirecting her thoughts. "Come here and let me re-bandage your hands."

"Do they look that bad?"

"Not bad at all. But there's this thick clear ointment—"

"That I didn't put on before the bandages."

"Yes."

Teresa went to get the ointment she had left on the dresser the day before.

"So that's how you knew I didn't put any on. The ointment was in there the whole time."

"And how did you know that?"

"Didn't you just pick it up? I heard it scrape against something. And you only moved four steps to get to it. It's exactly ten steps from the bathroom to the bed and you went in the opposite direction."

"Which is proof positive that you're adjusting to using your other senses," Teresa commented as she led him to the edge of the bed to sit.

"I am adjusting." He sobered, adding, "I'm also hoping to regain my sight. Tell me the truth, Teresa. Do you still think that's a possibility?"

"I don't want to give you false hope. I'm not a doctor, but from my experience as a nurse, I wouldn't rule it out. We'll have to get you to a hospital as soon as the snow melts so that a doctor can give you a more definite answer."

He nodded and sat quietly as she rubbed ointment onto his hands. Teresa noted how much they had improved in the last few days. His skin was no longer moist and seeping. With the aid of the ointment, his body was healing itself nicely. He must have been in excellent health before the crash. She wrapped his hands once again and held them between her own.

"Last night I was thinking," Trey said a moment later.

"I guess that means you do more than wander around at night."

"It's a long night with no company, more than enough to cause a man to think."

"What if I had kept you company?" Teresa asked without thinking.

"I would have been thinking *and* acting."

"Let's go back to what you were saying about thinking," Teresa redirected, unwilling to finish what she had started.

"If you insist." He let out a huge breath before going on. "Anyway, lying in this big bed, I found myself praying to God. I realized not long after I first woke up that I do believe."

"That's good."

"Well, I prayed. I prayed for everything under the sun. I started to have this deep conversation with God and found myself making all kinds of promises, mostly bargaining for my sight and memory to return.

"It doesn't usually work that way."

"I realized that, and then it occurred to me that I might regain one and not the other. God might decide that one was enough to gift me with. I thought about that, projecting what my life would be like without one or the other. I weighed the pros and cons. Life without my memory versus life without my sight. And you know what I decided?"

"No, what did you decide?"

"If I had a choice, I would have to choose to have my sight back."

"Why is that?" Teresa asked, once again amazed at the practical and calm manner in which he had been analyzing his life, his future. He should be angry, upset, and frustrated.

"There's a ton of reasons, the main one being you."

"Me?"

"Yes, you, Resa. I want to see you. Forget the memories. I can always make new ones. Hopefully, a few with you."

The idea wasn't as strange as it should have been. Teresa herself found that making memories with Trey was something she wanted to do, more than anything else she could think of at the moment.

"Seeing your face when you sing or smile or when your arms are folded as you tell me what I can or can't do. Being able to watch you when you're deep into your reading or just after my lips have had a taste of your own. I want that. I want that more than the knowledge of who I am. I can learn that again," he said aloud, silently adding, *because, I have a feeling that I am so much more with you.*

"I can understand why you would say that," Teresa told him, not because she didn't know what else to say, which was true, but because she truly did understand why regaining his sight was so important to him. She had the advantage of seeing his expressions. The raw emotion that showed on his face was so honest. Oh, she was falling harder for this man. Way too hard and much too fast. "Let's not stress about any of it now. Time will tell, and I'm sure that you'll have the strength to deal with whatever life has in store." Teresa had no doubt of that. Trey was a strong man who would use his head to direct and guide him. He would be able to accept his fate, whatever it would be. "Come with me."

Teresa led him into the spacious den. Angelfruit perked up from her resting place before the banked fire, bounding toward them when she saw Trey. "Calm down you crazy dog. Careful or you'll knock Trey down."

Of course, the words had no effect on the excited dog as she jumped around them bumping them both, her huge paws knocking Trey in the chest. Teresa somehow grabbed hold of him. They landed on the rustic sofa instead of the floor. Angelfruit joined them on the sofa until Trey firmly commanded her off.

"The military man image definitely fits," Teresa commented, shifting herself so that she wasn't lying directly beneath him. "Did she hurt you? Those ribs of yours aren't a hundred percent healed yet."

Trey let out a huge breath, leaning his entire upper body against her. "I'm fine. She didn't do any damage." He called the dog over and gave her a firm talking to. When he was done, Angelfruit settled her face in his lap. His hand scratched her behind the ears.

"You're a softy."

"No, I'm fair. I laid down the law, made sure she understood the command, and ended by praising her. Now she'll follow orders."

"Military all the way."

"Air Force, Navy, Marine, I don't know which, but one of them has got to be right. I just wish I knew more."

"Don't try to push too hard," Teresa advised, finding her hand straying to his hair, which was growing longer. The buzz cut he'd had when she found him confirmed his background. "Forcing what your mind's not ready to release can make matters worse."

"I'll try not to. Something like that could push me into an even longer recuperation period. You'd be stuck with me a whole lot longer than you anticipated."

Teresa smiled, liking the idea way too much. Eventually the snow would let them off the mountain and she would have to see about getting him to a doctor, which would mean bringing him in under his real name. But Travis Labranch seemed so wrong. She shook her head, erasing the name from her brain.

"Speaking of military men, you were telling me some interesting facts about a group of African-American military pilots trained to fight in WW II."

"The Tuskegee Airmen?"

"That's them. They were trained at the Tuskegee Institute founded by Booker T. Washington, right?"

"You've been paying attention."

"And why wouldn't I? This stuff fascinates me almost as much as you do."

Teresa had no answer to Trey's comment. She was becoming accustomed to hearing him express his feelings for her in an almost matter-of-fact way, as if he were totally sure about what he felt for her and had no problem voicing it. Could he really have such deep feelings for her? Weren't her own deepening? Honestly, yes.

"Tell me more about the airmen," Trey said. I'm guessing, but I think I'm a history buff. Don't you think it's important to know and understand where you came from? It's especially critical when your memory's not what it should be."

Knowing how well Trey read her, Teresa tried to hold in her surprise. How ironic it was that the history he sought was of a people he might hate. She briefly wondered if she should tell him that he was white. She pushed the thought aside. Black history was everyone's history. If he enjoyed it, she would share it with him.

"Move over, Angelfruit. Let Resa get her books."

"But I've already read you everything I had on the Tuskegee Airmen."

"How about something else? Poetry. What about those poems you read by Langston Hughes?"

Teresa found her book of poetry. They read and discussed the meaning behind the poems "Mother to Son" and "Dreams" before settling into a short story about a young black woman in a predominately white homestead town in the western part of the United States.

"That was a sad story," he said when she finished. "She should have been free go away with her boyfriend, get married, and raise a family."

"Technically, she had a family."

"The people she worked for? That's not the same. She was their maid, a black person who worked for them, someone they liked, not true family."

"Their daughter was like her own."

"A replacement for the one she lost."

"She still loved the daughter, and they all cared about her." Teresa found herself defending the white family.

"That's not the same as having a family of your own with the person you choose to be with. She was denied that by society's closed-mindedness. Race should not have been an issue"

"You're right," Teresa nodded. She'd never had such a conversation before with a person who wasn't of her own race. She found it to be refreshing. The injustices he referred to reflected an unfairness, the denial of a basic human right to love and be loved.

They fell into a silence that lasted until Angelfruit insisted on going outside.

"I'd better let her go out to do her business."

"How is it out there?" Trey asked, reluctantly standing. He had enjoyed leaning against her, feeling Resa's warmth beneath him. He reached out a hand for Teresa, and she took it. He silently gritted at the pain in his ribs but the feel of her hand in his own made it worthwhile. "Take me there."

"Angelfruit might if we don't get to the door fast enough."

Trey followed Teresa, his free hand trailing along the sofa, finding a table standing as high as his hip. His hand hung in the air until it connected with what felt like a bunch of smooth branches. Further investigation indicated that it was freestanding piece of furniture, perhaps a hall tree of some sort. Seconds later, he heard a knob turning and then a frigid wind rushed over him, providing a clue as to what it was like "out there." "It's freezing!"

"Which would explain why the snow hasn't even begun to think about melting."

"Still, it's refreshing. Why don't we go out and chop up a chunk of that stubborn snow."

"And do what with it?"

"Have a snowball fight."

"A snow brick fight would be the more appropriate term," she said as Angel barked and the door slammed, cutting off the chilling wind. "You're not going out there to catch a cold or get pneumonia after I've gotten you back on your feet."

"This would be a perfect time to use my feet," Trey told her, doing a strange little side step. He released her hand and reached for the door he knew had to be only a few feet away.

"Don't even think about it."

"Then give me a distraction." His hand searched for and found the doorknob in a phony attempt to get by her. "Create another memory with me."

"What exactly are you angling for?"

"A powerful memory." He shrugged his shoulders as if he were asking for the simplest thing in the world.

"I heard once," Teresa folded her arms and leaned against the door, "that the most powerful memories were those connected with strong feelings. Fear, happiness, intense pleasure."

"Intense pleasure, that sounds like a winner. Distract me with a few intense, pleasurable feelings, Resa."

She didn't say a word. Trey waited a second, then two, wondering if she would follow his suggestion. Just as he resigned himself to accepting that he was asking for too much, a hand landed on his shoulder, so softly Trey wondered if he were imagining it there, until the other followed. Damn his eyes! This was one of those moments when he would give his life to see her. Her fingers trailed a path down one of his arms, her touch already stirring a few intense feelings inside him. Trey didn't move. She had initiated this. Well, almost. He had suggested it, but Resa was touching him on her own. That thought shot another intense feeling right between his legs.

Resa's fingers reached the hand still gripped around that branch-like thing he didn't realize he was still holding. She slowly peeled one finger at a time away from the object, holding his hand within her own as if it were some sort of prize. Trey didn't move his fingers. He forced himself not to squeeze them, not to use them to crawl up her arm and pull her toward him. This was hers, all hers, to give and direct. He felt her fingers on his other hand, which she carefully freed from the doorknob he had found earlier. She held his wrapped hands for a moment, turned them over in her palms, then slowly lifted them. She placed both of his palms on her face. Her palms remained on the outside of his hands briefly before dropping to his shoulders. She was allowing him to know her better. He couldn't see her but she was making it possible for him to *see* her. Trey didn't move for a few moments, savoring the warm chills going through him. His fingers leisurely moved across her face, discovering the shape of her eyes, her cheeks, the bridge of her nose, every feature. Her full lips he traced slowly, lingering on the journey. She was beautiful. But he already knew that. His hands moved down, resting on her shoulders. He waited.

And then…

And then Teresa took his mouth. It was no small press of a kiss given and drawn away. Teresa took his mouth, his tongue, seriously intending to sear a memory into both their brains as her hot breath mixed with his, her tongue gliding across his like a plane moving through the sky. He felt free, as if he were flying through the clear blue sky with Resa by his side. She pulled away slowly, deliberately, and rested her head on his shoulder. He felt as if they had both landed in a safe, solid place.

"Resa," he said, holding her tight, feeling a sense contentment deep inside him spread until his entire body was one huge relaxed blob of happiness. He held her to him, knowing that at this moment, not being able to see her was not as important as feeling her in his arms. His mind relaxed, along with his body. He was immersed in the joy he found in her arms. Then pictures: a flash of blue sky and white clouds, the interior of a plane, a landing. His body tensed.

Teresa lifted her head from his shoulder. "What's wrong?"

He heard her voice and understood the question, just as he missed the heat of her body that had been pressed against him before he pulled away from her. He was suddenly cold. Despite that, his forehead broke out in a sweat when he realized what the images in his mind were.

"Trey?"

"M-mm?"

"Something happened just now, didn't it?"

Trey nodded, then took a step back, his arms moving in excitement as he tried to explain. "It was you. Holding you, kissing you. It felt so good, so wonderful. My mind and body just relaxed into you, and it came!"

"It came."

"A memory came. While I was making a memory, an old one came back!" Teresa was thrilled for him and watched as he moved around as if he were bursting with energy. "Tell me about it," she said, grabbing one hand in an attempt to calm him down before he rammed into something.

"They were flashes actually, like pictures in my mind. Pictures, ha! I'm blind, but I saw pictures or felt them or something like that." He walked two steps one way and two the other.

"About?" Teresa asked, trying once again to get a hold of some part of his body.

"Flying! Me! I saw myself flying. Not my face, I mean, but the controls, and I understood everything I saw. The sky was beautiful with fluffy white clouds. I felt free and on top of the world. Just like when you kissed me. You brought it back for me. Thank you, Resa." He turned, arms outstretched, moving in the wrong direction.

"Trey," she called just as he let out a loud groan.

"I know this isn't you all bony and hard. Is it some kind of weird coat tree?" he asked, running his hands over it.

"Right, one made with deer antlers."

"Come save me." The antlers had snagged his bandages and he pulled, unable to get free.

Teresa rescued him, allowing him a perfect excuse to thank her. Trey paused and got his bearings before wrapping his arms around her. "Resa, you are wonderful. Do you mind if I imprint a memory for you."

"I don't mind at all," Teresa answered, feeling curious and excited, happy and leery. All revolved around Trey or Travis Labranch. If he was beginning to remember, then he would remember who he really was, which person he was…

And then she forgot it all, feeling only surges and need as Trey held her for a full minute before using those amazing fingers of his to find and trace her lips and then imprint a kiss that told her who he was: a man she was falling in love with.

CHAPTER 8

The memories would come at odd times. When he was quiet and still, when he was wandering around the cabin at night, as he listened to Teresa read, or like now, just as he woke up. Bits and pieces of who he was had begun to fall into place this last week.

He didn't have a complete picture of the man he was. He didn't even have a full name. Trey didn't know what his family name was or if he had a family.

Family.

That was a piece he'd remembered today or almost remembered. There were no faces or images, only feelings, which seemed to revolve around the man Trey assumed was his father. In his memory he'd seen pride and a respect in the man's face suddenly shift into shame and disgust. With whom or what?

Was his father ashamed of him? Was he ashamed of his father?

Trey lay absolutely still on the bed, willing the memory to return. Angelfruit's paws sliding on the hardwood floors did nothing to distract him. Her bark and bid for attention as she partially leaned on the bed to lick his hand did nothing to pull Trey away from his determined goal. He vaguely heard the dog whimper as she scurried away.

There was something important, some key fact about his relationship with his father that would make it all clear. He was almost there. It was something he knew, but it lay hidden so deep inside that he couldn't pull it out.

It was important. Trey had to get it out; he had to know what it was.

Long agonizing moments of concentration produced nothing more than a steady pounding in his head. Trey allowed the blankness to cover him. The sweat that had poured out of him began to dry on his forehead. He felt nothing beyond that until...

"Tell me about it," Resa said as a cool towel rested on his forehead.

Trey swallowed. "This remembering thing is harder than I thought it would be."

"I noticed."

He said nothing else for a long time, savoring Resa's presence and the coolness of the towel on his forehead. "My dad, I remembered him," Trey finally said.

"And?"

"I felt this tremendous outpouring of respect and love that I had for him, that he had for me. It was mutual."

"That's good."

"Not so good. It turned into a horrible feeling of disappointment and disgust."

"Go on," Teresa urged when he didn't say more.

"We must have had a falling out. It must have been terrible. I felt something close to..." Trey paused, trying to put the feeling into words. "Rage," he said, "bordering on hatred. How can that be, Resa, after feeling so much admiration?"

"In a way, it makes sense." The towel left his forehead.

"No, it doesn't. Why should my feeling for him have changed? Was it something he did? Was it something I did?" He sat up, his hand reaching wildly for hers until she connected with him. "How could respect turn to disgust?"

"It's possible, Trey."

"How?"

"When someone loves greatly, the opposite can occur."

"Do you think I hate my dad?"

"What do you think?"

Trey was stumped. She had thrown the question right back at him. She said nothing while he mulled it over. She gave his hand a squeeze and waited some more. "I think I respect and love him, but something divided us."

"And that's more than you knew before last night."

"You're right, but what happened?"

"I suppose that's to know another day."

"That's easy for you to say."

"No, no, it's not Trey." Her hand left his, and a moment later he felt the warmth of her hands on his face. Her soft lips grazed his own before saying, "It's not easy watching you struggle."

"Oh," was his only reply. Was he being selfish? He had been so focused on his reactions to his memories that he had not considered how all of it might be affecting her.

"I admire your strength," she was saying to him. "You have handled yourself very well."

"I'm barely muddling through all this."

"You're doing a bit more than that. How about muddling out of this bed? I've got a surprise for you."

"That sounds like an incentive." Trey felt her shift to stand. "Wait." He grabbed her wrist.

"What is it?"

"Thank you."

"For what?"

"For being Resa. More importantly, for being on this mountain to save me." He leaned forward and aimed for her lips but landed on her chin, making his way up until he found his prize. His kiss was more than a grazing of lips, but he didn't take it any deeper than a gentle caress. "I love finding your lips," he said, leaning back.

"You do?"

"Yeah, when I miss, it gives me a chance to taste other parts of you. I guess I could consider that an advantage of being blind."

"I suppose that could be considered an advantage."

"A definite advantage," he told her, realizing the pounding in his head had disappeared. "You help make it all better."

"If you get out this bed, we can discover something else that might make things all better."

"Give me five minutes."

Teresa went into the closet and found a heavy jacket that had to belong to Dr. Ramsey and threw it on the sofa in the den. Going into the kitchen, she poured two mugs of hot cocoa, adding marshmallows to each. Before she could turn around, Teresa heard Trey walk into the room, causing Angelfruit to jump up, and bark a loud greeting as she circled.

"What's the surprise?" he asked, giving the dog a scratch behind the ear.

Walking across the room, she grabbed the jacket. "You'll have to put this on first." She guided one arm through a sleeve, then the other.

"This *is* a surprise. You mean I get to go outdoors? I'm no longer at risk of catching a cold or," he paused dramatically, "pneumonia?"

"No, and you'll see why." Teresa shoved a pair of large leather mittens onto his hands.

"The bandages are gone only to be replaced with mittens," he commented as she hooked an arm around his to guide him outside.

Teresa smiled at that. She had removed the bandages from his hands two days ago. They were almost perfectly healed and had minimal evidence of scarring. Opening the front door of the cabin, Teresa led Trey onto the porch. Angelfruit dashed out ahead of them, barking and running toward the back of the cabin. "What do you feel?"

He said nothing at first. Teresa felt his upper body rise and expand as he pulled in a deep breath. He turned in the direction she knew he'd face. His expression changed as he took it all in. "The sun."

"Yes, the sun. It's back, a little weak, but making itself known just the same." Teresa guided him to one of the huge rocking chairs on the porch. "Be right back," She dashed inside to grab the mugs of cocoa. She put her mug on the railing and placed the other between Trey's mittened palms before settling into the rocking chair next to him.

"I feel honored."

"That the sun decided to make an appearance? Don't feel too special too soon. It'll have to shine a whole lot brighter if the snow's ever going to melt."

"The sun had nothing to do with this. I feel honored that you've invited me to share in your morning ritual."

"My ritual?"

"Yes, don't you drink a mug of cocoa on the porch every morning?"

"Yes."

"Isn't that your special time alone?"

"If you call having a nervous dog checking on me every five minutes alone, then yes."

"Then I feel honored that you're sharing this time with me."

"Don't give it another thought," Teresa said, truly hoping that he wouldn't. He was extremely intuitive and seemed to understand the meaning behind almost everything she did. He didn't respond, simply turned his eyes in her direction in that way of his which seemed to look straight through her without even being able to see her. He took a slow sip from his mug and turned his face to the sun once more.

Teresa sighed, relieved that he hadn't said more. This *was* her alone time, but she had thought about sharing it with him on more than one occasion. And she knew exactly why. She was finding that she wanted to share a multitude of things with Trey. But how could she expect to even consider sharing any more than what they would have on this mountain when his entire life and future was a huge question mark?

"What are you thinking?" Trey asked.

"About the future," she answered, not even considering avoiding the question. What good would it do? He had to be thinking about the future.

"The soon-to-be-melted snow future? Your future research? Your future books?"

"No."

"What then?" he asked.

She gave him a sideways glance, knowing from the expression on his face that he knew what she was thinking. "You."

"Me, my future?" he asked.

"Us."

"Ah, us. Then our future." He nodded. "I believe I've been having some similar thoughts."

"Which means?" She stood and turned away from him toward the mountains to ask, wanting to know his answer, but leery of hearing it just the same.

"We'll build it as we go."

Placing the mug on the rail, Teresa spun around to ask, "Build what, Trey? A relationship, a life together?" she whispered, sinking to her knees before him.

"A foundation. Anything good needs a foundation," he leaned into her to say. "I know that," he whispered. "Not just as a piece of something I learned. A foundation means something important to me. Why is it important, Resa?"

Teresa took the mug from between his palms and placed it on the wooden porch. She leaned her forehead against his. "I don't know why because you don't know why. Which is exactly the reason I'm not so sure that there should be an us. You have so many cracks in your foundation, Trey."

"Not cracks." He pulled back, cold air immediately replacing the warmth of their shared breath. "Holes that can be filled." He laid his mittened palms over her hands, which were resting on his thighs. A second later, he used his teeth to pull the mittens off. Slowly, he moved closer. Teresa stilled, knowing that he was going to kiss her, wondering where his lips would land. Her nose received a soft peck, then a rub with his own just before he found her lips in a lopsided kiss that straightened and deepened. His tongue caressed hers, his lips lingering one second, then two, everlasting moments that surged through her, turning her desires into a solid substance that could fill any hole. He kissed her once more, his lips moving upward to land on the bridge of her nose before saying, "Holes can't stop us from building a brand-new foundation. Together we can fill them with what we have."

Teresa stood, needing to be away from Trey and all the surges which were beginning to make her believe that it was all that easy. She took a couple of steps backwards.

"Resa," he called, his head turned in her direction.

"It's not as simple as all that." Teresa took another step back, the rail stopping her from taking yet another. "What if you're involved in some secret job or undercover mission for the military?" She folded her arms as she waited for a response.

"What if I'm not?" was all he said, his face as intent and serious as when he had just kissed multiple surges through her.

"What if you're involved with someone else?" She stared at him, waiting for his expression to change, sure that he hadn't thought about that.

"What if I'm not," he said again.

"But you could be!" Teresa shouted, closing that distance she had created between them a few seconds ago. "You could even be married. What if you're married?"

One second Teresa was standing in front of him, the next she found herself sitting in his lap. "What if I'm not?" he whispered someplace close to her ear, his warm breath flowing across her skin, an instant surge starter. This way he had of nearly finding her body parts was more arousing, she was sure, than if he actually found the part he had been aiming for.

Breathing hard from surprise, then deep and long because she was where she wanted to be, Teresa stopped herself from pulling in just one more deep breath and said into his neck, "It can't be that simple. You can't ignore that possibility. You can't ignore your past."

"And I can't ignore what I feel for you, here and now. What good would it do to pretend that I don't care for you, that you don't care for me?"

"Because getting involved with you could mean that I could be hurting someone else." Teresa pushed away from him and stood. "I shouldn't be sitting on your lap. Your ribs are still healing."

"There could be no one else to hurt."

"Until I know that for sure, we can only be—"

"Don't say friends."

Teresa paused, not knowing how else to describe their relationship.

"For now, we're a potential item," Trey announced.

"An item?"

Trey stood, nodding. "A hot item. A future item. An item full of so much potential all aspects will have to be itemized and categorized."

Teresa laughed, exactly what Trey wanted her to do. Despite the laughter, she was serious and had to let him know that. "But for now, a cool item." Teresa wrapped an arm around his waist to guide him back into the house.

"For now," he agreed, allowing her to lead. "Ow!" he yelled a second later.

"Sorry." Teresa snickered, trying to hold back a laugh as she watched Trey fight with the coat rack again. The scene released the tension she felt from their very serious conversation.

"Teresa, aren't you supposed to guide me away from potential hazards?"

"Yes, it's just that I turned my head to call Angelfruit back into the house, and didn't realize I walked you into—"

"—the antlers from hell," he finished, unhooking his sleeve and batting at the coat rack. "Not a problem. I can adjust." He pulled himself closer to her, making a sideways shuffling motion away from the offending object.

"It's safe, Trey. It won't attack you again."

"Good, now give me some room. I've been practicing finding my way around these last couple of nights. I'll wash up, and then I'll help you make breakfast."

"You will?"

"If I have any hopes for our status of potential item evolving into hot item, I need to investigate what other potential talents I might have."

"Cooking?"

"Cracking eggs to be exact. I've got a feeling that I can make a mean omelet, but I'm willing to start off slow. Meet you in the kitchen in a few minutes."

Teresa pulled off her jacket, watching Trey make his way across the room, noting his confident steps. Not once did he look as if he didn't know where he was going. At the door of the bedroom, he pulled off the jacket and slung it across his shoulder, a perfect picture of a male model. Teresa laughed out loud.

"Something funny?" he asked without turning.

"Just you."

"Wait till you see my next performance."

"I can hardly wait," she told him, going into the kitchen to wash her hands and pull out the eggs, ham, and cheese for the omelets they would have for breakfast.

And a performance it was. Trey managed to crack the eggs with one hand, landing them all in the bowl, along with a few bits of shell that she extracted as best as she could, but obviously not completely since they both discovered a few in their omelets.

They laughed, throwing most of the omelets away, and resorted to toast and jam as a substitute. The laughter was a substitute for the kisses she knew they'd be sharing if there wasn't so much unknown between them.

"So much unknown," Teresa whispered to herself. There was one thing she knew and should have shared by now.

"Did you say something?" Trey asked.

"No, just talking to myself."

"That was some delicious toast."

"Glad you liked it. It came from a recipe handed down from generation to generation," she joked.

"I wouldn't have one of those, but I could probably track one down if I knew my family name," he laughed.

Teresa wondered if he laughed to keep himself from breaking down into despair. Not remembering had to affect him more than he let on.

"What's your family name, Resa?" he asked.

"Lewis."

"Lewis. Do you like it?"

"It's a name," she answered, not sure about the direction he was going.

"Well, I'm sure I've got one, and I'm sure it'll come back to me in time. After all, I remembered my father. Not his name, but you've got to start somewhere."

This was the moment, Teresa knew, that she had to tell him at least that much about himself. Somehow before, it hadn't seemed important. Not as important as his getting well, and now that he was well, and was remembering and needing to know, then maybe by telling him he would remember who he was and…"Your family name is Labranch."

"Pardon me?" he asked, his hand braced against the sturdy wooden table where they had eaten breakfast.

"Your last name is Labranch."

He was silent for a long painful, moment, his face serious and emotionless. "It sounds right. It feels right. How do you know this?"

"I saw it on your driver's license."

"My driver's license?"

"It was in your wallet."

"My wallet?"

"I found it in your pants, along with a few other things, including a phone number that I called before my cell phone went out. But it turned out to be a pay phone. Then there was some money, a card…" Teresa trailed off.

"Why didn't you tell me this before?" His expression turned from serious to chillingly cold.

"It never seemed to be the right moment. I mean, I was more concerned about you getting well, and after you decided that your name was Trey, well, things just went on that way."

"Things just went on that way until you finally decided to let me in on some important information about myself?" His fists hit the table. "I have been racking my brains trying to remember my family, and you had a name all along. Labranch." His chin fell into his chest after whispering the name, only to bounce up as he said, "Travis Labranch Sr. is my father's name. And I'm…"

"Travis Labranch, Jr. I'm sorry, Trey. You didn't seem like the man in the driver's license picture. He had a stern, hard look. To me, you're Trey."

"But I'm not." He stood. "And at this moment I feel pretty hard and stern. I need to think. You were right before, Resa. The past *is* coming between us."

"You're angry with me."

"Yes, and disappointed. I thought I knew you, but I really don't know you. And you can't really know me. I don't know myself."

"That's not true, Trey."

"Teresa, you can't have it both ways. How can you know me without knowing my past?" He turned and made his way back toward the bedroom, bumping into a small side table. "I knew that was there," he whispered loud enough for her to hear.

She couldn't let him walk away like this. He had been so positive about his problem and her stupid decision to keep his name from him had completely changed his outlook on the entire situation. "Trey!" she called out to him.

"It's Travis. Travis Labranch Jr," he answered without looking back.

CHAPTER 9

Trey was sulking, and he knew it. But he felt that he deserved a good sulk.

He was blind.

His memory had so many buckshot holes his brain might as well be Swiss cheese.

The beautiful woman he was crazy about had refused to simply let things happen between them and worst of all, had lied to him.

Not exactly lied, but had kept some very important information from him. And since then, he hadn't remembered a speck from his past. Though he had become accustomed to bits of ideas and facts surfacing to his consciousness at odd times throughout the day, for the last twenty-four hours, his brain had shut down.

Shutting himself in his bedroom and refusing to talk to Teresa hadn't done much to ease his mind into letting go of pertinent information. He had barely slept. And now he found himself tired of his own thoughts and his own company. Trey sat up, deciding that sulking wasn't in his nature.

He needed to talk to Teresa.

Hearing her move around in the kitchen, he went first to use the bathroom, hoping to join her on the porch and talk this thing out with her in order to find out why had she kept his name from him. For someone so worried about his past, why had she kept that simple fact from him? It didn't make sense.

Coming out of the bathroom and using his hands to scan the furniture, Trey found the jacket Resa had given to him to wear yesterday and made his way to the front door, successfully avoiding the coat rack. "Teresa," he called as he pushed opened the screen. He got no answer and called her again as he stepped out onto the porch. When nothing but complete silence greeted him, Trey realized she wasn't there. He knew she wouldn't be so cruel as to not answer and there was no way Angelfruit would have held back from bounding into him. But where could she have gone? The snow was still an obstacle. At least, that was what he assumed. She couldn't have gone far and would be back soon, he was sure.

He went back inside, deciding that getting some sleep might help to put him in a better frame of mind to talk to her. After lying in the middle of the bed for a good ten minutes with no hope of sleeping, Trey opened his eyes, then quickly closed them again in shocked surprise.

An image.

He had seen something.

Or had he? In his memories, he had seen images. Maybe he was remembering again. Maybe he had fallen asleep and didn't realize it.

He opened his eyes again and kept them open for a full minute. A fuzzy light, that was what it looked like. Trey stared at it a long, long time, praying that he wasn't imagining or dreaming it. He poked himself in his still sore ribs and groaned. He was awake. Closing his eyes again, Trey formulated an experiment to see if he was actually *seeing*. He turned his head to the right and counting to five, opened his eyes toward the large chair he knew should be there. A vague shape appeared, some parts darker than others. It was like looking through the lens of an unfocused camera. Trey got out of bed and moved toward the chair, stretching his arms to touch it. He saw movement. When he waved his hands in front of him, undefined shapes sped across his vision. Those undefined shapes had to be his fingers!

He could see. Not perfectly, but he was going to get his sight back.

"I can see!" he yelled into the empty room. He spun around once and laughed out loud. "I can see!" he repeated, waving his hands in front of his face. He walked to a large, blurry object he knew had to be the dresser and stood over it. Noticing the many fuzzy shapes, he reached for one, picked it up, and placed it back. "Don't know what that was," he told the empty room, "but I *saw* it with my own eyes, picked it up, and *watched* as I put it back exactly where I found it."

Resa! He had to find her. He had to tell her the good news. Trey walked through the den without the deliberate, careful steps he usually took and out the front door, avoiding contact with the dark objects he could now see.

"Resa!" he yelled, walking across the porch until his hands caught and held the railing. Hearing no answer, he yelled again, loud enough to cause an avalanche and not caring much if he did because that would mean that they would be stuck even longer on this mountain, giving him extra time to spend actually looking at Resa.

"Resa!" he yelled again. A loud bark answered his call, and the sight, the actual sight of a hazy Resa, held him immobilized. She was coming to him. His heart jumped.

"What's wrong? What is it?" he heard her say as she stomped toward him, the crunch of boots on snow reaching his ears. The dog beat her by a few seconds.

"What is it?" she asked again when she reached him. She was all over him, checking his forehead, his pulse, his hands. "Why are you yelling?"

Trey grabbed and held onto her flying hands. "I'm yelling because—" he paused, his hands releasing her and reaching up toward the blurry outline that he knew to be her face. Placing both hands against her cheeks, he peered into her face, and even without the sharp clarity he hoped would come later, she was a beautiful sight. He swallowed. "Resa, I'm yelling because I can see," he urgently whispered.

"You can?" she gasped and pulled him into a tight bone-crushing embrace. She pulled back to look at him, then hugged him again. "That's simply wonderful, Tr—"

"Trey," he finished for her. "Sitting alone in my room and feeling sorry for myself, I realized that whatever name I was born with, I'll always be your Trey."

"Are you sure?"

"I'm sure. I don't know why you didn't tell me my real name. You can explain that to me after you forgive me for losing my temper."

"There's nothing to forgive. You had a right to be angry."

"Maybe, but no right to make us both miserable for a whole day."

"But not anymore. We're ecstatic because you can see. How many fingers am I holding up?"

Trey stared at the blob that must have been her fingers but shook his head. "I can see, but not that well. Everything's blurry shapes and movement."

"I'm sure it'll get better. Come inside. You must be freezing. Where's your jacket?" she asked, hooking an arm into his and leading him inside.

"I sort of forgot it in all the excitement."

"Are you hungry?"

"No, just lonely. I wanted to talk to you. Where did you go?"

"For a walk, just to see how far I could go up the path."

"So soon? You need to be careful, you could fall off the mountain."

"I had Angelfruit with me."

"Correction, then you'd trip off the mountain right over her back while she barked an 'I'm sorry' behind you."

Teresa laughed as she pulled the jacket off her shoulders.

"Come lie with me," Trey whispered.

"Sure," she told him, pulling him toward the spacious sofa where they'd spent many long hours. Pushing her body to one corner, she sat with one leg on the floor, the other stretched along the back of the sofa before guiding him down between her legs.

Trey leaned into her, wishing he could wrap his arms around her and hold her between his legs, but this would do for now. After all, ribs did eventually heal. Simply being with her after twenty-four long hours and being able to see the outline of her hand resting on his chest was enough. Feeling content and relaxed, Trey knew that staying awake to talk was an impossibility.

"Trey?" he heard her say.

"We'll talk after we rest a bit. You were out in the snow, you have to be tired. I'm tired. Let's talk in a bit. Okay?"

"Okay," she answered without a qualm.

Awaking sometime later, Trey opened his eyes, his sleepy gaze landing on Resa's hand still lying across his chest. In the haze of someone who hadn't got enough sleep, he raised her hand to his lips, absently noting the long, slender, brown fingers. The warmth and comfort he felt didn't allow him to think beyond her.

Resa.

He slowly sat up to simply to look at her. And as he looked, a thought blew across his cloudy brain. Resa had to be uncomfortable the way she was half-sitting, half-lying on the sofa. Trey stood, pulled her legs onto the sofa and gently scooted her over, placing himself into the corner of the sofa. Elevating his legs on the coffee table, he guided Teresa's head to his lap. Satisfied, he once again fell into a sound sleep.

Abruptly, his eyes opened. Trey didn't know how long he had slept. He blinked and waited for his eyes to focus. Clear across the room he spotted a mug, fuzzy around the edges, but still a mug, sitting on a hazy-looking table in the middle of what couldn't be anything other than the kitchen. He scanned the room from his viewpoint on the sofa, taking in the pots that hung from the ceiling, the huge stove, a sink area. If he could pick out the outline of a mug and cooking utensils, he thought, why was he wasting his time looking at them?

Trey looked down. Finally, his eyes had landed on the sight they were meant to view. He had said so often that she was beautiful, but as he watched her sleep, her head resting on his lap, her face turned toward him, he realized that she was more than that.

She was gorgeous.

No—gorgeously beautiful, if there was such a thing.

And he took in her every feature. Her eyebrows were full, yet not too thick, just perfect, framing her eyes at just the right angle. He bet that her eyes were dark, a deep, dark brown, soft and smooth, like her skin. Not being able to help himself, he touched her cheek. She had a heart-shaped face. With his index finger, he pushed a path into the short, tight curls of her hair, captured a curl and twisted the soft, coarse strand around his finger. The bouncy curls fit her face perfectly. When a picture of long hair and pale skin flashed through his mind, Trey shook it out, not knowing where it came from, preferring the perfect picture lying before him. His eyes drifted to her full lips. They were parted and waiting for his own.

He leaned forward, ignoring the sharp protest in his side, to lay a kiss on her lips. It was an I'm-in-awe-of-your-beauty kiss that woke her. And she responded, her arms wrapping themselves around his neck as she pulled herself closer.

"I have no idea how we changed positions, but I like it," she whispered, looking up at him.

"Me too," he said, intently staring down at her. "And you know what else I like?"

"No, tell me."

"Your deep, brown eyes, your silky, smooth skin, your lips." He kissed her again. "Your luscious lips."

"You sound like a character in a corny romance movie."

"That's because I've got some romance cooking inside my head."

"You do?"

"Yes, I do, but only because I'm falling for you."

"And because you can see."

"Because I can now see your lips—and various other parts I want to sample. I can read the expression on your face and in your eyes. Romancing is definitely on my mind." Holding her gaze, he questioned, "How shall I begin?" He paused as if in deep thought. "Drinking in the sight of you is a good start. I could then describe every detail these eyes of mine are lucky enough to take in."

"Poetic and romantic."

Trey shrugged. "I'm saying it like I see it."

"It's good to know that you like what you see," Teresa told him, a part of her relaxing, a very tense part. She felt the instant relief in her shoulders and neck, and in her spirit. She felt free. Could she still have had that much anxiety about Trey and how he would react to her once he could see, even despite the evidence that he couldn't be a racist? It would explain why she had been so careful about developing a deeper relationship with him. But now, now all Teresa wanted to do was sit like this with him for hours, listening to every corny, romantic word that came out of his mouth.

"I do like what I see." His eyes scanned her from head to foot. "I adore what I see. As a matter of fact, this is the best place my eyes could have landed."

"I'm all you've been looking at!"

"Not true. I spotted a mug on the table in the kitchen. Didn't keep my interest at all." A loud rumbling came from his stomach before he could say more.

"Hungry?" she asked, knowing food would get him focused on something else. And as much as she was enjoying this moment, there were a few something elses they needed to discuss.

"Hungry, definitely hungry. Do you know what I want right now?"

"Food?"

"You. I've suddenly got hungry eyes. I want to see all of you."

Trey's eyes peered into hers, deep and intent, tempting her to stand and disrobe, give him what he wanted despite her modesty. Instead, she pulled her gaze from his and stood, saying, "You'll have to settle for watching me move around the kitchen while you help me make breakfast."

At first he felt immensely disappointed, especially after reading an almost "yes" in her eyes. Then Trey smiled and turned his eyes toward the kitchen. The idea of cooking with her, of watching her as they moved around the kitchen together, spread a warm, homey feeling inside of him. "All right," he told her.

"All right? After so many lines of poetic music, all I get is an all right?"

"I have to save up for future romantic moments."

"Please do, we might need them later. I still want to talk to you about your name."

"Why don't we have that discussion on a full stomach?" he suggested, wrapping an arm around her and guiding her towards the kitchen.

"Agreed," she said as they stopped at the fridge.

"Let me take a look at what our choices are."

"Sure," Teresa said, backing up to sit on the bench at the big oak table in the middle of the kitchen. She watched, her chin resting on her entwined hands as he searched, bent over, giving her a lovely view of his very firm rear end. A remarkably firm rear end for someone who had been idle for weeks. He started putting things on the table. "Eggs again? Are you sure you want to do that?"

"Not just eggs." He twisted around. "Do we have potatoes?"

The "we" made her smile. Her old Trey was definitely back. The last twenty-four hours had been miserable for her. "Yes," she told him, going into the pantry.

"I don't know why I want it, but I'm craving a french fry and egg sandwich."

"I've had those before. My grandmother used to make them."

"For all I know my grandmother made them for me, too."

Teresa doubted that. Although they were both from New Orleans, the french fry and egg sandwich, she was pretty sure, was an African-American kind of dish. Which brought to mind the other something they needed to talk about. Trey hadn't said a word about the difference in their race. She had already come to realize how little it mattered; maybe he felt the same.

"So I don't lose a finger, why don't you cut the potatoes to make fries while I rise to the challenge of cracking eggs and toasting bread?"

"That could work," Teresa said, deciding that both somethings could be handled on a full stomach. "This won't technically be breakfast, you know," Teresa told him, going to the cabinet to find a chopping board and getting a knife off the counter. "It's eleven-thirty."

"Brunch, then," Trey said, closing his eyes and becoming very still.

"Another memory?" she asked when he opened them a few minutes later.

"Mmmmm, tons of food, omelets made to order, Belgian waffles, crawfish étouffée, gumbo, jambalaya, champagne, mimosas—"

"And?" Teresa asked, feeling as if he were about to say more.

"It had to be the best New Orleans-style brunch the city has to offer," Trey added, shaking his head to rid it of the picture of a long-legged blond he had seen in his mind. The woman couldn't compare to the brown-skinned beauty sitting across from him. Had he been obsessed with white women before the accident? If that was the case, his taste had definitely changed. Trey cracked and beat the eggs without adding roughage in the form of eggshells. Finding the oil and a cast iron frying pan, he heated it just in time for Resa to add the fries.

"You're pretty handy in the kitchen."

"And other places."

"Ah-ha." She smiled at him as she tossed a few potatoes into the hot grease, the sizzle imitating the surge brought on by his words.

They moved around the kitchen in companionable silence, settling down to a plate of french fry and egg sandwiches. Teresa watched as Trey sat beside her sniffing the air.

"Mmm, aren't they beautiful? I can't wait to take a bite of one of these."

"Beautiful?"

"Yes, but never as beautiful as you."

"Trey," she laughed, "if I didn't already know how much you love food, I would take that as an insult."

"It's a good thing that you know me so well then. Now, let's eat."

"Wait a minute."

"For what? French fry and egg sandwiches tend to get cold fast."

"How do you know that?"

"I don't know I—" Trey paused for a second, lost in another memory, "—just do."

"You do."

"I just got a flash of someone saying the same thing to me. I don't know who she was, but she was a sweet lady. She was tall and thin, with brown eyes and skin, almost the exact shade as yours."

"I'm almost jealous. At least I've got two out of three on her. There is no way I can be considered tall and thin."

"I'm not attracted to tall and thin women," Trey said, shaking away the blond who suddenly appeared in his head again. "Besides, this lady was older, a grandmother type. Beautiful and shapely is more my style." He winked at her before taking a bite of the sandwich. "Delicious!"

"I told you to wait."

"Easier said than done."

"Don't touch that sandwich again until I come back."

"Good thing I'm also attracted to bossy women, huh?" he said as he put the sandwich down.

Teresa went to the attached shed where the generator that supplied them with electricity was stored. In a corner of the room was a wine cellar which kept a supply of wine at just the right temperature. She found a bottle of champagne and dashed back into the kitchen. Finding a cork, she handed it to Trey and went in search of the wine flutes she had seen when she first unloaded her supplies. Had that been just two weeks ago?

"Champagne," he said, immediately opening the bottle with an ease and confidence that showed that he had done this many times before.

"Correction. Mimosas," she said half-filling the flutes with orange juice.

"Brunch with style," he said, topping the glasses with champagne. He patted the seat beside him. "Come, let's eat."

"Is it my company or the food you want more?"

"This meal would be nothing without you."

"Good answer."

"Smart answer." He tapped her glass with his and took a sip.

They ate and laughed their way through three sandwiches (her one, Trey's two) and half a bottle of champagne.

"Should we drink the rest? It'll probably go flat." Teresa held the bottle up in the air. "Personally, I've had enough."

"Same here. We'll risk re-corking it and see what happens for linner."

"Linner?"

"Lunch and dinner makes linner. We've already had brunch, the next meal is linner. What shall we mix with the champagne to accompany our next meal? Some cola to salvage the bubbles?"

"I don't think so."

"Seven-up, we'll have spritzers."

"Whatever you say. If you can get that cork back in the bottle, then go for it. I'll clear the table. You can meet me in the den."

"My God!" Teresa heard Trey call out before she could make her way to the sink with the plates they had eaten from.

Turning to see what was wrong, she got a quick flash of Trey running into the bedroom, then an, "I can't believe it!" flew at her as she went to follow him.

"Resa!" he was calling before she could make it into the room. He stood framed inside the bedroom door, a look of shock on his face. "I'm white! You didn't tell me I was white."

"I thought you knew," Resa told him, finding it hard to keep a sober face.

"I'm white!" he said again, throwing his fingers on top of his head. "No afro, I should have realized I don't have an afro."

"There's not much hair there at all. You have a true military cut. At least you did when you got here."

"And it's blond!" he told her, yanking at the short strands of hair.

Gently taking his hands within her own, Teresa guided him to the bed, sat, and pulled him down to sit beside her. The thought of laughing completely left her. "You really didn't know?"

"How could I have known? I couldn't see myself before today. I couldn't see you before today. And even before that I assumed—I thought."

"You thought you were black?"

He eyes bore into hers, "Yes."

"Why?"

"I don't know. The songs you sang to me, the stories and poems you read—Resa, I felt a sense of pride and connection to the history you revealed to me."

"There's no reason why you shouldn't. As it's said, 'Black history is everyone's history.' "

"That's true, I guess, but—." He glanced down. "Look at my hands. I hadn't even noticed my hands. They could have told me what I am."

"What are you?"

"A white man obviously. Why didn't I notice?" His eyes connected with hers again. "Oh yeah," he sighed, "I only had eyes for you."

"And food," Teresa added, trying to break the tension she felt in him.

"But mostly you." Trey's hand went to her face. The contrast of white skin on brown startled him at first. He'd imagine his skin to be as brown as hers, but as he caressed her face, the picture became less startling, simply turning into what was. "Do you mind?"

"I stopped minding a long time ago."

"But you minded at first."

"It wasn't so much that I minded. Being attracted to you was unexpected."

"Not distasteful."

"Not at all. There were only two things about you I found distasteful."

"Only two?"

"Both had to do with your name and why I kept it from you. In that picture," Teresa plunged on, "on your license, you seemed like such a hard man. Your eyes were cruel slits. At first, I brushed it off as an attempt at a macho man image guys usually aim at when they have a picture taken. Then I found something else."

"What?" Trey asked when she didn't go on. He could feel her nervousness. If this thing was upsetting her this much, it needed to be out in the open so that they could get past it. The entire name issue seemed so unimportant to him now.

"It's something I found in your wallet with your license. I'll just show you." She stood. "I'll be right back."

Trey didn't have long to wait. She came back into the room with what looked to be a small, white business card in her hand. Resa handed it to him. He stared down at the blank card. He was suddenly nervous, but only for a second.

"You have to flip it over."

Trey nodded turning the card over. The words '*White power, the only power*' shouted at him. Something stirred inside of him. A hatred, a dark feeling of disgust. His eyes lifted. Resa's arms were crossed, her hands gripping her sides. Looking up into her eyes, Trey tore the card in two. "That's what I think about that idea." He stood and wrapped his arms around her. "The only power we have to concern ourselves with is the one between us." He kissed her then to demonstrate, just in case she might have forgotten.

Relieved, Teresa took a step back. "It felt so good to see you rip that card in two. It worried me so much, especially before you woke up. When I found it and your license, it had me imagining all sorts of horrible things."

"You thought you had saved a bigot."

She nodded. "Until you woke up. I immediately realized that you couldn't be what I thought. But then I couldn't call you by the name of the man in the picture. I already thought of Travis Labranch as a bigot."

"But I am Travis. That man in the picture is me. I'm also Trey, and we both adore you."

"Both you and Travis, huh?"

"Definitely, but call us Trey."

"Whatever you say." Teresa leaned into him, wrapping her hands around him. "Now that I'm done worrying about my white boyfriend possibly being a bigot, I've got to be concerned about him losing his mind."

"Not my mind, my heart."

"Romantic words again?"

"You are due a few."

"What now? Do we try to call your family?"

"No wait, Resa," he told her grabbing her hand to keep her in the room. "Stop. Take a breath," he said, pulling her back to the bed. "Don't feel that you have to fix things. I don't blame you for reacting the way you did. You were alone and scared and had no idea who you were stuck with in this cabin. Besides, I'm not sure I'm ready to contact my family yet. At least not until I remember more about them."

"But they might think you're dead. They'll be worried about you."

"I hadn't thought about that. Okay, then how about a little time? Until the snow melts."

"If you feel comfortable with that."

"I'm not sure what I feel comfortable with. I don't feel comfortable in my own skin. I thought it was at least a few shades darker. I don't know who I am. How can I be comfortable with me or what I am to other people?"

"Are you comfortable with me?"

"You, Resa, are the only comfort I feel right now."

"All right, then, come with me." Teresa stood and led him to the closet which she opened. She stood before the full-length mirror with Trey behind her. Wrapping his arms around her waist, she looked at him in the mirror. "What do you see?"

"My beautiful lady and her white boyfriend."

"Try again."

"A couple who looks very different."

"Once more. Look into my eyes; look into yours. What are they saying? What do you see? "

"A couple of people crazy about each other."

"Are you comfortable with that?"

"Yes, and I get it. I shouldn't worry. The rest will come." He kissed the top of her head, nuzzling the tight curls with his chin and resting it there. They stood that way for a long time staring at the picture they made. "I could stand here forever," Trey said a few moments later.

"I feel… peaceful, don't you?"

"Peaceful, yeah," he agreed.

"Angelfruit!" they said in the same instant.

"That's why it's been so peaceful! Where is she?"

"I haven't seen her since this morning," Trey said.

"She didn't even have breakfast, and now it's afternoon. Do you think something has happened to her?"

"Come on, grab your coat. Let's see if she's outside."

Trey and Teresa called for Angelfruit, peering around each side of the house and walking up the short path Teresa had managed to make that morning.

"She isn't anywhere. I'll feel so bad if something's happened to her. What will I tell Mr. Gray?"

"Your neighbor? He's the dog's owner, right?"

Teresa nodded, calling for her.

"I'm sure she's okay. She's an animal after all. She probably went back home where I bet she's safe and sound."

"I hope so," Teresa said, realizing how much she had come to care for the animal.

"I know so. Angelfruit got outside and instinct took over. Come back inside. You've got to be freezing."

Teresa shivered. "I am."

Trey led her back into the house, stoked the fire and helped her to shrug out of her jacket before taking his off. A few minutes later, Teresa found herself with a mug of coffee between her freezing palms.

"Can't make cocoa, but I can make a mean cup of coffee."

"Thank you," she told him, taking a sip. "This is good."

"Warm enough yet?"

"I'm getting there. The fire's nice. Angelfruit loved to sit right there." She pointed to the empty rug near the hearth.

"I'm sure she's fine, Resa."

"I hope so. She saved my life, you know."

"She did?"

Teresa nodded and told him about the night he had crashed and her reaction to the card he had torn in two.

"She led you back to the house, and you sat up all night with a rifle to protect yourself from a man with a concussion?"

"Yep, and after realizing how silly that was, I put the rifle away."

"Do you even know how to shoot the thing?"

"Mr. Gray showed me how to load it. I've never actually fired it."

Trey shook his head. "What were you going to do? Point me to death?"

"Scare you into obedience, I hoped."

"It's a good thing you didn't need it."

"Good thing." They were quiet for a while, the silence lingering as they drank coffee and enjoyed the fire. The popping of a log broke the stillness. "What are you thinking?" she asked.

His gaze, both lazy and sexy, landed on her. "Two things."

"Which are?"

"We could spend the afternoon on this sofa with mounds of sexual tension growing by the minute, which will eventually lead to me peeling the other layers of clothes off your body as easily as I removed your coat or…"

"Or?" Teresa asked, his bluntness surprising her, though it shouldn't have. Trey usually said what on his mind, and she was having similar thoughts herself.

"Or we can explore the cabin. I could use the diversion."

"Me too," Teresa said as she quickly stood, leaving the half-finished mug on the coffee table.

CHAPTER 10

Exploring the cabin wasn't diverting enough, Trey found. He would have done better at reining in those sexual urges if they had stayed by the fire with the flames to distract him.

Following Resa around this huge mansion of a cabin, hearing her laugh and smile at him when they discovered a buck's head with huge antlers in the game room, and watching her hips sway in a tight pair of jeans was doing him in. At least the top half of her was covered in a fleece-like sweatshirt.

"How about a game of pool?" she asked, her hands sliding across the green cloth table to the balls encased in a triangular rack.

"Pool? That sounds like fun." Trey went to the cabinet just beneath the buck's head to get a couple of cue sticks. He needed to be occupied with some physical movement and activity that did not involve stripping—.

Trey turned to find Resa pulling the fleece thing over her head. The top half of her body, which had been covered so nicely, flaunted itself before him in a pink, stretchy thing that clung to her breasts, molding and shaping the most perfect—.

"Trey!"

Trey's eyes lifted to where the loud, muffled sound of his name had come from. Resa seemed to be stuck inside the fleece thing. Shaking his head, Trey took the three steps to reach her and laid the cue sticks on the pool table. "What do we have here?" he asked, allowing the laughter instead of the heat to show in his voice as he enjoyed the tempting view up close.

"A woman in need of help," her voice called from inside the sweatshirt.

Unable to resist, Trey's hands went to her sides. "Should I move up?" he asked as his hands slowly rose from her waist, grazing the sides of her breasts, stopping just beneath her arms. "Or down?" he asked repeating the caress, his hands pausing a second as they slid past the full, soft mounds and down her sides once again.

He stood quietly, waiting for an answer. Her arms were still above her, giving his blessedly seeing eyes free access to the rapid rise and fall of her breath, the movement bringing her breasts closer to his chest.

"Up," she said on a sigh.

Trey's hands moved up once again, the heel of his palms pausing as they encountered soft, firm flesh. His fingers itched to cover, to hold her. Instead, he pulled back, his hands moving upward and slipping between the sleeve of the fleece and her arms. Resa's arms came down and rested motionless at her side. Her head was still inside the sweatshirt. Trey pulled it down, freeing her head. He didn't know what to expect. Her eyes were a deeper brown, soft and sexy as hell.

"I should have said down. I didn't unzip. That's why I couldn't get it off," she rambled, revealing her nervousness. "But if I'd have said down, then I would have missed…"

"My hands on you?" he said as she ran out of steam.

Her eyes said yes even before she nodded.

"Trey, you know how I feel about this."

"And you know how I feel about you." He unzipped the sweatshirt and pulled it over her head. The stretchy thing had a deep neckline that dipped into a V between her breasts. Trey pulled her into his arms in an attempt to hide temptation. He took a deep breath, and as much to assure her as to remind himself, said, "We won't do anything you don't want to do, okay? I won't touch you anywhere you don't want to be touched."

"That is so sweet and—I probably shouldn't say this."

"And?"

"And terrifying."

"Terrifying?" Trey pulled back to look at her face.

"Absolutely." Resa took a step back. "Because right now, I want you to touch me everywhere."

"Maybe you shouldn't have said that." Trey rubbed his hand across his face, his fingers in no way hiding the view of Resa so perfectly outlined in that top. "What *are* you wearing."

"A body suit. Why?"

"The way it molds to your body makes my body mold in its own way," Trey told her, his finger tracing the neckline, dipping into the V.

"I should have left my fleece on."

"But you were hot; we both were. How about we try to ease the fire a bit?" With that thought in mind, Trey's hands found her hips and lifted her onto the pool table. He kissed her with a gentleness that surprised him. He wanted to pull the body suit thing to her waist, but he also only wanted to take what she was willing to give. So, slow was the pace he set for himself as a trail of kisses brought him to the V in the suit. The rapid breaths and deep sighs coming from her were turning his body rock hard. He wanted to be inside her.

"Resa," Trey said as his lips grazed the swell of her breast. His teeth pulled at the neckline. "Are you still terrified. Should I stop?"

"Right now? Trey, I'd be terrified if you did stop."

Sleepy, sexy, brown eyes confirmed her words. "Being able to see in your eyes what you feel makes me love you even more, Resa." Capturing her lips, Trey leaned into her until Resa's back lay across the pool table. He positioned himself between her long legs that hung down the side of the table until he grabbed them to rest against his hips. "Cross your legs; hold me to you. Let go when you, I mean, *if* you want me to stop." Not giving her a chance to respond, Trey took her mouth once again and slowly pressed his hardness into her, giving in to the heat that had followed them through the cabin, claiming her tongue and lips as he wanted to claim her body, suckling her lower lip before tracing it with his tongue, then entering her mouth.

They moved as if in slow motion.

His tongue stroked hers, his hips pressed against hers. Forcing himself not to grind like an animal into her, he laid his head against her chest. Feeling her fingers running though his scalp, he looked up at her and asked, "Should I stop?" At the blatant desire in her eyes, at her hesitation, Trey answered for her. "I'll take that as a no."

His lower body flush against her, Trey leaned back just far enough to look down at her. "I want to see you, Resa. I want to feel your breasts in the palm of my hands to hold and squeeze, to tease and make ready for my lips."

"Trey." She squirmed, rubbing her lower body against him. "Show me," she whispered.

And he did, his hands at her waist moving upward, grazing her breasts, tracing the neckline to each shoulder, peeling the fabric down to bare the beauty beneath.

Inch by inch.

Trey kissed the swell of one brown-skinned breast and used his teeth to gently peel the stretchy material away from his treasure.

Treasure. That was how he felt about Resa and every part of her. His eyes feasted on his treasure, and he blew his warm breath on the raised nipple dark as a berry. His tongue tasted her, a quick, barely there caress.

"Trey!" he heard her say, and he smiled, blowing a farewell breath across the hard peak as he moved to uncover her other breast.

"Trey!" she said again between a sigh and a moan.

"Resa," Trey said, breathing her name against one nipple, then the other.

"What are you doing to me?"

"Making you want me."

"I already do," she told him, raising up on her elbows, her breasts pressing against him. "More than that, Trey, I love you."

"You what? Oh, the hell with slow. I love you, too. You know that I love you!" Trey took her mouth and laid her back onto the table, his lips traveling down to her bare breasts, treasuring her as he intended with his tongue and his lips, pulling her nipple into his mouth, squeezing and molding her as she pressed against him.

"Ahh, Resa." He paused to look into her eyes. "Look at me and tell me again."

"I love you, Trey."

"You do. I can see it in your eyes. I love *seeing* in your eyes the words I'd only hope to hear. You're my treasure, Resa. I love you."

"I can pretty much see things are going okay over here."

"What?" Trey said, turning at the sound of a deep male voice behind him. "Who?"

"Mr. Gray," Resa squeaked, sitting up. Trey hugged her to him, knowing that she would be more mortified than she already appeared to be if this Mr. Gray saw her half-naked.

"Mr. Gray?" Trey asked. "Mr. Gray who pulled me out of the plane?"

"That'd be me. I called out, got no answer, and thought I heard a noise up here. I'll go check on the generator. Probably no need to run it with the heat I found building in this room."

"Oh, Mr. Gray, I'm so sorry, I'll be down in a minute."

"Nothing to be sorry for," he said heading back down the stairs. "He healed up pretty good from the looks of it."

"Yes, I did. Uh, thanks," Trey told the man, wanting to show his appreciation in some way without exposing Resa.

"Nothing to thank me for," His voice trailed away.

"I can't believe what just happened," Teresa said, her hands covering her face.

"It's okay," Trey told her, moving her hands and lifting her chin to look into her face. "We haven't done anything wrong."

"But I've never. This is so embarrassing. He must think I'm some kind of bed hopper messing around with my patient."

"I'm not your patient anymore, Resa. And I don't think anything but good about you. Hey, I love you, remember?"

"Yes, but…"

"That's all that matters. He caught me loving you." Trey's hands went to her breasts that were still exposed.

"Trey! He's right downstairs."

"I know," he said, kissing one nipple before covering it. "That's why I'm reining in my desire to show you how much I love you." He kissed the other before covering it. "Until he leaves."

"I do love you," she said, laying her forehead against his and wrapping her arms around his neck. "I've never felt this way before. No one has ever touched me, not my heart or my body. And you know what I think?"

"What?"

"I think the mountains sent you to me."

"Then I thank the mountains."

A loud barking had them both turning toward the stairs.

"Angelfruit!" Teresa shouted, hopping off the pool table.

"Let's go see."

Trey followed her down the stairs to where Angelfruit stood barking at the screen door.

"Told that darn dog that she had no business in the house. She seems to think otherwise."

"Well, she saved my life, Mr. Gray, and rode out the storm with us until she disappeared this morning."

"That's because she met me about halfway down the mountain. I was makin' a path going up, and she was coming down trying to get to her man."

For the first time Teresa noticed the big black dog standing beside Angelfruit.

"I wouldn't open that door unless you want eight giant paws running around this cabin."

"No, I don't but I have to see her. I have to let her know I missed her." Teresa went out onto the porch and hunched on her knees to give the dog a hug and received a kiss in return from both dogs.

"Hard to believe she was scared to death of those dogs when she first got here," the old man told Trey.

"That's not hard for me to believe. She's a strong woman with a big heart."

"It's like that, is it?"

"Yes, it is."

"Good. It's not my business but I like her and don't want to see her hurt."

"She won't be. Not by me. But speaking of hurt, thanks for coming to my rescue. I wouldn't have made it out of the plane and up the mountain if it weren't for you."

"As I said before, no thanks necessary. Teresa would have gotten you out and up the mountain. She had a sled ready to carry you."

Trey simply shook his head in wonder at his luck in finding such a woman.

"I'm so relieved to see that she's okay." Resa slid through the door before the dogs could find a way inside. "I would have felt so bad if she had gotten hurt." With a final bark, Angelfruit ran off the porch, the black dog running beside her.

"That fruitcake of a dog is fine. How about you?"

The look Mr. Gray gave her seemed to convey a double meaning. "Um, we're okay. Trey needs to see a doctor to confirm what I suspect."

"Which is?" Trey asked, wrapping an arm around her.

"That you're perfectly healed," she said, stepping away from him, giving him a smile of apology. Teresa didn't know why, but Mr. Gray made her feel as if she had been caught fooling around by her dad. An image of her own father's face full of rigid disappointment with her mother right alongside him shaking her head in disapproval shot into her mind. It wasn't a feeling she was comfortable with. Her parents had never caught her fooling around because she had never fooled around. She had been serious when she told Trey that she was saving herself for marriage. She had concentrated on school, her career and community service, and only went on an occasional date, but nothing serious.

Trey.

Now Trey was something serious. He smiled back at her in understanding, giving her a wink before walking toward Mr. Gray.

"You mentioned something about a generator. I hadn't thought much about how this place was getting electricity. I take it the storm blew down power lines."

"You take it right. You would have barely noticed a difference. Doc Ramsey had a Generac Guardian generator installed."

"And you're right. We didn't notice a difference. Still, we've been sticking to staying downstairs, reducing energy consumption."

"Until today," Mr. Gray said.

"Until today," Teresa repeated. "We were exploring. Trey just got his sight back."

"Trey, is it?"

"Actually, it's Travis Labranch Jr. Resa calls me Trey."

"Resa, is it?"

"Yes," Trey said.

Mr. Gray looked at him and nodded his head before saying, "Let's have a look at the Guardian."

They followed him to the shed. He peered at the machine and checked a few readings. "It should keep running until the power's back up. Then, it'll switch to electrical power."

"When do you think that'll be?" Teresa asked.

"A week or so. The energy company's dealing with power in the city first. They'll make it up here last. The road's still blocked anyway."

"Oh, I had thought that since you made it here that the roads were clear."

"Nothing's clear but what I cleared myself."

"Maybe I can help," Trey offered.

"Maybe you can. My sons are all grown up and gone. My plow gave out a quarter of the way up, and I've got nobody to help me shovel."

"No, you're not well enough for strenuous work like shoveling snow," Teresa said.

"I'm sure I can do something."

"Those ribs won't let you. I won't let you. He's forbidden, Mr. Gray."

"Sorry," Trey shrugged. "I'm forbidden. But I'm willing to help out any other way I can."

Mr. Gray responded with a deep chuckle. "I understand. I have a woman at home who I'm heading back to. Plows won't come up here to clear the highway leading out for a couple more days at least. You two continue where you left off. I'll see you in a few days, tell you where to find the closest hospital."

He was out the door and on the path before they knew it. With a whistle, the dogs came from behind the cabin. Angelfruit turned to give them a farewell bark before following.

"Angelfruit's got her man. Mr. Gray's going back to his woman. I've got mine. Isn't the world a wonderful place?" Trey asked, wrapping his arms around her.

Turning to him in amazement, Teresa asked, "You really feel that way, don't you?"

"Lucky to be alive, to have a woman that loves me? Yes."

"Despite not knowing all there is to know about yourself."

"As long as I can have you in my life, nothing else matters."

"I understand what you're saying, and I love you just as much."

"But?"

"The unknown worries me. What if there's something in your life that would interfere with us being together?"

"Why worry about something we may or may not have to deal with?"

"What you're saying makes sense, and it's pretty similar to what I've been saying to myself."

"But you're going to worry anyway," Trey said, pulling down her arms which she had folded below her chest when the discussion began. He took hold of both her hands, entwining their fingers.

"I'll try to temper it."

"That's all I can ask. Now, I have another question," he said, his hands moving up her, his thumbs stretching to caress nipples that instantly hardened.

"What?" she asked, the surges spreading from her breasts and moving down to throb between her legs, forcing her to speak in a voice she barely recognized as her own.

"You said that no one's ever touched you like this before."

"No. I mean, yes, that's right," Teresa said, feeling excited and guilty all at the same time. She wanted his touch but she'd made a promise to herself. One she'd made and kept since she was thirteen. One that she would have probably broken if Mr. Gray hadn't interrupted them.

"Would you view the experience as an unknown?"

"Not so much now." Teresa sucked in a deep breath as he bent, his hot breath at her breast an instant before his entire mouth. Teresa couldn't say a thing as his tongue swirled around her nipple, amazed at the feel of it through the thin cloth.

"You were saying?" he asked a long time later, his hand replacing his mouth as he leaned into her to kiss her lips.

Taking a moment to think and remember what they were talking about, Teresa finally answered. "Not so much, especially when you do something like that."

"Does this unknown worry you?"

"Yes."

His forehead pressed against her own as he let out a moan.

"And no."

"Then we should do as Mr. Gray suggested and carry on from where we left off."

"No. I don't want to regret making love to you, Trey."

"You would have made love to me when we were upstairs if we hadn't been interrupted."

"Yes, but I would have regretted it."

"Then you'll just have to marry me."

"Is that a proposal?"

"Sort of. Not very romantic, was it? Erase it and meet me in front of the fireplace at six P.M."

"Two hours from now?" she asked, glancing at the clock on the mantle.

"Exactly. In the meantime, why don't you do something nice for yourself? Take a bubble bath. Paint your nails."

"Take a cold shower?"

"That would be me."

Teresa laughed. Could she love him any more? "I just need to say that no matter how old-fashioned I sound, I still intend to wait for wedding vows."

"Vows that will come sooner rather than later, I hope."

"Soon as we contact your family."

"My family," he said as a sudden scene flashed in his mind's eye: the man he had assumed was his father, a woman he immediately recognized as his mom, and a petite dark-haired young woman who smiled up at him with a look of adoration.

"Trey," Teresa whispered in his ear, her arms around him, the soft touch of her fingers as they moved across his back comforting him. Why did women keep popping into his brain. And who was this new one?

"Trey, are you okay?"

He nodded, barely registering that Resa was talking to him. This new face worried him more than the blond. She could be anyone. A relative? A sister? A cousin?

A wife?

Trey shook himself. He couldn't have a wife somewhere in the world, not when he was so in love with Resa. Putting his arms around her, he held her tight and breathed in her scent. "I'm okay. When you said family, I just got a good glimpse of mine."

"You saw someone other than your dad?"

Trey nodded. "My mom." He couldn't say more until he knew more. Maybe Resa had good reason to worry. Maybe she didn't. It wasn't enough to stop him from planning a romantic proposal, though. "Go relax for a while. I'm making dinner."

"Maybe you should be relaxing; you just got your sight back today."

"I'm not shoveling snow. I'll only be lifting meat and vegetables."

"Okay." She kissed him and whispered, "I love you," before heading into the bedroom.

Trey watched as she walked away from him and despite knowing that in two hours she would be walking back to him, he felt as if her departure was a premonition. Would she be walking out of his life forever? "Nope, that couldn't be true. Don't worry until you have to," he whispered to himself. Trey grabbed his jacket and went onto the porch and sat in a rocking chair, the same one he'd sat in a few mornings ago. He forced his mind to go blank, but found it extremely difficult to clear both the last hour and

Resa from his thoughts, especially since a remnant, still as hard as a rock lay between his thighs. Finally, after many long minutes, he was able to tuck the images into the back of his head.

Usually, memories came unexpectedly, mostly when he was relaxed and happy. Trey took a few deep, slow breaths, forcing himself to relax. "One, two, three," he counted as he inhaled, doing the same as he exhaled. Over and over again. The rhythm relaxed him. He felt as if he were on the verge of dozing off.

Images fast and fleeting began to run through his brain.

A compound or some kind of base, men marching, a camouflage-wearing speaker ranting in a loud voice fast-forwarded inside his head. His parents, the dark-haired woman again, a phone, he was talking on a phone.

Faces of people he couldn't identify flashed at him and then nothing.

Trey sat for awhile welcoming the nothing. The images were a collage of confusion, the only significance being the dark-haired woman who constantly smiled at him.

Trey shivered as the cold air hit his face which was now drenched with sweat. He stood, stumbled a bit, but made it to the front door without a problem. Going into the cabin, he headed straight to the bathroom, wanting to wash his face. He froze in the doorway at the sight of Resa submerged in bubbles, candles lit around the rim of the bathtub. "You took my suggestion," he said, forcing himself to walk straight to the sink.

"I took it as an order." She pulled the shower curtain closed before adding, "I've been soaking in this tub for at least half an hour, doing nothing but relaxing, you'll be happy to know."

"Good." Trey splashed his face before ordering himself to leave the bathroom. "Soak as long as you like." He had a lot to do, having wasted a half an hour trying to identify the dark-haired woman.

Searching the kitchen and den, Trey collected everything he needed to create a romantic atmosphere. He stoked the fire, placing more logs near the fireplace, replaced the rug Angelfruit had used as a bed with a huge bearskin he dragged from one of the rooms upstairs. The table he covered in a white tablecloth, the centerpiece a huge candle that smelled like vanilla, which he lit as he searched for possible food choices. From the looks of the contents of the fridge and freezer, he would be lifting cans instead of meat and vegetables. Shopping would be another thing they would have to do as soon as the road to the highway was cleared.

Settling on two cans of tomato soup and a box of biscuit mix, Trey got busy. He opened and poured the cans of soup into a pot and put it on low to simmer. Then, following the recipe, mixed a batch of biscuits, grated cheese, and folded it into the dough which he rolled into balls and placed on a cookie sheet. Having no clue where these ideas were coming from, Trey took a handful of vermicelli and broke it into little pieces which he threw into the simmering pot of soup.

Food almost ready, Trey found the flutes from that morning and the bottle of champagne he knew was certainly flat because it had been impossible to re-cork. He filled the flutes halfway with the flat champagne and placed them in the freezer, along with a two liter of 7-UP he found in the pantry.

There was only one thing he was missing.

A ring.

And he had no way of getting one. He would have to be creative. Trey surveyed the room, his eyes landing on the champagne bottle. Maybe this could work.

Taking the wire that had secured the cork to the champagne bottle, Trey went to work dismantling it and creating a ring. He measured it on his pinky finger, hoping it would fit Resa's. Carefully peeling the gold foil from the outside of the bottle, Trey measured and wrapped it around the wire, twisting a small piece on top. Trey molded this piece into the shape of a soli-taire, the gold foil resembling a gold nugget instead of the diamond he would have preferred. "Crude, but romantic," he whispered, hoping Resa would think the same. He placed the cork on top of the cham-pagne bottle. "Almost ready," he said aloud, taking in his handiwork.

Not wanting the biscuits to be ready before Resa, he went into the bedroom to peek. She was sitting in the huge chair by the bed wearing a thick terrycloth robe and probably nothing else. Trey tried not to dwell on the possibility, staring instead at her feet propped up on the edge of the bed where her toenails were in the process of being painted.

"Following another order?"

"I just happened to find nail polish in the vanity over there. The only color that wasn't dried out was fire engine red. I hope you like it."

"If that's all you have to wear, if that's all you *do* wear, I'm sure I'll love it."

"That's pretty much what I expected you to say." She smiled up at him.

"So I'm becoming predictable."

"Nope, you're becoming a man I know very well."

"Your man."

"My man," she said. "So when will dinner be ready, my man?"

"In about—" The lights flashed, then went out completely. "I was going to say ten minutes but due to technical difficulties, dinner may be delayed."

"Not necessarily. The stove and oven are gas-powered. You can finish cooking. I'll take a look at the generator. There's a flashlight in the top drawer of the dresser."

"I'll take a look at the generator." Trey went into the bathroom to retrieve a candle which he relit. "You finish painting your toenails, find a beautiful dress to wear, and be ready in fifteen minutes."

"Yes, sir." Resa saluted him. The gesture and words seemed familiar. He nodded to himself as he retrieved the flashlight. That would make sense. He must be an officer. He popped the biscuits in the oven, stirred the soup, and went into the attached shed. Having no success after playing with the generator, banging a few things, and pressing a few buttons, Trey realized that he had no idea what he was doing and went back into the house.

Going straight into the kitchen, he took the biscuits out of the oven and tossed them into a basket he had set on the table. The soup he poured into two brown crocks, carefully covering them with large ceramic bowls he had warming in the oven. And he did it all without burning himself. He must be something of a chef, Trey figured, taking a step back to view the scene he had created.

Romantic.

He turned and headed toward the bedroom just in time to see Resa standing in the doorway. She was wearing a black dress that clung to her body, flowing out at the bottom in ripples of material.

"When I packed this dress, I had no idea why I would need it."

"Now we know."

"Yes, now we know. No luck with the generator?"

"None whatsoever. We'll have to make do."

"Maybe I should—"

"Follow me into the bedroom to help me find a coat. Do you think the doc has one I can borrow? I need to look at least half as gorgeous as you."

"Only half. You're looking mighty fine in those jeans and that plaid shirt. Real lumberjack fine."

"Not good enough. I'm counting on being finer." Putting his arm around her, he guided Resa into the room.

"Oh." Teresa led him to the huge walk-in closet. "More poetic words?"

"Poetic, romantic, and absolutely necessary for a certain question I have to ask my beautiful lady."

"Does this jacket go well with that plaid?" She held up a brown tweed jacket with leather patches at the elbows. It had seen better days, but was the only jacket in the closet.

"No, but this shirt does." Trey reached from behind to pull out the only white dress shirt hanging in the closet. His arms circled her, and his lips grazed her neck. "Mmm, I couldn't resist taking a taste. I was getting kinda hungry."

"For dinner?"

"No, you, but dinner is going to get cold. Give me a minute to dress and don't leave this room." Trey spun her into the bedroom and proceeded to change in the closet.

"Whatever you say," came at him as the plaid shirt fell to the floor. Having changed his upper body in two minutes flat, Trey found a bottle of cologne on a shelf and patted his face and neck.

As soon as he stepped out of the closet, Resa walked up to him, nuzzled his neck, leaving a path of kisses down to the open V of his shirt. "Mmm, I couldn't resist. You look fine. Professor-like fine."

"Thank you." Trey looked down at her, feeling a sense of urgency to ask her to marry him, to commit to him. He couldn't have loved anyone this much before. It wasn't possible. "Dinner's getting cold," he said, leading her into the kitchen. "It's a bit simple. Our cupboard's almost bare."

"So you've noticed?"

"We'll make groceries when the road's cleared," he told her, pulling a chair back for her to sit.

"Make groceries, Trey? You are a New Orleanian, born and bred. We are the only people in the world who *make* groceries. Other people buy them."

"Same difference, right?"

Resa nodded.

"And we'll be making them together."

"That sounds very domestic."

"I want to be domestic with you." Feeling as if he might plop down on his knees and pop the question right then and there, Trey forced himself to step back and announce, "Dinner is served." He uncovered the crock of soup and offered her the basket of biscuits. "The fare is simple but guaranteed to be delicious."

"Everything's beautiful. The table, the candle—"

"The food. Tomato soup *avec* vermicelli and biscuit *avec formage*."

"French food?"

"American food with a French flair. And let us not forget the champagne."

"The flat champagne?"

"The champagne that will be revived with a clear refresher."

"You have an interesting way with words."

Teresa laughed as Trey took two frosted flutes from the freezer. The liquid inside was an icy slush. He added the 7-UP in each glass and took a sip. "Just like new. No, better than before." He held the glass out to her, turning it to the spot where he had sipped. "Taste," he offered, his eyes a sexy enticement.

Resa opened her mouth. The drink slid past her taste buds and down her throat. It tasted like Trey or maybe she imagined that it tasted like Trey. "Delicious," she told him.

"There's plenty more where that came from. Let's eat."

Teresa ate her soup *avec* vermicelli and her biscuits *avec formage* and drank her flat champagne *avec* refresher but only had eyes for Trey. Without reservation, she knew her answer to his question.

"Shall we adjourn to the lounge?" he asked after a multitude of poetic words that involved her ears and neck.

Smiling a yes, she leaned to blow out the candle at the exact same time as Trey. Their breaths collided, extinguishing the flame together. They took advantage of the moment and gave in to a soft kiss that held a promise.

"You get the glasses. I'll bring the champagne and the refresher?"

"Are you sure we need it?"

"Positive."

"I can get a fresh bottle of champagne. We can replace anything we take. "

"No, this one will do quite well."

With the generator out, the only light in the entire cabin was from the fireplace. The mood was truly romantic. They sat before the fire holding hands one moment, a head brushing against a shoulder the next, lips pressing a kiss on a bare shoulder, fingers making a trail up and sometime later, down an arm. They sat this way for a long time, content and sure of each other.

They both knew the question that would be asked, and they both knew the answer.

Trey laid a kiss on her forehead, less fleeting and more purposeful than those before. "Would you like some more champagne?"

"Sure, I'm starting to like the flat version."

"With refresher," he said, pouring the 7-UP into her flute and handing it to her.

Teresa sat up with a shiver, losing the warmth of Trey's body. Holding the champagne bottle in his hand, Trey pulled at the cork, which was just sitting on top of the bottle.

"What do have we here?" he asked, suddenly serious.

"A cork?"

"Not the cork, but what's beneath it, made with my own hands, a symbol of my love and commitment to you." Trey pulled the ring from the top of the bottle, slid off the sofa, and knelt beside her. "Even though this ring is made from simple materials, my love for you is not as simple. If you take this ring, we'll build something together more valuable than gold or diamonds. Marry me, Resa. Build a life with me; make memories with me."

Not needing a second to think and completely swept away by his words and the beautifully simple ring he held in his hand, Teresa told him, "We'll make thousands of memories." He slid the wire engagement ring onto her finger.

CHAPTER 11

"Trey," Resa called out sleepily as a cold draft hit her. She stretched an arm for his warmth, only to find soft fur.

The rug.

They had fallen asleep on the bear rug.

After Trey proposed.

He had promised her romance, and he had delivered.

Her hand went to her ring finger. The wire ring had somehow slid off in the night. She sat up and searched under the Indian blanket Trey had used to cover them.

"Looking for this?" he asked holding up the ring.

"I thought I'd lost it." Teresa took it from him thinking that she should feel silly panicking over a piece of wire, but she didn't, and Trey obviously didn't think she was being silly. "Where did you go?"

"About three feet away from you to restart the fire. Get back under the cover. It's freezing out here with the generator broken."

"Why didn't you answer when I called?" Teresa asked him, snuggling back under the cover because it *was* cold out there.

"I wanted to hear you say my name again in that soft, sleepy voice of yours. It's very sexy."

"It'll be yours to hear every morning. Come back under the covers before you freeze."

A few seconds later, Trey snuggled in with her, shivering even though they were both fully clothed, Trey minus the tweed jacket. "So, what are our plans for today?" he asked, nuzzling the side of her neck.

"I don't know, got any ideas?"

"How about a hike down the mountain to get some advice on how to fix a generator?"

"In your condition?"

"And what condition is that?"

"Weak."

"I'm insulted!" Trey said, feigning outrage. "How, exactly, am I supposed to build up my strength? I'm only talking about walking, Resa, not shoveling snow."

"Okay, gravity will help you down, but I don't know if you'll have enough strength to climb back up."

"Definitely," he told her, wearing the same determined look on his face he had when he first fed himself a bowl of gumbo *after* she told him he couldn't do it on his own.

"A gumbo feat, is it?"

Confusion clouded his eyes for no more than a second before he hugged her even closer and laughed. "A definite gumbo feat."

"Since I have no way of controlling a gumbo feat, I guess we'll find out if you can handle it the hard way."

"If?"

"Yeah, and if we accomplish nothing else, we'll get Mr. Gray to help us with the generator. I can deal with not having light, but another cold night, especially one without your warm body to snuggle into, is going to be too much to deal with."

"And why wouldn't you have my warm body to snuggle next to?"

"You'll be too sore and achy for me to lay a hand on you."

"From walking?"

"From tumbling down a mountain."

Trey laughed some more, kissing her on the forehead. "It's a good thing I have faith in myself. If not, I probably never would have told you that I was—"

"Addicted to me?"

He nodded. "And that I love you, or asked you to marry me."

"If I haven't learned anything else about you, Trey, I know that you're not lacking in confidence. Without it I wouldn't be doing what I'm doing right now."

"Which is?"

"Kissing you senseless." Teresa proceeded to do just that.

Coming up for air a few minutes later, Trey lifted her chin, looked into her eyes, and told her, "Stop trying to change the subject. We have a mountain to descend!" He stood and surprised her by pulling off the white dress shirt and letting out a huge Tarzan yell. "Me make coffee. You make ready for journey."

"It's a mountain, not the jungle!" Teresa smiled, wrapping the blanket around her as she stood. Life with Trey was going to be like a pot of gumbo.

Full of everything.

Full of flavor to spice up her life.

Later that night, Trey stood over the bed, a hot mug of tea in his hand, worry on his face as he looked down at Resa.

"I hope you're not gloating," she told him.

"Of course not. It should have been me. I challenged you to an uphill race."

"I accepted, and I would have won."

"Maybe," he told her, placing the mug on the end table and sitting on the edge of the bed.

"I should have seen that patch of ice."

Trey nodded, holding back a whopper of a laugh at the pitiful expression she wore.

"And I should have noticed that the branch I reached for was old and rotted."

Trey's head continued to bob as if in agreement.

"At least the snow bank broke my fall."

Not wanting her to see the grin that split his face, Trey took her in his arms. Now that she was safe and dry and relatively unhurt, the picture of Resa's arms and legs flying as she stepped on a patch of ice, sliding and slipping until she was able to grab onto a branch to steady herself, only to land in a huge snow bank when it broke in two had him unable to hold the grin inside. A few moments later, when he felt more in control, Trey leaned back, fluffed her pillows, and handed her the mug of tea.

"Go ahead and laugh, Trey. I know I looked like an octopus trying to hold on to air."

The octopus reference brought the image to mind. That and the fact that she herself was laughing set Trey off. Putting the tea back on the table before he spilled it all over the bed was a challenge.

"Come on in," she invited when the room grew quiet. "I'm not too sore for you to put your arms around me."

"I wish I could have grabbed you before you made that fall."

"You were too far behind."

"That was strategy. I was attempting to lull you into a false sense of victory."

"You succeeded. How about we simply lull ourselves to sleep?"

"Only sleep?"

"That's the deal."

Trey carefully eased himself into the bed and put his arms around her. Sleep was going to be hard. Though he readily accepted her terms of no sex before vows, that didn't mean his body took too kindly to what his mind had accepted. He inhaled, taking in the sweet scent of her. She smelled like vanilla. He had run a hot tub of water for her and squirted some vanilla bath stuff into the tub. That mixed with her natural scent and her warm, curvy body next to him was going to keep him awake.

But not her.

Resa was breathing deeply and soundly.

They had had a long day. The trek down the mountain had been easy and had only taken them about twenty minutes. The day spent with Mr. and Mrs. Gray had been pleasant and relaxing. The older couple invited them to lunch. They played around with the dogs for a while, and Mr. Gray came up with them to check on the generator, beating them to the top by a good fifteen minutes.

Mr. Gray had fixed the generator and was heading back down the path by the time Trey and Resa had made it to the cabin with Resa limping and hanging on to him.

"You all right, I take it," Mr. Gray said.

Resa had insisted that she was.

"Just had to have a turn at gettin' hurt," he said before going back home.

Trey let out a deep breath. It was a good day. He had gotten exercise, fresh air, a good meal, and had the love of a wonderful woman. Except for…

Trey rubbed his hand across his face. Except for the dark-haired woman who continuously popped into his head at odd times throughout the day. A restlessness, a sense of urgency began to fill him whenever he thought about her.

Could it be his mind's way of telling him that he'd made a mistake in asking Resa to marry him because he was already committed to someone else?

No.

He didn't want to believe that.

He couldn't believe that.

There was another explanation, he told himself.

Trey forced himself to relax, taking in deep breaths that filled his nostrils with Resa as he tried to clear his mind. With nothing but high hopes for their future, he finally drifted off to sleep a long time later.

Trey groaned, his voice deep and angry as he twisted in the bed beside her. He mumbled something under his breath, words she couldn't hear.

Teresa turned her head toward him, lying still and quiet. Trey had moved so much that he had made his way to the other side of the king-size bed as he fought with the covers. Instinctively she knew that he was wrestling with a memory as much as he was wrestling with the covers tangling his legs.

Unsure of what he'd said and unwilling to interrupt him, Teresa waited, hoping that he would speak again.

A few minutes later he did, this time in an urgent whisper. Lassie? Did she hear him say Lassie? Maybe he was remembering a pet he had named Lassie that had died.

Teresa crawled over to the far side of the bed where he lay restless and frustrated. She leaned over him to place a hand on his forehead, hoping to calm him.

"Cassie. I have to save her. I have to make her see the truth," Trey said loud and clear.

"Shhhh!" she told him even as the name, a woman's name sailed though her head. Was this a woman she should worry about?

Cassie?

Was she a sister? A cousin? A niece?

Could Cassie be his wife?

Worry about it when you have to, Teresa reminded herself.

"Shhhh," she said again to Trey, her hands running through the short hair on his scalp. "Cassie's fine; you're okay. Go back to sleep." Teresa spoke to him as if he were a baby, her voice soft and gentle. And like a baby, he soon became calm and drifted back to sleep.

Teresa couldn't. Despite her own reminder not to worry, she did. She lay beside him, twisting the wire ring on her finger. She lay quietly listening to Trey breathe deeply and evenly one moment, only to grunt or mumble the next. Her touch seemed to calm him, so she lay, with her body close to his, wide awake for an hour, then another before he stirred. His eyes opened slowly, full of new knowledge and an awareness of something he didn't have before.

"Who's Cassie?" She had never pushed him to share his memories before, she'd never had to, he simply did, but Teresa didn't want to give him the option of possibly not telling her.

"My cousin."

An intense feeling of relief pushed out of her. She felt like a balloon that had lost all of its air in an instant.

"My only cousin," he added.

"What were you trying to save her from?" Teresa asked, remembering his words from last night.

"A bad marriage."

"Oh?"

He rolled onto his back and looked at the ceiling. "I don't know why it was bad, but I was angry and I needed to save her. I felt as if I almost hated her husband."

They were quiet for a long time before Trey finally said, "That was a pretty wild memory."

"What makes you say that?" Teresa rested on her elbow as she turned more toward him.

"We're at the edge of the bed. This is a big bed, and I know we started in the middle." He suddenly sat up. "I didn't hurt you, did I?"

"No, I'm fine. You were more restless than anything."

"And angry. I remember being angry."

"Yes."

"I'll be back," he said before heading into the bathroom.

Trey was gone so long, Teresa felt herself falling asleep. She opened her eyes sometime later to find him sitting on the edge of the bed, the picture of her extended family in his hands.

"Who are these people?" he asked.

"Most of my family."

"There are a few people who look like me mixed up in this bunch."

"Yeah, a couple of my cousins couldn't help who they fell in love with. Neither could I."

Trey smiled at her in a fleeting, preoccupied way. "Me either," he said, staring at her, then the picture once again. "Why didn't I see this before?"

"Let's see, you've had your sight back for only two days. You've been pretty busy staring at me, cooking, eating, proposing, and climbing up and down a mountain."

"I've been busy. I'm feeling…"

"Tired," she finished for him, sitting up with her knees rising to her chest as she reached out a hand to grab one of his.

"No, more like battered and bruised."

"That would be my body that you're describing."

"Your body, my brain."

"You had a hard night."

"A lot of things were running through my head. I need to sort them out." He stood. "I need a shower." He looked around as if he expected the shower to pop up in the middle of the bedroom. "I need to take a walk."

"I'll go with you," Resa moved to follow him.

"No," he told her, a huge breath causing his bare chest to rise and fall. He had taken off his shirt the night before, wanting to get closer, he had said. "I love you, Resa," he told her, "but right now, I need to be alone."

Teresa nodded, scooting to the edge of the bed. "Would you like something to eat before you go?" She stood and headed out of the room into the kitchen.

"No," he said, then again, "no, I'll be okay."

The words stopped her in her tracks.

"You weren't expecting a no to that question, were you?"

Teresa shook her head. "You never turn down food. Are you sure you're okay?"

"I need to think. I'll take a walk to Mr. Gray's and back. Maybe I'll sit on a ridge or something for a while. I just need some time to think."

⁓

Thoughts.

Were the thoughts he was having based on fact or were they the product of his mind? Could he be mistaking dreams for memories? Trey wondered. Not when the evidence was staring him right in the face.

A short laugh shook his upper body. Twinges of pain in his ribs were a faded reminder of his accident. Trey took out the picture he had taken from the house without Resa knowing. He had stashed it in an inside pocket of his borrowed jacket.

Teresa's extended family. He knew these people, at least half of them. That is, he knew who they were, their names and their relationship to each other. And in the midst of them, in the center, was the dark-haired woman—his cousin Cassie.

Trey's fingers touched her face. What had he done to her? Was she safe? Alive? Did she have her baby?

Silent tears streamed down his face as he sat on a ridge of rock. He had trudged up the mountain barely a quarter of a mile before piles of unmelted snow had stopped him from going any further. He'd gone up because he had told Teresa he would go down. He didn't want her to find him. He couldn't face her right now. He could barely face himself.

He had awoken with a repugnance for the scenes that had gone through his mind as he slept. Initially he had categorized his dreams, no, his nightmares as just that, nightmares.

Despite realizing that the dark-haired woman he had been remembering was his cousin Cassie. Despite admitting it aloud to Resa as soon as he opened his eyes. Trey had spent an hour or so in the bathroom, staring at himself in the mirror, searching his brain in an effort to determine if his nightmares were real.

How could they have been memories of things he had done? He was not that kind of person. When he had finally convinced himself that his mind had created these terrors, Trey had gone back to the bedroom to find Resa sleeping.

Seeing her resting so peacefully, he had wanted to gather her in his arms, hold her to him, and love her for the rest of his life. Going to the bed, his eye had caught sight of the picture he now held in his hands. It had sat on an end table next to the bed. He hadn't seen it before, yet it had seemed to call out to him. Trey had picked it up and couldn't take his eyes off it.

The people in his dreams, in his nightmares, were there. But they were smiling. And there in the center was his cousin Cassie. She was standing close to a man Trey knew was Daniel, her husband. He didn't know him personally, but he knew everything someone could know about someone from reading a file. He had yet to recall whether or not he had met Daniel, but he knew he had hated him. Trey had been trying to save his cousin from what he thought was a bad marriage, just as he had told Resa.

That was why he had been flying in the middle of a snowstorm.

He had been trying to save his cousin from Daniel, not because he was an abuser or a drug addict or a criminal. He was trying to save Cassie because he— no, not him. He hadn't been Trey then. *Travis,* the man he was beginning to hate, the man he had once been, didn't want Cassie to marry a black man.

Trey had remembered all of this from his dreams. He hadn't wanted to believe they were actually memories, pieces of himself he did not care to remember, but he held the evidence of the truth in his hand.

It was all too real.

And what made it worse was that the people Travis had hurt, resented, and hated were related to and no doubt loved by the woman he had come to love himself.

A black woman.

He was—he *had* been a racist.

Worst yet, one of the leaders of a white supremacy group.

Tucking the picture back into his coat pocket, Trey covered his face with both hands.

The irony of it all squeezed his heart and twisted his gut with a sense of hopelessness that consumed him. He didn't feel the cold wind that blew past his ears or, an hour later the weak rays of the sun. It was only at the rustling sound of an animal moving in a nearby bush that his senses became attuned to what was happening around him.

Trey turned his body away from the view of majestic mountains towering before him. The snow-covered path he had taken up the mountain still held his footprints. He needed to go back. Resa would be worried about him, now even more than she had been this morning.

He raised his face to the sun, feeling its heat just as he had that first day Resa had taken him outside. The sun was stronger, and he could only guess, brighter. The despair that had taken hold at the discovery of who he was began to melt as he thought of Resa. He had loved her from the beginning, before he could see, even before he was fully conscious. He had fallen in love with Resa the woman. Race had nothing to do with it, but now that his memory was returning, race had *everything* to do with everything.

Would she still love him after finding out about his past? Knowing that the white card he had torn in two was his even though Trey hadn't known it at the time? He hated that it was, but fact was fact. His life as a racist was fact as well, and he hated that more than anything else.

"White power, the only power." Trey remembered the chant well. He had participated, had led the masses of young men in repeating the words. Their brains had been just as poisoned as his. The words had been repeated and internalized, believed and used to make one race feel superior to all others. Knowing the thoughts of that group, Resa had reason to be afraid. She had been so relieved to see him tear that card in half. If only he could tear that part of his life away as easily.

A squirrel darted out of the bush that had rustled earlier and up into a tree. How long, Trey wondered, had it sat in the bush before darting out and moving to that tree because he had been there? How long could he sit here and feel sorry for himself before deciding to move forward and do something? Could he be as brave as that little squirrel?

His other self, the man he was before, had taken action, but action in the negative form. Trey was still a man of action. Hadn't he hated Resa feeding him and risen to the challenge of doing it himself? Hadn't he stayed up nights wandering around his bedroom and the cabin to find his way around without stumbling? Hadn't he done all he could to convince Resa to marry him?

Trey was a man of action, but more.

He was a man of principle.

A man similar to but completely different from the man he once was.

Trey had to take action. Needing to get beyond the despair that had taken over, he stood. He would talk to Resa, tell her everything. Well, almost everything. Some thoughts and images had sent waves of disgust through him. He would share only the things that concerned her family.

Family.

Cassie.

Trey had to find out what had happened to Cassie. If those two goons he had sent to kidnap her, supposedly for her good, had hurt her, he wouldn't forgive himself.

First step, find out what had happened to Cassie.

Next, talk to Resa.

Then turn himself in to atone for the crimes and sins his other self had committed.

And hopefully by doing all of this, keep Resa in his life.

Descending the mountain by way of the path he had created on his way up, Trey walked with a determined stride past the cabin, knowing he couldn't see Resa. Not yet. He continued down the path,

Angelfruit meeting him before Mr. Gray's house came into view. He stooped to hug the dog, just as Resa had done the day before yesterday. Had it been such a short time ago that everything in his world had seemed perfect?

Standing, he gave the dog a final rub and continued down the path with Angelfruit dancing around him and barking with joy, the other dog meeting them and following suit with Trey stopping long enough to give him a rub behind the ears. Mr. Gray came out of the shed and stood waiting for him to approach.

"Generator stop working?" he asked.

Trey paused in thought. "It's fine as far as I know."

Raising an eyebrow at that, Mr. Gray repeated in a slow, casual way, "As far as you know."

Trey nodded as he stood there, not wanting to explain himself and not knowing exactly what to say.

"You need something?"

"To use the phone if I can."

"Just got service today. It's right inside. Help yourself."

Trey quickly thanked him, wanting to get away from his knowing eyes. Mr. Gray had a way of assessing a person and situation in an instant. Could the older man see what he once was? "Mrs. Gray," Trey called as he entered the cabin.

"Is that you, Thomas?" she asked from the kitchen. "I'm baking bread for supper."

"No, it's me, Trey," he said, relieved to find her busy. He didn't want her kind eyes on him. He felt unclean, undeserving of something as simple as kindness. "Don't let me stop you," Trey added, not wanting her to come into the room. "Your husband allowed me to use the phone." Trey picked up the phone and froze. Who would he call? Who should he call?

"Hello, dear." Mrs. Gray, clad in an apron and a ton of flour said at the door leading to the kitchen. "Nice to see you again. You go ahead and call whoever you need to call. I'll get you a mug of coffee as soon as I get these loaves of bread into the oven."

Before Trey could tell her not to bother, she was gone. And suddenly a number popped into his head. His father's work number? Yes, it was. Area code? 504 eased into his brain. Not wanting to lose the number, Trey quickly dialed it and waited as it rang. What would he say to his father? What did you say to a man who raised you one way only for you to turn out another?

"Labranch Architects."

It was his dad. The sound of his strong, friendly voice went straight through Trey, triggering in rapid fire speed a number of conversations he had had with his father over the phone in the last few years.

"What's going on with you, Travis?"

"Father, you don't understand. You wouldn't understand."

"Father? What happened to dad?"

"You no longer deserve the title," he had said after a deep, long, condescending sigh. *"A dad teaches his child the superior quality of his race and supports his own, not the mud races. From now on, you are Father to me."*

"Hello?" his dad said on the other end of the line. Trey's voice refused to work.

"So, my cousin is married? Father, tell me, did she marry a man of pure white blood?"

"I'll tell you nothing."

"Which means I'll have to find out for myself."

The dial tone echoed in Trey's ear but the sound did not stop the memories from coming.

"Travis, leave Cassie alone. "She's had trouble enough during her pregnancy."

"Yes, Father, I found out about her carrying that mud baby. I'll have to save her from such an infection. Don't worry. Unlike you, I take care of my own."

Trey could feel the phone being taken out of his hand. Then he heard Mr. Gray ask, "Problem?"

"Many problems," Trey found himself saying.

"Come with me," he told Trey, leading him out of the house and back toward the shed. "Stay, you fruit-cakes," he told the dogs as they tried to follow them inside. The older man sat on a sawhorse and pulled up another for Trey. "Sit."

"Thanks," Trey somehow managed to respond.

Mr. Gray sat quietly as Trey pressed his fingers against his forehead in an attempt to stop the horrible conversations from replaying inside his head. When they finally disappeared, Trey felt a huge adrenaline rush. He hopped off the sawhorse and began pacing up and down the drafty room.

"Problems come and go." Mr. Gray's voice came at him unexpectedly. Somehow Trey had forgotten he was there.

"True," he turned toward him, "but some are hard to deal with."

The older man nodded. "And you've got yourself a big one, I take it."

"Mountain-sized."

"That happened pretty quick. You were happy enough yesterday. Something happen to Teresa? Know that if it did, you'll be in some trouble. Unlike her, I can use a rifle just like the one I left her."

"No, nothing's happened to Resa. It's me, all me."

Mr. Gray gave him an assessing look before saying, "If you say so."

"There you boys go." Mrs. Gray came in with two mugs of steaming coffee on a tray with a couple of sandwiches. "I put yours in your favorite mug, Thomas." She handed him a mug in the shape of a grizzly bear. "And Trey, I fixed yours just like you had it yesterday, two sugars and a touch of cream."

"Thanks," both men said in solemn tones.

"I'll leave you two to talk. Don't disappear without saying good-bye, Trey. I'll have some fresh baked bread for you to take back to Teresa."

"Thank you, Mrs. Gray," Trey nodded, picking up the other mug. He gazed at the coffee. A touch of cream. He stared at the rich liquid, a deep brown, as deep as Resa's eyes, as deep as the color of her smooth, soft, skin and let out a derisive laugh. "I take my coffee the way I like my women."

"You got a problem with that?"

"No, not me, my old self." Trey took a sip, the liquid spreading through his body, physically warming him inside the way that Resa warmed him emotionally.

"That's the problem?" Mr. Gray asked.

"Yes, my memory's returning, Mr. Gray."

"Yesterday, I recall you wanting that to happen."

"Well, yesterday I didn't know what a horrible person I was before the accident."

"Before? Does that mean you're not anymore?"

A tremor of disgust rolled through Trey. "No, never again."

"How's that?"

The question gave him pause. He'd had no intention of saying so much to Mr. Gray, but somehow the man's face of experience and his no-nonsense words had Trey talking and thinking. Why had he changed? Why did he want to stay the way he was now? "I'm not sure. The accident. The knock on my head. Resa. Falling in love. It all must have had something to do with changing me. I don't want to go back to what I was before."

"So where's the problem?"

"Me—my other self. I've done things I'm not proud of."

"Does Teresa know?"

Trey shook his head.

"Can you fix it?"

Trey nodded.

"Then stop whining and fix it. Problems come and go."

Trey stared at him for a long minute as understanding dawned. This problem was here, huge, nearly devastating. It wouldn't simply go away. "I intend to," he said, realizing that he had needed a push toward a decision he had already made, and Mr. Gray had given it to him.

As Trey headed toward the wide shed door, Mr. Gray stopped him. "Don't you have a phone call to make and a loaf of bread to fetch?"

"Yes, sir, I do," Trey went back into the house, this time to actually talk to his dad in order to complete phase one of his action plan: find out what had happened to Cassie.

Phone in hand, he dialed the number that came quite easily to his fingertips. "Labranch Architects," his dad said in a preoccupied but friendly tone.

"Dad, how's Cassie?" Trey quickly asked before losing his nerve.

"Travis, is that you?"

"Yes."

"Did you call me *Dad*? What kind of joke is this?"

"No joke, you're my dad and…" Feeling his throat begin to close, he stopped. "…You always will be." Recalling the snippets of conversations from the past, Trey understood the meaning behind his dad's question. Now wasn't the time to repair their relationship. There would be time later. So he forged on, asking, "How's Cassie?"

"Why do you want to know?"

"Is she safe? Did she have her baby?" Trey's heart felt as if it were beating double time as he waited for his dad to answer. The pounding of blood in his ears seemed to become louder and louder as the silence grew.

"Dad?"

"No thanks to you and your friends, Cassie and her baby are safe and sound."

A five-pound weight lifted away from the five hundred that remained on his shoulders, but he felt the difference. "Thanks, Dad," Trey whispered into the phone, wanting to say so much more but having no idea how to say it. "I'll be in touch."

"I hope I won't regret knowing that." His dad paused for so long Trey thought he had hung up until he heard a whispered, "Son."

Trey held the phone to his ear, the dial tone letting him know that his dad was no longer there. He looked down at his hand gripping the receiver as if his life depended on him holding it as tightly as he could. Forcing himself to replace the phone, Trey looked up to find Mrs. Gray staring at him with concern.

"Everything's fine, I hope."

"Everything will be," Trey told her, accepting the warm bread and smile before finding his way to the path and Resa. If he hurried, he could make it back up

to the cabin before nightfall. She was probably
worried sick about him by now. No sense in making
her worry about him falling off the mountain in the
dark.

CHAPTER 12

The day had gone by, and Teresa couldn't remember much of what she had done with it. Her attempts to keep from worrying about Trey and whatever memories he was wrestling with had thrown her into a robotic mode. She wandered around the cabin but couldn't remember what she had done. She sat for awhile with a book in front of her but had no idea what she had read. She had cooked and even eaten without actually tasting the food she had prepared. She had spent all her energies trying to remain calm, trying not to make assumptions and jump to the wrong conclusion, in essence; "not to worry until she had to."

But now the day was gone.

The sun was leaving.

And Trey hadn't come back yet.

Despite the cold weather, Teresa stepped out onto the porch and leaned against the rail. The snowdrifts piled as high as five feet in some areas reflected the waning sun which did nothing to melt the snow drifts.

Turning toward the path leading to Mr. Gray's, Teresa set her focus there. Trey would be coming up the mountain. Around mid-day she had seen him walking past the cabin as if someone or something were chasing him, which was the same way she had seen him head up the mountain early this morning. What demons had Trey been running from? Why had he been so interested in her family photo? Why had he taken it with him?

Darkness took over the sky as she kept her eyes trained on the path. But it was her ears that caught Trey's approach. Boots trudging on ground made muddy by the slush of melting snow and the rustling of a tree branch announced his arrival. As she saw him coming into view, she realized he was moving with a firm, purposeful stride.

Spotting her, he paused mid-step before finding his stride again.

Despite not being able to see his face, Teresa could tell that he had somehow sorted things out. It was obvious in the way he moved. He seemed determined and focused and he was making his way back to her. Earlier he had said he needed to be alone.

Now he needed her.

By the time she stepped off the porch, he was there, his arms going around her.

"I love you. No matter who I used to be. I love *you*, Resa. Love me back."

His words and the way his arms wrapped around her without any indication of letting go anytime soon dissolved her worries. "Of course I still love you."

A long moment later, he released her to look at her. Pressing his mittened hands on her face he said, "You are amazing and beautiful. I don't deserve you, and I can't believe that I almost missed having you in my life."

"I know what you mean. If I hadn't been awarded the grant, if Dr. Ramsey hadn't let me use his cabin, and if your plane hadn't crashed, we might not have ever met."

"No, Resa, it's so much more than chance. I'm talking about something inside me that had built a dividing wall so thick that I wouldn't have been able to see *you* even if that wall were as transparent as glass."

"Trey, what are talking about?"

"A part of me I wish I had never remembered." His face transformed into a look that was a mixture of disgust, sadness, and resolve.

"Tell me about it."

"I will. As much as I can anyway. I—" He stopped, at a loss for words, it seemed, nowhere near the poetic, confident man of yesterday. "I just hope that you still love me after—"

"After?" she asked when he didn't go on.

"After. You'll understand." Saying that, he began to climb up the wooden steps.

Teresa held on to his hand, forcing him to stop. She stood two steps below him and waited until he turned to look at her. "Whatever you've remembered won't change the way I feel about you. You're the same man who woke up this morning, Trey. Memories are your past. They don't dictate who you are today."

"Depending on what those memories are, your past can haunt you. It can even wreak havoc on your future."

"Then all we can do is deal with the present together. If not, we won't have a future."

Trey shook his head as she walked up the two steps to stand beside him. "I won't hold you to that. Listen to what I have to say first."

Teresa leaned forward to place a kiss on his lips. She whispered, "It won't matter. I know the man you are now."

In answer Trey pulled one arm to her side and the other around his waist. He led her, realizing that he had no idea how to begin this conversation which could very well change the way she looked at him, how she felt about him.

Suddenly he couldn't do it.

He couldn't tell her that he had been the leader of a group bent on destroying and degrading anyone who wasn't a pure, white American—at least anyone the group felt didn't fall into that category. Trey had eaten, drunk, and socialized with those who found Resa or anyone of her heritage inferior beings. They had targeted, at his own request, members of her family. He couldn't do it. He couldn't see her love turn into distrust and hate.

"Trey?" Teresa's hand on his shoulder forced him to focus on her. "Do you want to sit?" she asked him.

Trey nodded, taking a seat on the sofa where they'd spent many hours. He looked over at the fire softly crackling, so similar to the one they'd had when he proposed to her. He looked down at her hand. Her hand, one of her beautiful, brown hands was caressing the ring he had given her. No, he couldn't risk losing her. Maybe he could tell her some small piece without revealing too much. Then he could repair the damages, somehow make amends, and come back to Resa to explain it all after he had atoned for his sins.

"Tell me about it, Trey?" she prompted after they sat in silence for far too long.

"I can't. A least not everything."

"Are there holes?"

"Too many." Why had he been involved with those crazy people? Why hadn't he been able to distinguish right from wrong? How had he allowed stupid, blind ignorance to control a decade of his life?

The feel of her soft, warm fingers tracing his hairline and moving down his cheek got his attention once again.

"I've done some things I'm not proud of, and I have to make amends."

"We've all done things—"

"I'll need to leave," he jumped in, not allowing her a chance to make him feel better. He couldn't feel better, he wouldn't feel better about himself until he made things right.

"Okay," she said softly, her arms wrapping around her waist as she obviously held in whatever else she wanted to say. "But you don't need to leave alone. I'm going with you." She stood over him in all her bossy glory, her love for him huge and strong and peering down at him. This was how he was going to think of her when he was gone. Loving him, bossing him. Trey gently pulled at her arms before standing and wrapping her in his arms, kissing her. He needed to get his fill of her. With that in mind, his lips met hers, so different from his, but not. They drew from each other exactly what the other needed.

"Is this a nice way of telling me you don't want me to come?"

"Yes."

"You need to do this by yourself."

"Yes, I do."

"I don't like it."

"I know," Trey said, kissing her once more briefly, softly, before guiding her back to the sofa.

"You can't go anywhere until you've seen a doctor."

"I knew you'd say that."

"And I'm coming with you for that."

"I knew you'd say that, too." Trey's arms squeezed her, drawing her closer to him, savoring now the love she showed him, just in case he couldn't find a way to make…

Negative thoughts breed negative results, he reminded himself, and forced his mind to move in a positive direction. "If the road's clear, we can probably go into town tomorrow. But Resa, I can't use my real name. I don't want to be traced. Some people are out there looking for me."

"Then you're in trouble."

"A bit, but I intend to set things right for me and… for…others."

He looked left, then right, then settled his eyes on his booted feet, for the first time since she'd known him, avoiding looking at her directly. Even when he was blind, he had looked at her dead center. A cloud of shame seemed to surround him, and an awkward silence fell between them. Unsure of what to do or say to get them past it, Teresa sat, waiting for his eyes to lift and find hers again. When they did, she was thrown by the torment she found in them.

"Resa, I can't talk about it all right now. Knowing it and feeling it has torn me up inside. Can we do this tomorrow, after the doctor?"

Teresa nodded, pulling him into her arms and resting his head on her shoulder, her fingers running through his hair. "That feels good," he whispered, his fingers making their way through the tight curls behind her ears. Taking one of her hands, he laid it against her hair and then his own. "Our hair is one difference," he told her, entwining his fingers in hers. "And look at our hands, so unlike each other in color, but fitting so perfectly together. Our differences aren't extreme. Resa, they can't be stronger than the way we feel about each other. Tell me that I'm right."

"You're right," Teresa answered, not as anxious now to know what memories were tormenting him. She could wait another day to know whatever it was. They couldn't be more powerful than what she felt for Trey, what she knew he felt for her. Nothing could be serious enough to take from her what the mountains had given.

The next morning found Trey up early. The warmth of Resa by his side during the night had been both a comfort and hope for their future. Resa was awake, too. She hadn't said a word; she didn't need to. The change in tempo of her soft, even breathing was enough of a clue. And enough assurance that she was just as aware of him as he was of her. If he wanted to, Trey knew he could convince her with the touch of his hands and the feel of his lips, to give in to the awareness, the need simmering inside them, and take it to its natural conclusion.

But he loved her too much.

If he persuaded her now, Resa could later see it as a ploy to use her, possibly making it harder to forgive him later on when she finally knew all there was to know about him. It wasn't worth the risk. What he needed to do was create positive memories, anything to help his cause. Trey's lips grazed her forehead, lingering only briefly lest the sweet caress ruin his good intentions.

"Trey?" she whispered, twisting her body toward him.

"I'm going to take a look at your Jeep. We'll need to dig it out if we're going anywhere today."

"Your ribs."

"I'll be careful." Anticipating the physical labor, Trey was out the door a few minutes later, throwing on his borrowed jacket as he went in search of a snow shovel. A quarter of an hour later, Resa was at his side working quietly beside him. In another half hour, the snow surrounding the Jeep had been removed, and a path leading to the road Mr. Gray had shoveled a few days ago was cleared.

"I left a pot of cocoa warming on the stove," she told him as he took the shovel from her hands.

Her brown eyes bore into his, probing for answers. Unable to give them, Trey offered a quiet, "Thanks," meaning more in that one word then he could say at the moment. He was thanking her for loving him, for rescuing him, for being so patient and understanding when all he could offer her at this moment was disappointment and evasion. If he could keep all that he had remembered from her he would, but it was impossible. Trey had to admit who he was. He had to turn himself in and hope that Resa would still love him afterwards.

Coming back into the kitchen, he found her sitting at the wooden table. "The cocoa's hot. Come sit with me."

This could be my last cup of cocoa with Resa, he thought, sitting in the chair opposite her.

They had sipped without talking for all of two minutes when Teresa realized she couldn't tolerate the quiet sadness enveloping him. Without thinking about what she was going to do or say, she jumped up from her chair, banging the mug onto the table and splattering the last drops of cocoa across the table on Trey.

"She hates me already," a voice whispered inside of Trey's head before Resa's drowned it out.

"Stop it, Trey! Look at me," she almost yelled when he didn't so much as flinch at being splattered.

Trey did, taking her in all her angry glory as she stood there with her arms folded and eyes boring into him.

"You will not sit there looking ashamed and depressed. I have no idea what's going on inside your head, and I won't push you to tell me just yet. I'm giving you the time you asked for, but I won't spend it with this feeling of doom and gloom surrounding you. If you have to leave, I want to enjoy this last day with you. For the rest of today, forget the past," she demanded. "Don't worry about the future. Spend the entire day with me and think about nothing else."

"How can I do all that?"

"The same way that I can wait for you to tell me these memories that are eating you up inside. By loving you enough. Love me enough to forget about it all for one day."

Forget about it all. Her advice was simple, but not easy. Still, it made sense. He had wanted to remember who he was and the details of his life before he lost his memory, and now that he had, he wanted to forget it all so that he could be with her. The irony of it all added another ache to the pain he was already feeling.

"You do love me enough." She leaned forward, kissing him. "I know you do," she said, resting her elbows on the table, nearly lying across it to stare at him, refusing to let his eyes go. Teresa was looking for her Trey, and she was determined to find him beyond the pain and tormenting memories. She didn't have long to wait. His eyes remained focused on her as she peered into him. Reaching beyond the sadness, she found him.

"Of course, I love you." he told her.

"Then good or bad, don't let memories come between us. Give me back the Trey I fell in love with."

The Trey she fell in love with. Yes, he liked that person. Not himself as Travis or himself as the tormented soul he had become in the last twenty-four hours. "You can have him, but know that there's another side. If you can accept that when the time comes, I'd be honored."

"We'll deal with it when we have to."

"Then starting now, let's enjoy our day together," he said, reaching for and holding her face between his hands in Trey-like fashion. "You've got me," he told her, feeling alive and more true to himself then he had felt in hours. He kissed her, showing her how much he loved her and wanted to be there for her. She returned the kiss, twisting onto her back and taking him with her until they were both half-lying on the table.

"What do we do now?" he asked.

"Enjoy each other."

Knowing that her idea of enjoying and his own wouldn't coincide, Trey suggested, "Why don't we go somewhere?"

"We are." Resa sat up, twisting her body until she sat with her legs dangling on each side of him. "To the hospital."

"Can't we go to the hospital and play tourist at the same time?"

"In Del Rio, Tennessee?"

"That's where we are?"

She nodded.

"There's not much to do here, I take it?"

"Not really."

"Then how about going someplace like... Chattanooga?"

"That's over three hours away!"

"Three hours? Are you sure?"

"Chattanooga was my last stop before coming here. And you still have to see a doctor."

"There *are* hospitals in Chattanooga," he said, the idea taking root as well as the excitement of spending the whole day in Resa's company in the real world. For the entire day he'd have her beside him for any and everyone to see. It would be a first step toward thumbing his nose at the white supremacists who filled his brain with absurdities and hate.

"I'm sure there are. As a matter of fact, I remember seeing a hospital off Interstate 75 on the drive up here."

"So what's stopping us? Let's do it."

"I don't know."

"We'll go to the hospital first. I'll let them poke and prod me until you're satisfied, and then we'll have some fun together. Call it a last fling before I leave."

"Our only fling," she told him, her arms folded at the look of excitement in his eyes. This was the Trey she wanted. That decided it. "Let's do it."

While Resa washed the mugs and tidied up, Trey went into the bedroom and acting on impulse, packed a few pieces of clothing for both of them into a bag he found in a closet. If Chattanooga was three hours away, it didn't make sense to drive back tonight. A night spent at a hotel would top off the day.

"I thought I'd pack a few snacks and drinks for the trip but the pickin's were few. We'll need to do some shopping while we're out," Resa was saying as she walked into the room.

Food required money, and he didn't have much of that on him. A couple of twenties and a credit card from the wallet Resa had returned to him was all that he had. He didn't want to use anything with Travis's name on it. Not only because it left a feeling of distaste in his mouth but because he was sure there were people out there looking for him, and he didn't want to give them a way to find him. The thought of Resa paying for an outing that was entirely his idea was also distasteful. Money would be a problem, he realized, dumping the clothes out of the bag and onto the bed.

"I think we should stop by the Grays on the way down the mountain to let them know that we'll be gone all day," Resa was saying as she went into the bathroom.

Maybe he could borrow some money from Mr. Gray, if he left him something as collateral. Trey looked down at the watch on his wrist. He had never paid much attention to it, automatically taking it off when he took a shower and putting it back on every morning. It looked like real gold. He didn't remember buying it, but it could be considered something of value. The watch was all Trey had. Hopefully Mr. Gray would agree to a loan. It wouldn't hurt to ask, which meant he had to be prepared.

"Trey? Did you hear me?"

"Sure," he answered, repacking the bag and dashing to the Jeep to put it in the backseat. He'd surprise her with the hotel idea if he got the loan. It would be their last night together. Trey gathered all his personal belongings, his wallet and its contents and slipped it into the back pocket of the baggy, borrowed jeans he wore. Realizing he had no clue where to find the bloodstained jeans and sweatshirt Resa had shown him one day, Trey stood in the middle of the room. His eyes were drawn to the picture he had returned. Not wanting to start their trip with talk about him leaving, Trey decided not to ask her for the clothes. He'd wear the ones on his back or the spares he had packed. Walking across the room, he picked up the picture and stared at Cassie and her husband, Resa and all her relatives, and said a prayer that somehow he'd find a way to set things right. Cassie and Daniel looked so much in love. Did he look at Resa that way? Trey was sure that he did. Taking the picture with him, Trey dashed out again and packed it in the bag with the extra clothes, feeling that having it with them would somehow make tonight's discussion easier.

They were in the Jeep and on the road within the next ten minutes with Resa behind the wheel.

"I'll drive," he had offered.

"Sorry, not today, you've done enough strenuous exercise for the rest of the week."

Trey didn't press the issue and kept his mouth shut about the ache in his ribs that lingered from shoveling this morning.

Stopping at the Grays brought other problems. He dodged dogs bent on seeking extra rubs, avoided questions about a loaf of undelivered bread and twisted out of staying for a hearty breakfast. In the midst of it all, Trey found a moment to make his request to Mr. Gray, who gave a quick assessing glance at the watch and then Trey, before nodding and going somewhere inside the house. He returned with five crisp one hundred dollar bills.

"That's way too much," Trey protested.

"I'm getting it back," he stated.

"Yes, you will, with interest."

"That's not necessary. The only interest I have is when you're going to see a doctor. I was the one to carry you in. I know how bad you started out."

"Thanks again for that." Trey paused clearing his throat as this man's kindness washed over him. "We plan to go to a hospital today."

"Have you got insurance?"

"I didn't think about that," Trey admitted, knowing that as Travis he most likely had insurance. But he wasn't planning on using that.

"Hospitals don't take people in without insurance. Unless you go to county. It's sure to be crowded and real busy."

"I'm sure it is," Trey answered, wondering if he was going to spend the day stuck in some county hospital.

"You could see my doctor. I'll get Lily to call for you. Then you two can go see those sights you're so set on seeing. After that, see about getting your life back together."

"I appreciate that, Mr. Gray," Trey found himself thanking the old man once again.

"No thanks necessary. Lily!" he called to his wife who stepped to the door of the house with Resa standing behind her. "Can you call Doc Williams and ask if he'll see Trey today?"

Mrs. Gray nodded, and Resa came out of the house. The two dogs made a beeline for her. Trey and Mr. Gray watched Resa play with the dogs.

"I still can't believe she used to be afraid of those fruitcakes."

"Resa can overcome anything," Trey stated with pride, hoping that was true in his case.

"She's a special girl," Mr. Gay added before turning to Trey to say, "Why don't you make it a day? If you're traveling all the way to Chattanooga, stay the night at the Holiday Inn with that Chattanooga Choo Choo."

"The Chattanooga Choo Choo Holiday Inn? That's a lovely place," Mrs. Gray chimed in as she walked toward them. "Get a railcar room. It's so quaint. You each should have one of your own, of course, not being married and all," she told Trey, a stern look accompanying that suggestion.

Trey smiled at her. She would be pleased to know that sharing the same bed with Resa had been completely safe, well, almost completely. Holding her in his arms without having her as his own hadn't been easy, but much preferable to not having her there at all. Of course it also left him in a permanent state of arousal. A discomfort, but not enough of one to push the issue and make her regret making love to him. Besides, he didn't deserve her yet and was in too precarious a position to risk losing her. Sharing a hotel room wouldn't change either of their minds.

"The Chattanooga Choo Choo Hotel. That's the way to go," Mr. Gray repeated.

"Shhhh," Trey told the couple, glancing at Teresa still playing with the dogs. "It'll be a surprise."

They nodded and smiled indulgently. Mrs. Gray handed him a piece of paper. "These are the directions to Doc Williams' office. It's off Interstate 40. You can't miss it."

Finally getting away from the dogs, Teresa ran over. Trey told her about their appointment with the doctor.

"That's wonderful of you. I like that better than walking into some hospital and waiting for hours to have Trey checked out."

"You'll like Doc Williams," Mrs. Gray told them as they hopped into the Jeep. The couple waved them off. The dogs followed a short distance before turning back.

The drive down the mountain to the highway was quiet as Teresa concentrated on the narrow road. Turning west onto US-70, she released a huge breath.

"Not used to driving on mountainous roads, I take it," Trey stated, a bit of laughter in his voice.

"I've been doing a lot of things I'm not used to doing," Resa said, relieved to hear his good-natured teasing. He was making an effort to be more relaxed. "Like driving up this mountain to begin with."

"Four-wheel drive must have helped you with that."

"Yes, it did, but coming down's another thing altogether. Gravity and what nature left behind on that narrow piece of road had me scared to death."

"Well, you did a mighty fine job, little lady." Putting on a cowboy accent, Trey tapped her chin with his fist. "Scared or not, you done good."

"Why thank you, sir," Teresa told him, playing along.

"Being scared's a part of life, even for this lonesome cowboy." He made a clicking sound, causing Teresa to look over at him. His eyes held hers a moment. It would have been longer except that she needed to pay attention to the road. From the corner of her eye, she could see Trey, still in cowboy mode, tipping a pretend cowboy hat back. "And sometimes there's a lot of things out there to be afraid of," he added, turning serious as he held the hand she wasn't using to drive. "I've got a heck of a lot of those things running through my head right now."

"I realize that." She glanced at him, hoping he wouldn't fall back into the depression he had been feeling earlier.

"And there's nothing I can think of that's more scary than losing you." Trey lifted her hand, placing a soft kiss in her palm.

"I know what you mean," she answered.

"You're scared of losing you, too?" he asked, deadpan.

"Exactly," she answered, satisfied that he wasn't allowing himself to wallow in depression.

"Glad we feel the same."

"It's a good thing I love you."

"I thank God for that every day."

"Open up that piece of paper and tell me where I'm going, cowboy," Teresa told him. Following his directions, they pulled into the parking area of a small medical plaza fifteen minutes later. It was next to a clinic and across from a small hospital. Teresa turned the engine off.

"How do you want to do this?" she asked.

"I want to do this without telling anyone that I used to be Travis Labranch."

"Trey, you are Travis Labranch."

"Then why do you call me Trey?"

"I think we've had this discussion before. Because to me, you're Trey."

"And I refuse to be Travis."

"Who will you be then? John Doe?"

"That's probably the best way to do this. A few days ago I was John Doe. I'm just going to pretend that I'm still John Doe."

"Then you had better do all the talking. I'm not good at pretending; it feels too close to lying. I'm lousy at lying."

"Unfortunately, I believe that I was once very good at it," he admitted, sharing a small bit of what he now considered his dark side. Other fragmented thoughts, twisted and ugly, crowded his mind. He pushed them away with the same effort he once used to force himself to remember. "If this is going to make you uncomfortable, you don't have to come inside," he told Resa. She had been too good to him to be put in a situation that would make her feel uneasy or leave her with a negative memory of him to dwell on when he left.

"Oh, no, I'm coming inside. I want to hear first-hand what the doctor has to say."

Trey leaned into her, his lips grazing hers. "Of course you do." He smiled into her mouth, separating her lips with his own to deepen the kiss just enough to build a sweet memory for them both.

Trey was out the car and on the driver's side before she could unbuckle her seatbelt. He loved the expression on her face, the heat for him he found in her eyes as she stared up at him. He reveled in the fact that she couldn't lie because the truth he was seeing in her eyes was enough to carry him through whatever he would face to have Resa in his life forever.

Offering a hand, he pulled her out of the Jeep and kept her hand in his as they walked into the office. There weren't many people inside, and Trey went straight to the receptionist, giving Mr. Gray's name as a reference. He was given a clipboard with a number of papers to fill out and a black ink pen.

"How can I help you, ma'am?" she asked Resa.

"We're together," Trey told her, proud to say that for the first time.

"Oh, I'm sorry—. I didn't realize."

Trey wondered if she was sorry because she made a mistake or sorry because they were together. An image of a group of young white men sitting together in a room, nodding in agreement, flashed into his mind. Inside his head Trey could hear his own voice. Had he been speaking to these young men? He was sure that he had. Closing his eyes, he listened to himself. *"This world we live in nowadays is a tricky place. There is so much intermingling and acceptance that we must be careful in the way we represent ourselves. Subtle displeasure and censure is a way of getting our point across."*

Trey opened his eyes to find himself seated on a cushioned chair next to Resa. Had he just experienced subtle censure? How dare she? Who was she to judge who was fit to be in his company? She had no right to decide who he should be with, who he should love.

Trey gripped the clipboard in one hand and the pen in the other. He felt himself rising, his face hot with indignation. Feeling Resa's hand on his arm, he looked down at her. From the look on her face, she had no idea what she had just witnessed. Whether she knew or not, it was wrong for her to be judged or to be treated this way.

Never.

She was better than him. Better than that whole group of men he'd seen inside his head.

"Trey. What's wrong?" she asked.

The anger inside him consumed him to such a degree that he couldn't answer.

"Sit down. Talk to me."

Trey didn't want to sit down; he wanted to leave. Why would Mr. Gray send him to a place with these kinds of people? He'd wait a whole day in that county hospital before inflicting Resa to this sort of *subtle censure*.

Before he could open his mouth to tell Resa that he was leaving, the receptionist called a patient, a little girl with a huge bandage on her arm. She had a round, chubby face and wore two short pigtails. Her skin was a creamy dark brown. Her mother stood and took hold of her uninjured hand. "Coming to get those stitches out once and for all?" the receptionist asked the little girl in a friendly way. "You'll hardly feel a thing," she added when her only response was a solemn nod. "Then after it's all over, we'll have a treat for you," she continued, guiding them inside.

The door closed behind them but opened a second later. The receptionist stared as him curiously. "Is there something I can help you with, sir?"

"No," Trey said, shaking his head allowing Resa to pull him back into his seat. He stared at the clipboard for a long moment, not seeing any of the words on the form. Was this what his life was going to be like? Memories of his old self colliding with his new? Would he view anything he saw as suspect?

"Did she remind you of something?" Resa asked.

"Yes, and I got a little confused, but I'm okay now."

"Good. Let's fill out this form. There's only one person before us."

Trey looked over at the old, balding white man sitting across the room and found himself wondering if he participated in any special night time meetings like the ones sponsored by the group he'd once help lead. He shook his head. Not every white person in America was a white supremacist, he reminded himself. His cousin Cassie who had married a black man; his mom and dad. Scott, the white man who married Resa's cousin, was another, and he could list a whole lot more. Feeling better, Trey looked down at the chart. Resa was leaning over him and had already filled in the top line. *Doe, John.*

"I thought you couldn't lie," he whispered into her ear.

"Technically I'm not. I've got a feeling that some-times you are John Doe. Like just a minute ago. I lost you for a while. You weren't Trey, and you were fighting to keep yourself from being Travis. Basically you were in limbo, therefore better known as John Doe."

"Three people in one? That makes me sound sort of crazy."

"Not crazy considering the circumstances. Only confused."

"Which one will win?"

"That's up to you, but I'm betting on Trey."

"Then I can't lose."

"Goodbye now," the receptionist was saying to the now smiling little girl and her mother. "Take care not to get hurt like that again," she said. The next instant she was calling the patient who snored quietly in a chair across the room. "Mr. Frank, the doctor will see you now," she said to him. "Mr. Frank?" She gently went over to nudge the man awake.

The gentle manner in which she had handled the little girl and the old man put to rest the assumptions he had made about the middle-aged woman. Being white did not automatically make someone guilty of being a bigot. Trey would have to learn not to jump to conclusions. It would be difficult as his mind revealed inside knowledge, practices, and beliefs of the underhanded organization he had once led.

"Fill out the rest of the form, Trey. They'll be calling us in next," Resa prompted.

The next few minutes were spent filling out the various forms, marking only what they could since his medical history was a mystery. They decided to use Dr. Ramsey's cabin as his address. "I'll be back before you leave."

"I'll be here until the end of the summer."

"The doctor's ready to see you, Mr.—"

"Doe. John Doe," Trey told her, frustrated with the interruption. He hoped he could set things right by the end of the summer. He stood, reached down to grab Resa's hand and they followed the receptionist inside. Directing them to a small exam room, the older lady smiled. "Doc Williams will be with you in a moment," she said, closing the door behind her.

"I'm pretty sure everything's going to be fine," Resa was saying as the door opened after a soft of knock.

"If you're fine, then why are you here?" A cheerful young man, wearing jeans and a white lab coat came into the room. The thought immediately coming to Trey's mind was that he had the look of one of the organization's followers. Trey tossed that thought aside as the man, not much older than he, introduced himself. "I'm Dr. Williams," he said to Resa, then Trey, shaking each of their hands. "You're friends of the Grays?"

"Yes," Trey answered.

"Miss Lily tells me that you were involved in a plane crash just as the blizzard hit."

"That's right," Trey answered, just now realizing that he should have been somewhere nearby as the phone call to the doctor was being made.

"You sustained some injuries, lost your sight for a period of time, and you still have no memory of who you are?"

"Yes," Trey cautiously answered, wondering exactly how much Mrs. Gray had said.

Making a clicking noise, the doctor noted a few things on the chart he was holding and shook his head a couple of times before saying, "Trauma to eyes due to hitting your head during the crash most probably caused the temporary blindness. Your temporal and occipital lobe were most likely affected. I'll be asking you a few specific questions to see if there's any evidence of post-concussion syndrome. I'd say you had your run of bad luck, crashing during a blizzard and not being able to get to a hospital."

"I'd rather think I was pretty lucky. I crashed into the backyard of a nurse."

"Oh, you must be the lovely young lady who nursed Mr. Doe back to health." The doctor smiled at Resa.

"Yes, I did."

"Well, he's walking and talking. You must have done some serious nursing."

"I did what I could."

"Okay then, let's start this exam, Mr. John Doe—" He stopped.

"Something wrong, Doctor?" Trey asked.

"Not really, but it seems to me that Miss Lily called you by another name. What was it?"

"Trey," he jumped, in not wanting the doctor to dwell on names. "It's a sort of nickname I acquired."

"Some nickname, but it sounds right," the doctor said, placing the stethoscope in his ears. He checked every vital sign, prodded and prodded Trey before declaring, "You're looking mighty healthy for someone who survived a plane crash."

The room filled with sighs of relief.

"I'd like to ask you a few question, Miss—

"Miss Lewis, Teresa Lewis."

"Well, Miss Lewis, I'd like to ask you a few questions about Trey's treatment under your care. Then we can get a few x-rays and take a trip across the street for a visit with the sheriff."

CHAPTER 13

An hour later, after x-rays and a PET scan of his brain, Trey was cleared of any permanent damage to his brain. It was confirmed that the blow to his head had affected his temporal lobe and was responsible for his memory loss. Trauma to his occipital lobe had been responsible for his temporary blindness. Declining the doctor's offer to visit with the sheriff, they were back on the road again.

Hearing the word sheriff had struck fear into him. Trey was less afraid of being arrested and thrown in prison for his past misdeeds then he was of Resa finding out his past before he had the chance to tell her any of it or have the opportunity to set things right. It had not occurred to him that he might be required to report the plane crash to the local sheriff's office. Dr. Williams didn't press the issue but let it be known that filing a report with the sheriff's office could help him to find out who he was. The doctor meant well, but there was no way that Trey was going to have anything to do with any kind of police until he turned himself in. Unfortunately, Resa might. He would have to warn her. Someone was bound to show up asking about the crash and survivors. The blizzard was probably the only thing that had kept the authorities away this long. This entire situation was getting stickier by the minute, leaving more to worry about, more to talk about tonight.

Resa had been quiet since leaving the doctor's office. He was sure that she had drawn some of the same conclusions about the authorities that he had but was keeping her thoughts to herself, not wanting to ruin their day any more than he did. The silence inside the Jeep stretched and soon evolved into a comfortable, peaceful one as they turned on to Interstate 40, an hour later, veering south on I-75 toward Chattanooga.

The quiet didn't bother Teresa. In fact, it was soothing to know that they didn't have to talk. They were both experiencing an enormous amount of relief. Relief that Trey was well and healing, relief that they had avoided a visit to the sheriff's office. Anything else would come later. Their time together didn't have to be filled with noise, just each other. No talking was necessary. "Chatta about nothing," she whispered to herself, a curt laugh pushing pass her lips.

"What did you say?"

"Nothing." Resa smiled at him.

"Nothing?"

"It was silly, especially after dealing with all that tension at the doctor's office."

"Silly's good for relieving tension."

"Maybe."

"So you won't tell me."

"Nope." She shook her head, enjoying this trivial conversation about nothing while she could.

"Then I won't let you in on the surprise I've got planned."

"A surprise?"

"Don't ask twice. If you won't share, I don't intend to."

"Fine by me," Teresa laughed, deciding that the anticipation of a surprise was much better to dwell on. The next eighty miles were filled with moments of silence, teasing, a bit of playful prying, and an ease of affection. Often she felt a hand on her knee or fingers that lightly caressed her neck or shoulder. Teresa soon found herself following his lead, feeling free to express herself in the same way.

"Are you hungry yet?" Trey asked as they neared Chattanooga.

"Even if I'm not, I bet you are."

"It's way past lunch time."

"It's barely one o'clock."

"And all we had for breakfast was a mug of cocoa and a bit of food at the Grays. A man on the mend can't survive on that."

"You mean, *you* can't survive on that."

"Either way, I'm starving."

"Look, there's a sign and I literally mean a sign. Take the Chattanooga/Birmingham exit."

"You want to go to Birmingham to eat?"

"I'd die of starvation by then."

"Then Chattanooga here we come. Direct the way. This is your trip."

"But you're glad you came."

"So far, " she smiled over at him.

"Take that Downtown/ Lookout Mountain exit," Trey said a few minutes later. "There's bound to be food there."

"Check that out," he said, fake surprise evident in his voice. "The Chattanooga Choo Choo Holiday Inn. Pull in there."

A big sign in the shape of a black train engine high on top a red brick building proclaimed the words Choo Choo. The vivid green Holiday Inn logo on an awning identified the building as part of the familiar hotel chain. Pulling into the parking lot, she glanced at Trey. There was little-boy excitement on his face, telling her that this was his surprise.

Stepping out of the Jeep, Trey announced, "I smell food." Wrapping his arm around her waist, he nuzzled her neck. "Smells almost as good as you."

The grounds of the hotel held an array of businesses. There was a museum situated inside a railcar from the original Chattanooga Choo Choo, a shop that sold a variety of goods as well as providing old tyme photos. A trolley similar to the streetcars found in New Orleans ran up and down one of the streets near the hotel. Instead of being army green, the trolleys were yellow with red trim. This was definitely a tourist area, and where there were tourists, there were places to eat.

"Let's check out the hotel. There might be a buffet."

Walking into the spacious lobby, Teresa noted the airy feel of the atrium. Following his nose, Trey led them to the restaurant section of the hotel. "Lo and behold, a buffet." Resa laughed.

"Don't play with a man's appetite."

"I wouldn't dream of it."

Following Trey around the buffet, Teresa suddenly realized just how hungry she was. Her plate filled with a variety of dishes, she left Trey to make her way to the table they had been shown earlier. Later, having eaten her fill, she watched as he went back two more times before joining her for desert. "Where do you put it all?"

"I've got no idea, and I hope that I don't pay for this later. For all I know, I used to be a picky eater. At this rate I might turn into one of those fat guys."

"I doubt it," Teresa told him, reaching over to grip a bicep which he immediately flexed. "After all you've been through, you've still got muscles. I'd say you're used to eating enough to feed an army or air force or whatever you used to be part of."

Whatever he used to be part of. Funny how his past kept jumping out at him. Placing a kiss on the hand still gripping his arms, he moved to her lips, giving her a quick kiss there before offering her a piece of his apple pie, which she quietly accepted, her eyes relaying that whatever it was he was thinking she was here for him, with him now. An uneasy look came into her eyes as she shared the pie with him.

"You know, I just realized something."

"What?" he asked, offering her the last piece of pie. When she shook her head in refusal Trey popped it into his mouth.

"I think we stand out a little here. Not only are we the one and only interracial couple I've noticed, but I'm the only black tourist around."

Scanning the room, Trey noted the same thing. Except for the busboy and the woman working at the desk, Resa was the only black person around.

"Does that bother you?"

"No, I didn't even think about it until I got the feeling that people were staring at me. At us."

"Well, this is Tennessee, the home of the Ku Klux Klan," Trey stated as simply as if he'd named the first president of the United States.

"What? Are you sure?"

"Yeah, I read it somewhere," he told her, trying to downplay what he had revealed. He'd read it somewhere alright. It was a proud proclamation plastered on almost every publication produced by the organization, because it was based in Tennessee. That memory almost pulled Trey out of his seat. Instead, he stared at the people in the restaurant, in the lobby and others milling around. Some people paid them no mind, but others were staring, with daggers, it seemed. The look reminded him of the subtle censure he had, in his other life, directed others to use. Trey threw a bit of his own subtle censure right back at a young teenager lagging behind his parents to stare at them, and an old couple who almost ran into a wall because of their preoccupation with them.

"Do you mean to say people in this room might be Ku Klux Klan members?"

"Or of a similar organization. You never know, but most of the people here are tourists. I wouldn't worry." Trey kissed her long and deep, tasting the coffee she had been drinking with desert. "Most people are just nosy," he said, rubbing his nose against hers, wanting her to forget the people who stared. At least, he hoped he was right. What if someone from the organization came across him here with Resa? Trey shuddered with that thought. They would both become targets.

"Are you ready to go, John?"

"What did you say?"

"You are in limbo-land again. I'm going to the restroom. Why don't you find out what there is to see here in Chattanooga?"

"Will do." Walking with her until they reached the registration desk, Trey watched her until she entered the restroom, then scanned the room for familiar faces. Not sure who would be familiar, he searched nonetheless. As he looked around, a thought popped into his mind. No one would be around. They were all preparing for the Grand Action. "The Grand Action?" he thought. "What was that?" Training his mind on that thought, he focused, but got nothing. His brain shut down.

"Can I help you, sir?" the young girl at the registration desk asked.

"I'd like a room, a railway car room," he added, remembering Mrs. Gray's suggestion, "and any brochures on the sights in this area."

"This is your lucky day. There was a cancellation of a railcar room just this morning. The blizzard kept the couple away. We lucked out here, barely getting any of the snow that fell further north," she rambled. Then, "Will one king-sized bed be sufficient?"

"Yes," Trey answered. The transaction of money and keys caused him to absently compare their hands. There was a time when feelings of immediate dislike and superiority would course through him with even such a trivial encounter. Now all he felt was grateful. Grateful for the smile and the professional manner in which this young lady addressed him, the brochures she offered, and the availability of the room he wanted.

After waiting for Resa at the hotel entrance, he pulled her into his arms as soon as she was within reaching distance. "Mind if we check out that little shop I saw coming in?"

"The one for the old tyme photos?"

He nodded.

"I wouldn't mind browsing."

As soon as they entered the store Trey went to a cowboy hat hanging on the wall. "What do ya' think, little lady?" he asked, tipping the hat forward.

"Nice accent," a middle-aged woman behind the counter said.

"I was about to say the same thing," Teresa nodded.

"Would you care to try on a complete costume? How about you, too, ma'am? I can take a picture of you two together. You are together, right? I'll have you decked out Old West style, photographed, and out the door with a brand new souvenir in less than twenty minutes."

"What do you think, Resa?"

"Why not? I like the idea of a souvenir."

"Me too. Show us what you've got, miss."

Not long afterward, Trey was outfitted as a gunslinger and Resa a saloon girl. Standing in front of the mirror together, they both uttered a solid, "No!" The saloon outfit didn't fit Resa's personality and the dark gunslinger getup reminded Trey of Travis.

They spent the next thirty minutes rummaging through racks of clothes, finding, trying on, and discarding a number of outfits until Trey spotted a portrait on one of the walls. "That's the one," he announced, pulling Resa toward him.

The portrait was of an old western couple on their wedding day. The man looked stiff and uncomfortable in the dark suit and white shirt. The woman dressed in white ruffled lace didn't look too thrilled either.

"They don't look too happy."

"It was probably one of those mail-order marriages famous during old western times. Ours will be different. We'll smile and look happy."

"That's not the only thing that's going to be different," Resa told him. "This will be a true black and white picture."

"Making us unique pioneers."

Resa grinned up at him and they laughed at the truth of it.

"I've got another outfit for you guys to try," the lady called Marge announced. "Sheriff and deputy!"

"We've found what we were looking for." Trey pointed to the wall.

"So, it's like that, is it? Why didn't you say so? You two engaged or something?"

"Yes, we are," Resa answered for them, her thumb and index finger tracing the wire ring she still wore.

"I'll get the wedding outfits for you, and since it took more than the twenty minutes I promised, I'll throw in a complimentary picture."

"Thanks," they said together, following the woman to the dressing room.

Seeing Resa in the frilly white dress almost had him believing that it actually was his wedding day.

"You are looking mighty handsome there, cowboy."

"And you are beautiful. Marry me."

"I pronounce you man and wife," the lady named Marge declared. "Step right here in front of the camera."

Trey bowed to Resa, allowing her to pass. They stood side by side, their arms around each other and smiled at the camera. "According to Marge, we're married."

"Then kiss me," Teresa invited just as Marge shouted, "Get ready!" She snapped the first picture. A second later she looked up and said. "True love, I can see it. The camera never lies." Then she snapped the next picture and one more, for good luck she told them.

By the time they changed and came back to the front of the store, the pictures were ready. Resa went into her purse to pay for them.

"I've got it," Trey told her.

"But you paid for lunch, and I know that you don't have that much money on you," she whispered not wanting Marge to hear.

"I got a loan."

"A loan?"

"From Mr. Gray. I'm treating you today, not the other way around."

"Whatever you say." Teresa let it go. After all, she had promised him his day.

He paid for the pictures as she admired them.

"Pick out your two favorites. I'm keeping that last one to post, if you don't mind."

Trey didn't say anything for a moment. His tone was curt and firm when he answered, "I do mind."

"But you two are such a beautiful couple and the world, or at least the part that comes in here, needs to see it."

"I agree with that, but I have personal reasons for asking you not to post it. Here, I'll pay for the third shot." Trey threw a twenty on the counter, grabbed the portrait and walked out the door.

"Sorry," Teresa said to Marge, slowly following him out to quietly stand beside him.

"I didn't mean to do that," he told her.

"I realize that."

"I can't have my picture plastered around anywhere, especially here."

"I figured as much. Where should we go now?" Teresa asked, glancing at the brochures he had taken from his pocket, knowing that he was dealing with some more memories and she needed to pull him back.

"How about a ride on the world's steepest passenger railway at Lookout Mountain?" he asked, trying to sound enthusiastic.

"You don't want to do any sightseeing here?"

"No, we'll have plenty of time this evening. We've got a room."

"Ah-ha, the surprise."

"And just wait until you see it," he said, a bit of real excitement creeping into his voice.

⁓

"Impressive."

"I agree," Resa said her head turning in every direction in order to take in the surrounding mountains and valleys as they traveled down Lookout Mountain's Incline Railway.

"When they said steep, they meant steep," Trey said, peering out the window. "Take a look at that long line of track."

"Enjoy the view," she told Trey. "I bet you won't find one like it anywhere else." The sight of distant cities many miles away added to the awe she already felt for the mountains. They held a beauty she wished she could grab with her bare hands. Instead, she reached for Trey's, leaning into him as she peered over his shoulder, barely registering the train passing beside them at the halfway mark. Reaching the bottom, they exited the railway. Teresa pulled Trey along as they got in line for the ride back up the mountain.

"You enjoyed that, I take it."

"I love the mountains. They've got a hold on me, I think."

"I understand. I feel the same way about a certain someone."

"You and your compliments."

"They're more than compliments. They're the truth," he insisted, guiding her to sit by the window for the return trip up Lookout Mountain.

"This might sound a little crazy, but I'll let you in on a little truth I think I've discovered."

Trey's heart froze, then beat double time. Truth? What truth? Had she somehow found out about him? "Relax," he told himself. If she had, then she wouldn't be smiling.

"I told you that the mountains sent you to me. Well, I believe there's some greater reason, some secret to why you came into my life."

"I know why you came into mine."

She looked at him in question, her face now so familiar and dear to him. Her brown-eyed, brown-skinned beauty was a wonder. "You are my savior. You inspire more awe in me than any mountain and are more beautiful in comparison."

"Trey, why do you tell me these things?"

"Because they're true."

"Oh."

"And because they're inspired by love. I love you," he whispered into her ear.

"I love you, too."

"Just keep right on loving me for a long time, Resa. For a really long time."

She nodded, to show that she understood his meaning. "Worry when you have to," she reminded herself, focusing on the view just as the other car passed at the halfway mark. This time around, people waved and shouted from the other car. With a bit of encouragement from the driver, the enthusiasm spread to the passengers around them.

Trey joined in, grabbing one of Teresa's hands and raising it high to greet the neighboring car. Faces smiled right back at them, young and old and mostly white but all friendly—until the end. A little boy no more than seven or eight was energetically waving both hands in the air but froze at the sight of them. His little face turned into a mask of hate unusual on someone so young. His mouth twisted, and his tongue stuck out to blow a huge raspberry directed at them with the point of his finger. Resa stopped waving, her head shaking in disapproval. Trey simply stared at the boy, his eyes following the child who turned to face the back of the trolley to continue his insult. Trying not to let the towhead freckle-faced boy's insult throw him into making assumptions, Trey was ready to let it slide. Not every insult held a racial connection, he reminded himself. But before he turned back to Resa, a man sitting next to the child nodded and laughed, giving the little terror a high five. Trey wasn't sure but he could have sworn the man said, "Good job."

"What a brat," Resa said, leaning back into him.

"Yeah, a brat." Trey hugged her to him. Similar to the other brats the organization had begun raising to hate. Suddenly a clear image of himself appeared vividly in his mind. He was sitting in an office bare of everything except a desk and chair. He was on the phone. His voice, the tone he associated with Travis, filled his head. *"I'm going to be this baby's godfather. Raise him the right way, straight from the cradle. If you don't catch them young, they grow up with crazy ideas of equality."* He had been talking to Cassie after finding out she was pregnant, but before he knew that her husband was a black man. He had been hell-bent on taking Cassie's baby to raise exactly as that little boy was being raised. Feeling sick to his stomach, Trey followed Resa out of the railcar and back to the Jeep.

"You're not letting that little kid bother you, are you?" Resa asked.

"No, more like the Travis in me rearing his head to bother me. I have some serious issues. Are you sure you still want to marry me?"

"I haven't run away screaming yet."

"Okay, then, are you interested in seeing the world's tallest underground waterfall?"

"I'm game."

Two hours later, they made their way out of the cavern, away from the world's tallest underground waterfall. Taking hold of Resa's elbow, Trey muttered in her ear, "That was pretty anti-climatic."

"Ruby Falls is pretty, but it was anti-climatic," Resa agreed, turning to take one last look at the thundering, 145-foot waterfall that amounted to a heavy shower of water falling into a small natural pool. Colored lights shining upward in an effort to create a dramatic flare did little to transform the world's tallest underground waterfall into the spectacular display promised. Ruby Falls was beautiful Teresa had to admit, but after the buildup and hoopla leading to the viewing, the waterfall left one a little flat. They had found more excitement making their way through the cavern than actually viewing the waterfall.

"This day isn't exactly turning out the way I hoped," Trey mumbled.

"Not exactly, but I've had fun. I've had good company."

"When my brain wasn't lost in limbo."

"You're still recovering, Trey. Maybe spending all day out wasn't a good idea."

"Maybe we had better talk about the man we've been avoiding all day—Travis. I was happy with you until I remembered. I found you and fell in love and that was all that was important. Then he showed up. Avoiding talking about the man I used to be hasn't made him go away."

"And you want to make him go away?"

"Permanently. You'll understand when I tell you about him. Do you mind if we go back to the hotel? We can talk there."

"I was going to suggest that."

"Don't you mean fold your arms and tell me what I was going to do?" Trey threw at her in an attempt to lighten the mood. He didn't want her to hate him. Which was why he had attempted to ignore the issue all day.

"Not this time." She smiled at him gently. "This is your call. I promised to wait until tonight. If you want a few more hours respite, I'll give you that, but I do deserve some answers tonight."

Resa deserved a whole lot more than answers. "Let's go, then."

The ride back to the hotel was empty of sound though chock-full of emotion. His mind was a jumble of resignation, disgust, and most of all, *fear*. Resa was doing a good job of trying to remain calm, but he could sense the anxiety she was feeling. Parking in almost the exact same place as before, Trey turned to her. "Don't hate me, Resa," he told her, reaching to the back of the car to get the bag he had packed. He might not need the clothes, he could be leaving her tonight. But he needed the picture. It would help him to explain.

They walked down a lighted path across the beautifully manicured grounds to a line of railcars. Trey searched, found their railcar and led Resa up the steps to the door.

"This is where we're staying?" she asked.

"Surprise." He gave a sheepish half grin, not feeling as cocky about his surprise as before. "I thought you'd like this. Sleeping in a railway car is pretty unique and special. Like you."

Teresa nodded and whispered, "Like you, Trey." She reached for his hand and caught his wrist, stopping him from opening the door, not ready to hear what awful things Trey had supposedly done before the accident, before she had fallen in love with the man she knew as Trey. "Can this discussion wait? *I* want a respite. *I* want to enjoy the next few hours with you."

Thinking that forever would be better, though impossible, Trey settled for what he could get. "A few hours won't hurt."

"Good. Kiss me and open the door."

Trey glanced around at all the people still milling about. "What if I open the door and then kiss you?"

"That sounds even better."

Unlocking the door and stepping inside, Trey placed the bag on the nearest surface. Then he gently pulled her to him as he closed the door with his body. Closer to him than she had been all day, Resa's body rested flush against him. Her warm breath heated the skin on his neck. Trey leaned back, his hands lifting her face. He focused on her lips but that wasn't where this kiss would begin. He would get there. He would find her lips just as he had done before he could see. He had found what he was looking for, even when he was blind, and he would a find a way for Resa to be his.

Closing his eyes he leaned into her, his lips pressing against her chin. He nibbled and sucked before moving on, not up, that would be too easy. Eyes closed, Trey meandered his way across her cheek, his lips sliding and tasting as he went, across her eyelids, back again to move down the bridge of her nose to hover above her lips. He inhaled her sweetness before opening his eyes to find his prize.

"Trey," she breathed into his mouth.

"I love finding your lips," he said before hording her goodness, using his lips and tongue to pull her into him. He wanted all of her and she was giving herself to him until—

She pulled back and stared up at him with a look that left no doubt she was just as full of desire as he. Taking a step back, Resa maneuvered a hand under his shirt, her fingers warm and enticing on his bare skin. He had wanted a kiss, a real kiss, but Resa was telling him with her eyes that she just plain *wanted*.

"Let's go to bed," she whispered against his mouth.

"Oh. Oh noooo," unbelievably, came out of his mouth even as 'oh yes' sighed inside his head.

"But I want you." She took another step back, looking confused.

"But we can't, Resa." Trey moved back into her, his hand maneuvering its way under her sweater and up her back to pull her close, completely contradictory to his words.

"Why?"

"Because we're not married."

"We're close enough to being married." She smiled up at him. "Marge married us."

"No, Resa, that's not good enough."

"How about wanting you so bad that I—"

Shaking his head, he placed a finger on her lips. He knew what she was going to say. He felt the same way, had been feeling the same way for as long as he'd known her. He wanted Resa—so much that his skin craved her touch. "I know exactly what you mean, but you can't do this, Resa."

"What am I doing?"

"Giving yourself to me because you're afraid of what I have to tell you about myself."

"No." She moved away, folding her arms as she went. "That's not what I'm doing."

"I think that you are." Trey took one of her arms and pulled it down, then the other. "I can't let you do this. I'm not worth it. Not yet, anyway. I will be. When I deserve you, we'll come together. We'll be together. Please. Can you wait for me, Resa?"

Teresa had waited years for the love of her life. She had found him in the least likely place and from the least likely race. And if loving him as she did meant waiting, she would. After all, she had waited twenty-five years already, what could a little more time hurt?

"Waiting is something I know how to do. I've been doing it a long time."

"I know, and I'm honored—"

"—I want you to be more than that." At his raised eyebrow she continued. "I want you to be aware that I'm banking on you being worth the wait." Teresa kissed him with a sultry passion that brought to life the memory of a slow, hot evening in the middle of a New Orleans summer.

She slowly pulled away, came back for another quick taste of him before turning to a door behind them that she hoped was the bathroom. She had never been so bold as to become a seductress, or felt so hot that the cold shower she was about to take would no doubt create enough steam to fill the room the minute she stood under it.

Trey felt her move away from him. The warmth of her lips, the heat from her body pressed against his, left him completely. Shivering as a sense of bereavement went through him, he watched her move away from him, questioning his decision, his own sanity. He had had Resa in his arms, warm and willing and *he* had held back! She disappeared behind a door just as his feet moved to correct his mistake, only to stop at the dark paneled door. Blood pounded above and below as he took deep cleansing breaths. He had stopped for a reason, a very good reason, he told himself, as he searched his passion-clouded mind for the reason. A few deep breaths later, and the sound of the shower blasting sent traces of those reasons back into his brain.

"You don't deserve her. Not yet, at least."

"Not yet," he repeated, backing away from the door and plopping into a chair. "You hurt her family. You judged and demoralized her people," he reminded himself, head in his hand. "And you're not a free man." Feeling himself falling into the same depression he had begun this day with, Trey lifted his head. He wouldn't allow his last hours with Resa to end this way. His eyes landed on a pad and pen sitting next to the phone. Picking up the pen he found himself doodling. He drew a heart and a couple of stick figures, smiling to himself as he realized what he was a doing. This was something he had never done before, at least not something he had done in over a dozen years. He felt himself reconnecting with his young self, the person he had been before his heart had been trapped with hate and his brain washed with bigotry.

A plan grew along with the doodle. Trey wrote a message at the bottom of the pad, his heart lighter than it had been a few seconds ago. The shower still blasting, he propped the pad up in the middle of the bed and left to set a wonderful, memorable night in motion.

Teeth chattering, Teresa wrapped herself in a towel and peered into the room. Seeing no sign of Trey, she was both relieved and disappointed. Standing in a towel, cold, Teresa dug through the bag Trey brought, finding a pair of jeans, a light sweater and a pair of undies rolled together. Not caring much about what he had packed, she quickly dressed, intent on covering herself before he returned. Throwing the towel into a corner of the bathroom, she stood before the mirror running her fingers through the short curls on top of her head. She dug into her purse to find a small tube of gel she kept for hair emergencies. This would be one if she didn't tame her hair before her curls became frizzes.

As she rubbed the gel between her palms and then into her hair, she realized that Trey had been right. She had thrown herself at him because she wanted to make love to the man she knew, not the one she would soon know about. If she loved him, she would have to love all of him or at least accept who he had once been and at the same time appreciate who he was now. She had been scared. Teresa stared at herself. She was still scared. Placing the brush on the counter, she bent to find her shoes, wondering where they had gone off to. As she found them and slipped them on, she noticed a rectangular pad leaning against the pillows. A huge heart in the middle and two stick figures holding hands dominated the page. Teresa grinned at this new piece of info she had on him. He was a doodler. This was the kind of information she was content to know. At the bottom of the page was some writing.

Meet me at The Station House at seven.

Love,

Trey

Resa glanced at the clock radio at the bedside. It read 6:55. That didn't give her much time to get to, no, first to find what The Station House was. Taking a quick glance at herself in the mirror once more, she grabbed the key from the table on her way out. Walking across the grounds and back toward the photo store in order to get to the main part of the hotel, she spotted The Station House and headed toward it. Moving closer to the row of businesses, she discovered that it was a restaurant. Food. She should have known.

Teresa walked inside. It took a moment for her eyes to adjust to the dim lighting and her ears to take in the sound of a live band. A singer belted out the words to a popular song as she scanned the room for Trey. Intent on finding him, Teresa jumped when a young man dressed in a back and white uniform said to her, "Your table is ready ma'am."

"But I—"

"We've been waiting for you."

"Oh," was all Teresa could think to say as she followed the young man to the table.

Not long after she sat, someone laid a tray before her. On it was a green leaf from an oak tree and a red rose. Not knowing what to think as the waitress walked away, Teresa scanned the room once again, knowing that Trey was the only person she'd get any answers from.

The tune came to an end as she half-listened to the singer, "Once again, welcome to The Station House, home of the famous singing waiters and waitresses! As I leave you to serve more of the delectable dishes from our menu, my colleague has an oldie but goodie coming right at ya'!"

The young man who had directed her to the table went up onto the stage. Teresa turned her focus to him, absently picking up the leaf as she listened.

"Oh, this is an oldie but definitely a goodie, folks, but then again, much more than that. Though I love the old stuff, this particular song wasn't my choice. I'm singing by request of a gentleman for a special lady."

A soft melody filled the restaurant. The young man's voice deepened with a rough timbre, sounding as close as someone could get to Louis Armstrong's voice. The words to "What a Wonderful World" vibrated in the air. The significance of the leaf and rose was made clear as she listened.

This was Trey's doing.

So positive that he was the gentleman and she the special lady she stopped searching, closed her eyes and opened herself to the song, feeling the wonderful world described within it.

Blue skies, white clouds, roses, trees and a rainbow full of color, a human rainbow in a world with all kinds of people, people who cared about each other. A utopia? A possibility? Maybe a world they could have together? Teresa sighed at the possibilities.

" '...what a wonderful world'," Trey's voice rang inside her ear as his arms wrapped around her from behind.

"What a wonderful you," she told him, twisting to face him. "Thank you."

"Thank you for—?"

"A wonderful memory. Thanks for making this one for me."

Shrugging his shoulders, he caught her gaze and held it. "I thrive on making memories. For you. For me. For us. I need you to remember them while I'm gone."

"I won't have to do that for long, right? You'll be back."

"I'll be back. My world can't be wonderful without you in it."

"Then we'll have to make sure I'm in it."

"Agreed." He slipped into a chair beside her.

Time slowed as they lingered in their own little world. Lingering over the menu, over dinner, over dessert, over coffee. They lingered over every song as they danced, Trey convincing the waiter to sing their song again when every other customer left. He was certain that the waiter sang for no other reason than to get rid of them.

A slow walk back to room, the promise of a wonderful world more than a dream, neither one of them said a word. Talking would have shattered the memory they were creating, so fragile after a day of disappointments. They would have their wonderful world even if it lasted only a few hours.

Once inside their room, Trey guided her to sit on the bed. He helped her to remove her sweater, guiding one arm out, then another, folding it and laying it on a nearby chair. He unbuttoned her jeans and slid them down, tracing her shape, savoring her smooth skin against his palms. He gently tipped her onto the bed to pull off her shoes, one at a time. There was an underlying sexual tension between them, but more importantly, a sweetness of greater intensity and meaning than making love right now would be. What he felt was more tangible than the physical act of love. He needed more. He needed her love and respect because he might lose both later tonight. Not now, he thought as his hands lingered on her body until she took hold of them both.

Pulling his hands to his sides Teresa undressed him, savoring each moment, knowing that he would be gone soon. Each touch was precious to her, a memory to cherish. When they were in their underwear, Teresa pulled the covers back and invited him to crawl into bed.

Snuggled against him, Teresa didn't want to sleep, but long moments turned to contented slumber as she lost herself in his arms.

"Cass!" Trey felt the name rumble from his throat. A rush of urgency had him out of the bed and across the room before he realized where he was. A few moments of Resa staring at him as if he had gone crazy brought him fully back to himself. This was his last night with Resa. The last opportunity to hold her in his arms until God knew when. If she ever let him hold her again.

Trey moved back to the bed and eased under the covers, pulling her back into his embrace. She came, with some hesitation. The memory he had cultivated, their wonderful evening was over.

"Your cousin again."

"Yes."

"Your memories revolving around your cousin are why you're in trouble," she said, not asking but telling him what they both knew was true.

"Partly," Trey admitted, answering the question that was a non-question.

"My cousin Daniel married a woman named Cassie."

"I know. Cassie's my cousin," he answered sitting up. "It's warm in here," he told the room in general, throwing the blankets off. He stood and paced. Feeling her eyes on him and knowing there was no chance of avoiding the inevitable, he went to the bag he had packed and turned it upside down, emptying it onto the bed.

Out came the picture Teresa had found him staring at yesterday morning—Was it yesterday morning or the day before? She couldn't remember, the days were all running together.

They both stared at Teresa's family.

"Remember 'those others' I told you that I had to set things right with?"

She nodded, saying, "I'm guessing that 'those others' have something to do with my family." A surreal feeling began to overtake her. "Your cousin Cassie and my cousin's wife are one and the same."

"Yes," he said simply before a burst of information poured out of him. "Your cousin was the one I didn't want Cassie to marry. The marriage I was attempting to put an end to. Determined is more like it." As he stared down at the picture, he paused for a long, tense moment. "Funny, I know these people, but I don't know them. Now that some of my memory's returning I can tell you a lot about them. I know most of their names, what kid belongs to who, and where they work and live. I probably know even more, but that's where the holes in my memory come in. But if I really think about it, I don't know them because I don't know their stories, their history, their personalities. That was never important to me."

A chill ran through her as Trey spoke. Teresa knew that her cousins had experienced some trouble awhile back. Could the person Trey was before the crash have had something to do with it? How could he? But then again, how could he know or claim to know her family?

He was holding the picture in his hands, his gaze focused on the people framed before him. "These two are your parents, I bet."

"Yes," Teresa said, looking where his finger pointed.

"They have to be because I can't find a name for them, and I know just about everyone else's. You're tall like your dad but you look like your mother," he glanced up to say, catching her eye for a fraction of a second. "Beautiful," he said on a soft breath before his eyes flew back to the picture.

"Thanks," she told him, not sure how to answer. Not sure how she should feel as a numbness began to inch into her heart.

"You're not in the picture."

"I took the picture."

"That explains it," Trey went on, unable to stop himself now that he'd started. "There are Scott and Vanessa." He paused, clearing his throat as an image of his drunken self and his attempt to steal Scott's girls in order to save them from an unnatural environment flashed through his brain. He shook his head before going on. "There are Vicki and Megan, Scott's kids. Vanessa adopted them, you know. It all started with them."

"What started?"

"My interference in their lives; I was full of anger and was unreasonably jealous of Scott, who worked for my father. I tried to break up his engagement, you know." Trey sounded as if he were talking about someone he didn't know.

"Scott and Ness?" she asked, vaguely remembering some mention of trouble before they were married.

"Ness, I think I remember her being called that." Trey moved around the room again, the picture still in his hand. Putting it down long enough to pull on his jeans, he sat on the edge of the bed, picture on his lap, still as a statue.

Teresa waited.

"I tried to do a whole lot more to a few other people in this picture."

"Such as?" she prompted, wanting to know, thinking he might not tell her, and feeling that every word he spoke was harder for him to say than it was for her to hear.

"Ruin Devin's reputation. Sabotage his and Scott's partnership, attempted kidnapping. This list goes on but I won't color myself any blacker. I think you get the picture," he said tonelessly.

"I think I get the picture," Teresa answered, understanding exactly what he was telling her without allowing herself to truly take it all in. "You're saying that the card I found in your wallet was yours. That you believed what it said and acted accordingly."

"I once believed, but not anymore. I'm not that way anymore."

Teresa didn't want to believe any of what she was hearing. The man she fell in love with couldn't be the man he was describing. "Are you sure about all of this?"

"I'm sure. I wish I weren't as sure as I am at this moment." Placing the picture on the bedside table, he avoided looking at her as he spoke. He hadn't looked at her for a long time. "I'm sure because I remember the man I used to be. I remember Travis. I remember his hate and jealousy. I can almost taste it sometimes, and it makes me sick to my stomach." Trey paused, not wanting to say more but knowing he had to. Raising his head to look into her beautiful face, he said, "Why I believed what I used to believe and did what I did, I can't explain. Why did I change? A knock on my head and you in my life is my only explanation."

"Trey, this is all—" She stopped, her arms twisting the covers with quick, jerky movements.

She should have her arms folded, telling him to get out of her life. Something she had every right to demand. Something he was relieved that she hadn't done yet.

"Horrible. I agree. That's why I'm turning myself in." He stood and slipped a sweatshirt over his head, and stuffed his wallet into his back pocket. Standing beside the bed, he looked at her, really looked at her for the first time since this discussion had begun. "Don't hate me," he pleaded. "Hold on to our memories, the good ones. I'll come back when I've set things right. I hope you'll still be free, and that you'll have me."

Shoes in hand, he went outside. Teresa stared at the closed door, feeling nothing. In a state of disbelief, she scooted under the covers, telling herself, "This has got to be a nightmare." Nothing that left her so numb could possibly hurt so much.

CHAPTER 14

Trey sat on the steps outside, slipped his shoes onto his feet, went to the front desk, paid for the room, requested a taxi, and headed to the bus station—all without thinking.

If he thought, it would be about Resa and then he'd go back to her and she'd insist on helping him.

Or maybe she wouldn't.

He had no idea what she was thinking or what she thought of him. He hadn't asked. He didn't want to know.

His best course of action was to get as far away as possible so that he could make his way back to her. Hours spent waiting in the bus station, then three times as many on the road, blended into a jumble of events which led to the ones that he would have to live through to become worthy of Resa.

Getting off the bus at the combination bus and train station, he felt a sense of familiarity. He walked past the parked buses waiting for passengers. A memory eased into his mind as he stopped to take in the sight of the train that had just pulled into the station.

He remembered that he had been leaving New Orleans. A desperate panic had filled him, along with an intense sense of injustice and failure. He had failed. He hadn't taken Devin down, he hadn't ruined his reputation as he had planned and had almost gotten himself killed in a warped attempt to save Scott's girls from being raised by—

"Excuse me," a short, stocky man carrying a huge duffel bag said behind him.

Slowly coming away from the memory, Trey turned unfocused eyes on the man behind him.

"You might want to stand here all day, but I've got places to go and things to see. This is New Orleans, man!" The man reached around Trey, knocking him sideways to get to the exit.

"—mud people," his mind supplied. He promptly shook the thought away, sick to his stomach of the opinion and mindset of the man he used to be. Darting through the station and out into downtown New Orleans, Trey moved as fast as his feet would take him, past the main post office, the main library and onto Canal Street, all landmarks he knew but none he truly saw. Turning on the famous street and in the direction that would be less likely to cause him to mix with crowds of people, tourists and natives alike, he went in search of a hotel. He needed to clean himself, shower, shave. Resa had gotten into the habit of shaving him. He hadn't shaved himself since…

Since the morning he'd realized what a mistake it had been to send Red and Joe, two of his most ardent followers to "save" Cassie by kidnapping her. They'd screwed up. Trey didn't know how, just that they had, which was why he had flown out in the middle of a snowstorm, to get Cassie.

"Sir, are you coming in?" a doorman asked, holding the glass door wide. Nodding once, he walked past the man, wondering how long he had stood there looking like a fool. Trey prepaid for one night, hoping to get some sleep before going out the next day to see his dad, then maybe Cassie, to offer some kind of apology, and then to turn himself in to the police.

He took a shower, scrubbing at his skin in an effort to wash his old self away. He felt like *mud*, like a person tainted with evil. Feeling raw, he lay in the middle of the bed yearning for Resa, yearning to cleanse his soul as thoroughly as he had his body. Pulling the covers around him, he felt himself falling into an exhausted slumber brought on by twenty-four hours of wakefulness. He had hoped that would be enough to stop him from remembering.

But he didn't want to forget everything. Trey pulled out a memory of Resa on the day his sight had returned. They had fallen asleep on the sofa, her head resting on his lap. He had simply stared at her beautiful face. With that memory etched in his brain, he slept.

~~~

Many hours later, bright light shone inside the room. Hopping out of bed he felt a surge of energy.

Today was a new beginning. Resa's face swam in his mind as he once again dressed in the only clothes he had. The digital clock's red glow told him it was eleven o'clock. If he walked to the architectural office his dad owned, he could make it there just as he came back from lunch. His dad was man who followed a schedule just as surely as he was a man who followed the Golden Rule: Treat others as you want to be treated. Trey knew this rule, he had learned it, but somewhere in time he'd lost sight of it, of his family, of everything that had once held meaning for him.

"What day is it?" He stopped just before crossing the threshold at the entrance of the hotel, looking up to find the same doorman he had seen yesterday.

"Wednesday."

Wednesday, this was even better. For as long as he could remember, his mom ate lunch with his dad every Wednesday. They'd leave early and be back around twelve-thirty or so. He could sneak into the office and wait for him to return.

Plan set, Trey walked up Canal to South Jefferson Davis Parkway, turning toward Bayou Saint John where the office in which he himself had once worked was located. His pace was steady enough to show his determination but slow enough to reveal the uncertainty he was feeling.

A few blocks from the office building, his steps slowed even more. What should he expect? What could he expect from a man he had basically disowned. "No expectations," Trey whispered to himself, glancing left and right before walking through the doors of a place that was as much home as his childhood bedroom. The lobby was empty. Maria, the sweetest, most rapid Spanish speaker from Mexico, was nowhere to be found. He grinned in memory of his attempts to translate the rapid-fire Spanish she used to throw at him. Even in his fourth year of Spanish in high school, he had never been good enough to understand every word from her mouth. He hadn't talked to her in over a decade. His smile faded as the last words he spoke to her rang inside his head. She had shot a question at him, her words as quick as lightning. He had just come from a meeting of a new exclusive club a friend's uncle had begun. Having spent an hour hearing about the virtues of being white and the horrors other races brought into the white community, he had exploded with, "Don't speak that trash to me. If you want to talk to me, use English." He had leaned onto her desk with a superior sneer. Looking as if she might slap him, she'd responded with a slow, carefully enunciated, "No problem," and had never spoken to him again. Funny, that day, he had felt as if he had won, that he had showed his superiority. Instead it had been the beginning of his downfall.

A spat of Spanish syllables rushed to his ears. Trey dashed into his dad's office, standing behind the cracked door to peek into the lobby. Maria looked exactly the same, petite, slender and full of energy. She couldn't have been more than six years older than he, which would make her about thirty-five. A feeling of shame overtook him as the many snide, degrading comments he had thrown her way under the guise of jokes flooded his mind. He wanted to go to her and explain, to apologize. But now was not the time. She was sitting at her desk working just as hard as usual when she paused to exclaim, *"Hola! Es el bebe!"* The next minute she was twirling a baby in her arms. "Oh, Cassie, she is perfect. The cutest bebe in all the world."

"We like to think so." It was his cousin's voice. Using a tremendous force of will, he stopped himself from flinging the door wide and checking to see what damage those fools he had sent might have done to her.

"We know so." A deep male voice cut into his thoughts.

That was Daniel, it had to be Daniel.

"You say that because she is yours; I say it because it is true," Maria said as everyone laughed.

Everyone, Trey discovered, was not only Maria, Cassie, and Daniel but also his mom and his dad. He would recognize their laughter anywhere. They were both happy people, as he'd once been before he'd joined "the club."

"The club." A classmate, a boy he barely knew, had been passing out fliers to all the white kids at the all boys high school he had attended. The flier, Trey could almost see it in his hands, had consisted of a list of questions. One question from it stood out: Do you love your race? He had laughed at the question, telling the guy who had given him the flier that the human race was the only one he was worried about. But later that day, after finding out that Trey hadn't made the track team, just like he hadn't made the football or baseball or basketball team, the guy came back in his face. "I've been watching you, and I notice you can't get yourself on a team, and I know why."

"Why?" Trey had asked slamming his locker closed, already knowing that it was because he was a scrawny, weak kid who hadn't caught up to other guys his age.

"Black people took all the spots. Look at all the teams. Almost all black. Hardly any room for us white folks."

Trey had dismissed him as crazy. He knew half the guys on the team; most of them were his friends. But the classmate wouldn't leave Trey alone. He caught him at odd moments to whisper half truths in his ear until Trey started to believe them and eventually became ripe pickings for "the club."

The absence of noise made him aware that his dad was coming toward the door. He thought of hiding behind it but quickly tossed the idea aside. A huge plant in one corner of the room looked like a good place to hide, but a flash of him dodging behind a similar plant in his quest to rid Scott, a one time co-worker of Vanessa, his black fianceé, made the thought distasteful as well as cowardly. Besides, scaring his dad half to death wasn't his intention. In the end, he sat on the corner of the desk and waited. His dad entered, closed the door behind him, shrugged out of his suit coat, and hung it up before looking up to find him there.

His dad's mouth moved to form his name but Trey was relieved that the shock of seeing him stopped him. Trey could only associate evil thoughts and deeds with it, and he didn't want to hear his dad utter the name that represented all he now hated.

"Hi, Dad."

"What are you doing here?" his dad asked, going behind his desk.

"I'm here to turn myself in," Trey began, stopping when a knock sounded at the door.

"Who is it?" his dad asked.

"Cassie. I think I dropped Jessica's pacifier in your office earlier."

"Wait a minute," he called staring hard at Trey, relaying the message that he didn't want Cassie to know he was here, which was fine because suddenly he didn't want her to know either. Trey nodded, stepped behind the office door and waited.

"Come in, Cassie Bear," his dad called, standing next to the now open door and pressing his body against it to keep Trey there. Having no intention of moving, Trey peeked through the crack in the door, spotting Daniel walking up and down the lobby holding the baby. He had her on his shoulder. Wide eyes looked around, curly, dark hair crowned her head. Maybe it was his imagination, but she looked exactly like Cassie. She was darker of course and had to have some feature of her father, but all he saw was Cassie, and he fell in love. She was a beautiful baby. He and Resa could easily make one just as adorable.

"Are you anxious to get back to work?" Cassie's voice invaded his thoughts.

"No, not really," his dad blustered.

"It's okay if you are. I mean we enjoyed lunch with you and Aunt Margaret and all, it's just that you seem to be acting a little strange."

The baby's cry stopped her from questioning him any further. His dad visibly relaxed and closed the door as he called out, "See you later!" He locked it behind him.

The click of the lock startled Trey. A sudden knowledge that his dad had never locked his door before made it clear that he was deeply disturbed by his presence.

"What are you doing here?"

"Dad—" Trey stood in the corner taking in the tense shoulders and abrupt movements.

"You're not going to harm Cassie or that beautiful baby. You'll take yourself away from Cassie and Daniel's life, away from your mother's and away from mine."

"Dad," Trey said once again, holding his hands out in surrender.

"You won't hurt this family anymore. Leave or I'm going to call the police." The phone was in his hand, making the threat real.

"Dad."

"Stop calling me that. I am no longer your dad, remember."

"I remember telling you that, but I don't believe it anymore. I remember believing a lot of things that I don't believe anymore."

"What are you talking about?" his dad asked, the phone emitting a loud warning tone before a recorded message to hang up came through the phone.

"I'm not the same man I was before. I've come to turn myself in."

"What?" The phone fell out of his dad's hand and onto the desk with a dull thud. Trey picked it up and replaced the receiver onto the base.

"Sit down, Dad. I have a long story to tell you. Some of it I just remembered," Trey said, easing himself onto the edge of one of the wide, black chairs in front of the desk, apprehensive, uncertain. "Please, Dad, sit," he begged when Travis Sr. stood towering above him.

Slowly Travis Sr. sat, keeping a leery eye on him. "I have no patience for games, Travis."

Trey flinched at the use of his given name.

"If this is some kind of trick…"

"It isn't." Trey shook his head before going on. "I've done some terrible things."

"I know."

"I'm here to make it all right, to turn myself in."

"Why?" His dad caught and held his gaze. Trey couldn't look away. These were the eyes of the man who had raised him to turn out in a completely different way than he had. This was a man who had loved him, who still loved him. Trey saw it in his eyes beyond the anger and hurt that was most obvious.

"Because I have done things that are morally, ethically, and legally wrong. I have gone against what you've spent your life teaching and showing me by your example. I'm setting things right because I can't live with myself unless I do."

A long moment of silence filled the room before he answered. "I'm listening."

And Trey began with "the club", which was the beginning of it all, which led to the white supremacy group he had joined.

Trey talked, his voice the only one in the room as he went trough every detail of his life and its destructive path as best as he could recall. With pain in his heart, he confessed to the crimes he knew he had committed, hoping there weren't many more hidden in the back of his mind. The pain lessened, though it didn't completely disappear when he talked about Resa and how she'd saved him in so many ways. Voice hoarse, mouth dry, Trey ended with his journey to New Orleans.

"How do I know that this isn't all a lie?" his dad asked, his face blank of all emotion. "You have told hundreds of stories, thrown a ton of insults my way. Why should I believe what you're saying?"

"Because the man you raised me to be has finally evolved."

There was a knock on the door. "One minute," his dad called, going to unlock and open the door.

"You've been locked up in here all evening, Mr. Labranch. I just came to tell you that I'm leaving for the day."

"Thank you, Maria. I'll see you in the morning."

"Are you okay?" Trey heard her ask. He sank into the chair, not wanting to see her, or for her to see him.

"I'm fine. I'll see you tomorrow."

"Adios!" she called.

Turning to face him as he shut the door, his dad stared at him, his eyes intent as a decision became clear in his eyes.

"You believe me."

His dad nodded. "I'm not sure if it's because I want to or because I prayed for something like this to happen for so long that I'll believe anything."

"You're believing the truth, and I'll prove it to you. Take me to the police yourself. Stay with me while I turn myself in."

Grim-faced, his dad nodded.

The ride to the nearest police station took no more than ten minutes. The Third District Police Station was located right along Bayou Saint John. Before getting out of the car, Trey turned to his dad and took a good look at him. His dad had aged tremendously since he had seen him last, which couldn't have been more than a year ago. Trey wondered how much of his own actions contributed to the gray in his hair and the stoop to his shoulders.

When his dad switched the engine off, Trey laid a hand on his dad's shoulder to get his attention. "I've used many words to hurt you, and these words may not be enough to erase the ugly ones, but I need to say them."

"I'm listening."

"I'm sorry. For the rest of my life, I will do what's right. I'll make you proud." Tears clouded his eyes but he saw his dad nod in acknowledgement.

They walked to the door side by side, Trey towering over his father who he had passed up in height long before puberty was over, but who he was just catching up to in maturity.

A young, female officer sat behind a desk.

"Can I help you?"

"I'm here to turn myself in, " Trey said, relief filling his lungs as the words left his mouth.

Before the young officer could respond an older man joined her. "Mr. Labranch, what are you doing here?"

The man looked vaguely familiar to Trey. He had short brown hair and a wide friendly smile that Trey knew was one he wore often.

"I came with my son. He's here to turn himself in."

"T. J.?" The officer's head twisted toward him. His face changed from friendly to threatening. He was around the desk in a blink of an eye. Trey's hands were handcuffed and he was being escorted to the back of the building before he knew what was going on.

"Frank!" his dad yelled. "Wait a minute." Frank looked as if he would refuse the request but he stopped, turned and waited. "For the first time, in a very long time, I'm proud of you, Son."

Trey mouthed, "Thanks, Dad," before being twisted back around and pulled down a hall into a small, dark room where his rights were read to him in clipped, sharp phrases. Frank left, assigning another officer to stand guard over him.

"Mr. Labranch." The officer's voice echoed down the hall to Trey. "How did you get him to do it?"

"I didn't get him to do anything. He came to my office and told me he wanted to turn himself in."

"So, no one else knows?"

"Not yet. Could you not tell the family until he's told his story?"

"Fat chance. Soon as Randy gets here, the whole family will know. It's their right to know that he's been arrested. Scott, Devin, Daniel, they'll all want a piece of him. The FBI wants a piece themselves."

He was wanted by the FBI, too? Sweat beaded Trey's brow at the idea. What else had he done? And Randy? Who was Randy? The name sounded familiar. Trey was certain he knew Randy.

"All I ask is that you listen to his story. He's been hurt, and he lost his memory."

"That's his story?"

Trey heard nothing else as the door was closed and locked by the officer who had been guarding him.

He sat in the dark room counting, taking deep breaths to keep himself centered. He was afraid, but at the same time certain that he was doing the right thing. The door swung open. Frank was back and along with him, a tall police officer with dark skin, dark eyes, and an expression that confirmed that he was in deeper trouble than he'd known.

One second the officer was standing across the room, the next, he was in Trey's face. "Where the hell have you been, T. J.? Do you know how many people have been looking for you?"

"A hellava lot," Frank said as if Trey didn't get the message.

"I realize that. I would like to make a confession. May I have pen and paper?" Trey asked, his heart beating double time. He probably should have written the confession ahead of time but he hadn't thought of it. And he hadn't thought about having a lawyer present. If he was confessing, would he even need a lawyer?

"I'll get you your pen and paper," Randy pulled back to mutter. He was gone all of two seconds, returning to slap a pad and pen onto the small table where Trey sat. "Un-cuff his writing hand, cuff his other one to the table and let him write. I don't think I can talk to him without throwing him across the room and bashing his head against the wall."

"That'll probably upset the feds," Frank said nonchalantly. "Right or left-handed?" he asked.

"Right," Trey answered, recalling the hand he'd used to fill out the forms at the doctor's office, the hand he'd used to write a note to Resa and to sign the card he'd left for her. He wondered if she'd found it yet. The cuff fell off his right hand. He twisted it in an effort to get feeling back into his fingers. His body was pulled to the left, another click of the cuff, and he was attached to the table. He leaned sideways, half lying on the table.

"Go on and write," Randy said to him, his arms folded, his eyes drilling holes into him.

Funny, Trey thought, Randy was almost the exact image of the man he thought he had been when he imagined himself black. Taking a deep breath he wrote:

I, Trey…

He paused, drew a line through Trey and forced himself to write his real name. From then on the words poured out of him. Nearing the end of the first page, Trey's thoughts were interrupted by a commotion outside the little room.

"Sounds like your family's here," Frank commented to Randy.

"I told them I'd keep them posted."

"Did you really think that would keep them away?"

"No," he answered focusing on Trey. "My brothers-in-law and cousin are all after your hide, my friend, and I don't feel much like protecting it." He walked out, leaving the door wide open.

That's who Randy was. The cop who was Vanessa's brother. Scott's brother-in-law, Devin's brother-in-law, Daniel's cousin. He'd known it. Confession forgotten, Trey strained his ears to hear what was going on outside. From the sounds of it, Scott, Devin, and Daniel were out there, and they all definitely wanted a piece of him.

"I want to see him! I want to look into his face and spit it in. I want to *personally* warn him to stay away from Cassie and to keep his goons away from my family!"

That was Daniel. He deserved to do what he was asking. Trey himself wouldn't have considered doing any less.

"Kidnapping. He needs to be charged with kidnapping, slander, and assault. I'm here to make sure it sticks."

Devin could have charged him with more. He deserved more, Trey thought, remembering a time when he had snapped the back of Devin's protective goggles while he worked, nearly causing him to be blinded in one eye.

"Where is he?" Scott asked. "I want to give him a few nightmares. He certainly had no problem giving my girls their share."

Scott's words were the last distinguishable ones he heard before the station turned into a mob scene.

"Enough!" Randy's voice rose above the others. "We have him; he's writing a confession, and the Feds are on their way. There's no reason for you all to be here."

"They've got every reason to be here." Trey recognized his dad's voice.

"Uncle Travis? Mr. Labranch?" male voices said in surprise.

"You're hurting, you're angry and you have a right to be, but please let justice take its course."

All was silent for so long that Trey thought they had all left. Then female voices traveled to the back of the station, Cassie's voice the first he recognized.

"Daniel, what are you doing here?"

"You don't have to be here, Cass. You don't have to see him. I do."

"If you're going to stay, then we're going to stay," she said to her husband, reminding him of Resa.

A few other female voices made sounds of agreement, voices he assumed were Vanessa's and Monica's.

All had been quiet for a good ten minutes when Frank leaned over to whisper, "I hope a good healthy fear of the Lord is running through your blood."

Ignoring the officer, Trey turned to a new page and started a letter.

*Dear Cassie,...*he began, not stopping until he had begged forgiveness for every act, for every ounce of fear he had caused her. He also tried to explain what had caused him to be the way he was and how he had changed. It was important for her to know. He ended the note vowing to never harm her or any of her family ever again.

More commotion in the front part of the station led to Frank leaving. The door locked behind him. Trey tore the sheet out of the pad and folded the note. He stopped himself from putting Cassie's name on the outside, guessing what Daniel's reaction would be. He wrote *To Dad* and placed the note inside the pad, not even considering asking Frank or Randy to give the note to his dad. He'd have a better chance with the federal agents.

The door opened a couple of minutes later. Two men in dark suits came inside, along with an officer dressed in a white shirt who had to be the district's captain, Trey realized. Frank released the cuff from the table leg, re-cuffing his hands behind him.

"Come with us, Mr. Labranch," one of the men ordered.

"Trey, call me Trey," he answered.

The man nodded and led him out of the room. There was dead silence in the station. Walking out the door and facing the people he had hurt would take more courage than turning himself in. He wanted to hide, to stare at his feet in shame, but he didn't. His steps slowed as they came into view. All three couples stood with their arms around each other, a united force no power could disrupt. White power had no reign here, he thought at the sight of Scott and Vanessa, Cassie and Daniel. They rightfully belonged together as much as Devin and Monica. Trey made eye contact with each person, forcing himself to accept the revulsion and disgust he found there.

Feeling as if he had taken a million steps across the station, he paused to hold Cassie's eyes. "I'm sorry," he whispered as the agents pulled him out the door. Trey turned to see her standing at the door, her husband and his dad behind her.

CHAPTER 15

Teresa drove past the Grays' home without stopping. She couldn't face being in their company or answering any questions about Trey. There weren't many she could answer anyway.

Parking beside the cabin, Teresa discovered that she had to deal with company whether she liked it or not. A man and woman stepped out of a dark, four-door vehicle, badges in hand as they walked toward her.

They introduced themselves, gave their names and politely requested a few moments of her time to answer some questions.

Teresa agreed, leading them up the steps, barely making it onto the porch before Angelfruit came bounding up. She automatically gave the dog a big hug and a few rubs before guiding her company inside.

"I have no problem answering questions. I'm simply not sure I have many answers for you."

"We're only asking that you do the best you can," the woman said, glancing around the cabin. "Big place, very nice."

"It is. It's not mine. I have it on loan. Can I get you anything?" she asked.

"No, thank you. We'd like to get down to business—"

"So we can leave you in peace," the woman finished.

Teresa sat on the chair opposite the sofa she and Trey had often shared, and her visitors sat down on it, blocking out the memory of herself and Trey sitting there together.

"We understand that you had a visitor staying here with you during the storm, the survivor of a plane crash."

"Yes," Teresa answered, knowing all along the questions being asked would center on Trey.

"You housed him, nursed him back to health, and took him to a doctor, I understand."

"As a matter of fact, I'm returning from doing just that. Where did you get this information?"

"Your neighbors. We asked them a few questions."

"Who are you?" Teresa asked, remembering their badges.

"FBI agents. We believe that a suspect we have been tracking was the survivor of that crash."

"Oh."

"Tell us about him."

Teresa began by describing Trey, his image fresh in her mind. Giving them details about the crash and his recovery, his personality, his memory loss and temporary blindness. Not once did she question telling them all she knew. Trey had already decided to turn himself in. She even told them that.

There was a long pause as they took notes, conferring with each other. Her mind drifted to the card Trey had left for her at the front desk. It had a rose on the outside, like the one he had sent to the table. The outside read,

To have your love and knowing that I will one day be with you…

When she opened it, it continued,

…is all that I need in this world.

Then he added a few spaces down,

This separation is necessary for us to one day be together.

Yours always,

Trey

The card had quickly made her realize that she hadn't been dreaming and assured her that Trey truly loved her. However, it left her wondering about her family and his role in their troubles and how her love for him and her family could possibly mesh. She had tried to call her parents but they were still inaccessible on their cruise and weren't due back until tomorrow.

"Ma'am, we have a few more questions," one of the agents said.

Teresa glanced up.

"Were you aware that this man, Travis Labranch Jr., was a high level member of a white supremacy group?"

Teresa nodded, barely believing it herself. Her Trey wasn't. Travis had been. "He told me last night, before he left to turn himself in."

"Last night?"

"Yes, Trey and I... I call him Trey... It was a name we decided to give him when he couldn't remember who he was," she babbled. "We went to the doctor and spent the day in Chattanooga. He began to remember who he was and was having a hard time dealing with what he remembered. I don't know who he used to be, but he's not that man anymore. He's a good man. He's turning himself in."

"At least that's what he told you. Do you have any idea where he went?"

"If Trey told me he was turning himself in, then he's turning himself in. I believe that he was headed to New Orleans."

"We've got all the information we need." The man stood and the woman motioned to her partner to go ahead of her.

"I want to ask you one more question. You don't have to answer it if you don't want to."

"Go on."

"Did you become romantically involved with Travis Labranch?"

"Not Travis, with the man he became after the accident."

"Have you considered the fact that he might have been stringing you along?"

Teresa shook her head. "I would have known."

"Trouble is, sometimes we think we know." The woman looked as if she were going to say more but ended with, "We may need to get in touch with you again."

"This is where I'll be," she said. Teresa stood on the porch to watch them drive away, then sat in one of the rockers. Angelfruit quietly came onto the porch to lay her head on Teresa's lap.

As she looked about her, she saw that the huge snow drifts were slowly becoming slushy mounds. She heard birds singing, and there was a freshness in the air. A definite change was coming. Surely the mountains wouldn't take back what they had given her. She had found love, but this love couldn't interfere with the love she had for her family.

Twice she had thought to call her cousins or her aunt and uncle to get the story. What exactly had Trey done to them? How was he involved? Since the situation had always been a touchy subject, Teresa had never gotten specific details. Now she would have to wait until tomorrow to talk with her parents.

It was closing time. Teresa had no choice. She had to leave the library. She had lingered inside, using the Internet to research more information and find more books on aviation and the Tuskegee Airmen. What she'd found today, in addition to the notes she already had, would be enough for her to complete the books she planned to write. She had also spent hours researching concussions, amnesia, and personality changes due to head injuries. She had discovered a great deal of information about how concussions could lead to memory loss and personality changes or limited function. She'd seen accounts of instances where there had been changes in judgments. Could a concussion change a person's entire belief system or had Trey been putting on an act, just as the agent had suggested?

Impossible!

He was sincere, and he loved her. She would have known if he were lying.

The thirty-minute drive back to the cabin wasn't long enough. Not wanting to feel Trey's presence in the cabin, she sat on the porch. As the sun went down, the temperature cooled, but not enough to send her inside. Her cell phone rang. She caught it on the first ring.

"How many messages were you going to leave, little girl?" her dad's voice exploded over the phone.

"Hi Daddy. I missed you guys. You two were so far away and gone for so long I guess I started to worry about ya'll."

"You wouldn't have had to worry if you had gone to a place that had a real phone. Cell phone service won't reach all the way to Jamaica."

"I know, I know. How was the trip?"

"Here, talk to your Mama."

"So, you had a good time?" Teresa asked the question she knew she should, wanting to blurt out all the others she had tried to keep at bay. She listened to her mom talk about the beautiful beaches, the mansions, the food on the cruise, and the souvenirs she had bought until she was about ready to explode. Just as her mom was finally winding down to a point where she could get a word in, her mother's phone clicked, indicating that someone was calling in.

"That must be your Aunt Joyce. She left a few messages herself. Something about that horrible man who caused all those problems for her children."

"Go on and talk to her, then call back and tell me all about it." Teresa hung up and slipped the phone into her front pocket, wondering how she was going to stand the wait. Her mom could be on the phone with Aunt Joyce, her sister-in-law, for hours or minutes, depending on her mood.

Something crawling around in the bushes convinced her to go inside. Nervous energy had her in every room picking things up, straightening rugs and pictures. She was a nervous wreck. Realizing that she hadn't eaten all day, she decided to make a meal. Finding little else in the pantry beyond a can of tomato soup caused her appetite to disappear. As she was debating whether to leave the mountain to go grocery shopping just to have something to do, her pants pocket rang and vibrated.

"Teresa, you'll never believe what happened! That T. J. demon turned himself in. The whole family's relieved, but everybody's upset. You know that he's Cassie's cousin. They all went to the station because

Randy found out and let everybody know. I'm surprised they didn't—"

"Woman! Can you try to slow down!" her dad yelled in the background.

"Don't pay any attention to your dad. What I was trying to say is that we just got back into town and all hell's broken loose."

As her mom rambled on, not taking a second to slow down, a sense of relief filled Teresa as she realized that Trey had been true to his word. She hadn't needed the proof, had believed in him, but to have this assurance renewed her faith in there still being a possibility for them to be together.

"This whole family could use a vacation, Teresa," her mom ended.

"They could use a vacation," Teresa repeated, not knowing what else to say, having half-listened. An idea began to take shape. "A vacation, huh?" she repeated. "Why don't you all come for Easter?" she heard herself say. "The cabin's big enough, and nature has a way of taking people's mind off their problems."

"Easter's too soon. But the family would love the idea of coming up for a visit."

"Well, how about the end of May? School will be out, and everyone will have enough time to make arrangements to come."

"Good idea, you're almost as smart as ya' mama. I'll call Joyce and tell her the news. You get ready to have an army of company."

Disconnecting, Teresa wondered if she had lost her mind. Being an only child, she knew what it was like to appreciate solitude, but she had spent more than enough time at Uncle Cal and Aunt Joyce's, and been to enough holiday gatherings to know what it was like to have an endless stream of relatives around. Smiling, Teresa realized that she needed them as much as they needed her. Not just because she'd be able to get some insight on Trey and things he had done as Travis, but because they were family and she loved them.

Throwing all her energy into writing her books made the next month speed by. Focusing on her writing kept worry for Trey and her family at bay, at least until the wee hours of the night when she longed for his arms around her and his poetic words of love, and some assurance that the problems her family had were not solely Trey's doing.

The last Saturday in May brought family in droves, causing Mr. Gray to walk up the mountain to see if she was being invaded. Angelfruit and her companion bounded up just before him, running back and forth between the vehicles and then everything on two legs, finally focusing on the kids, initiating a game of chase.

Teresa found herself hugged a million times and kissed almost as many. It was all a welcomed distraction. Pulling in a deep breath and releasing a contented sigh, she smiled for the first time in weeks.

"Good to have family around, isn't it, little girl?" her dad said behind her.

Teresa turned, laid her head on his shoulder and wallowed in the huge bear hug she got. "Especially when you're here."

"You'd better include your mama in that or I won't hear the end of it."

"The end of what?" Connie Lewis turned to her daughter and her husband to ask.

"The end of nothing, woman! Come tell our little girl hello."

"Not before I get a how-do-you-do from my little niece," Uncle Cal declared loud enough for the mountains to shake as he pulled her away from her dad.

"With the two of you pulling her around like some kind of rag doll, I don't know when I'll get the chance to say much of anything."

"Much of anything? You Connie? Don't you mean *almost* anything or *every* anything."

"Hush now, and Calvin, let go of my girl so I can have a good look at her."

Teresa turned, leaning down to give her mom, who was a good five inches shorter, a hug and a kiss.

"Not so little anymore is what I'm thinking," she said as usual, the same thing she'd said since Teresa turned twelve and passed her in height. Her mom stepped back a second later to have that look. "We missed you, baby."

"Not little, but she's ya' baby, huh Connie?" Uncle Cal laughed before pulling his brother, her dad, away to search for the perfect spot to set up the horseshoes they had brought along.

"She'll always be my baby," Connie called to their retreating backs. "Now wait a second before you two go off and do your own thing. There are bags and boxes that need to be brought it."

"Bags and boxes?" her dad bellowed.

"We're letting the young people handle that," Uncle Cal declared. "Josh! John!" He called his two youngest, twins in college but home for the summer. "Organize these people and make sure everything gets inside."

"Sure, Dad," Josh said.

"I see we've been elevated to head custodial workers now," John joked.

"Well, if you two are delegating duties," Connie folded her arms to say, "let me delegate one your way."

"Oh-oh, look what you've done, Cal," Teresa's dad said in a loud whisper.

"Make sure you keep an eye on these kids," Connie ignored them to say.

"No problem," they agreed.

"I know you went shopping, but Joyce and I brought a few things, too," her mom was saying.

Teresa eyed the boxes of groceries and two ice chests that she was certain had seafood for gumbo. She could see that her mom's idea of a few things was only held in check by the amount of space in the vehicles they had come in.

"Now, tell me about your plans to entertain all this family for the next few days," her mom said, hooking an arm into one of hers.

Before Teresa could answer, a loud command of, "I don't want any of you kids falling off the mountain!" interrupted her.

"If they call that watching the kids, I think we're in trouble," Teresa declared.

"They'll watch them like a hawk. That little remark was for my ears. Those two are just trying to get to me."

Laughing, they entered the house. The huge den was full of baby cousins, older cousins, and cousin-in-laws. With the help of her mom and Aunt Joyce, Teresa provided everyone with their own corner of the cabin, be it a bedroom, the loft, or a corner in the den. Having five bedrooms helped. Her cousin Monica and her husband took over the master bedroom, the only room big enough to fit the three portable cribs she brought for their five-month-old triplets. Teresa gladly gave it up. She had been unable to sleep in it since Trey left. Her cousin Ness and her husband Scott settled into another bedroom with their twin boys. Cassie and Daniel were given a room to share with baby Jessica. All the babies being housed in a bedroom with their parents left the last two rooms for the elder adults, her mom and dad, and Aunt Joyce and Uncle Cal. Everyone else either claimed a space in the loft or in the living room.

An hour later, the cabin relatively quiet, the women slowly drifted into the kitchen.

"What's the plan for lunch?" Monica asked, one baby cradled in her arms.

"Hot dogs today, a feast tomorrow," Teresa told her.

"And do we have a feast planned," Connie said. "We're going to start off with a huge ham, stuffed crabs, macaroni, yams, and potato salad."

"Don't forget the gumbo."

"That's your specialty, Joyce," her mom said.

The discussion of tomorrow's menu went on without Teresa having much input. The mention of gumbo had her picturing Trey with the bowl of gumbo in his face and rice on his nose.

"Are you okay, Teresa?" That was Cassie, Trey's cousin. She had only met her once, when she and Daniel got married.

"I'm fine," Teresa answered, searching Cassie's face for some feature, some resemblance to Trey.

"You're probably just a little overwhelmed by all this," Ness said. "Remember when you used to come over to spend a week in the summer? That first day you always looked shell-shocked."

"Only child syndrome."

"But you got over it quick."

"How else could I have any fun?"

"And if this family isn't anything else, it sure is fun," Sonya, her cousin Randy's wife, added.

They reminisced, chipping in to get lunch ready. A ton of hot dogs lined up inside of buns later, three little girls came into the kitchen.

"MaNessa, we're star-r-v-ing," Megan said to her stepmom, her blond head bobbing with each syllable.

"And we want to eat before the boys," said Jasmine, Monica's daughter. Her pigtails moved side to side as her head shook in the telling.

"Because you're hungry?" Monica asked.

"Because the boys are hungry and not smart enough to stop chasing those dogs to come inside to eat," Vicki, an older version of Megan, answered for the three of them.

"And because we're a little bit hungry," Megan admitted.

Not long after, the boys came in to eat, followed by the big boys, who were smart enough to stop pitching horseshoes to eat.

Lunch was barely finished when the sound of muffled crying was heard. Monica, Ness and Cassie all lifted similar monitor devices to their ears.

"Sound like my boys are awake," Ness said.

"Jessica's needing something." Cassie stood, heading upstairs.

"And somebody's bound to be hungry." Monica left, heading to the master bedroom.

It didn't take long for their husbands to follow. "Those boys are good daddies, I see," Connie commented.

"When the kids outnumber the parents they have to work as a team."

"What's Daniel's reason?" Teresa asked, picturing Trey running behind her to take care of their child. "He and Cassie outnumber Jessica."

"Daniel's just smitten," Aunt Joyce answered.

"Yeah, with his wife *and* his kid!" Uncle Cal yelled from the other side of the room.

"Find the right man and you'll have the same," Teresa's mom said.

"One day," Teresa muttered, leaving them to talk as she laid the makings for smores as an after dinner treat. The evenings were still cool enough to light the fireplace without making the house a sauna. Her distraction of having her family here was leading her right back to her heartache.

The day went by quickly, dinner no more than soup and sandwiches, tomato soup not being an option. Her dad and uncle were engaged in a game of chess, the kids were all asleep in the loft from a day spent outdoors, the couples were all in their rooms or corners, and the kitchen had been taken over by her aunt and mother who decided that gumbo made the night before was better because all the flavors had time to blend overnight.

Talk about blending. This family had some serious blending going on. Their lives stated, marry who you love. If only it were that simple for her. It had been, at first.

Rubbing the homemade ring on her finger, Teresa decided that a bit of fresh air was due. The darkness beyond the porch light was a bit of comfort that soon edged into loneliness, so when someone stepped out onto the porch she welcomed the invasion. It was Cassie wearing Teresa's jacket.

"Hey," she said, sitting across from her in an over-sized rocker. "I hope you don't mind me borrowing your jacket. I forgot to pack one but I didn't want the cold to keep me from enjoying a bit of mountain air."

"No problem. I don't need it. My fleece is keeping me warm."

"Oh, so this is where you are," Daniel said, coming out on the porch. "Share that rocker with me. You can hop on my lap."

Teresa watched as Cassie stood. Daniel settled her on his lap, rocking them both. It was obvious that they were in love and happy.

"You two make a cute couple," Teresa said.

"Thanks, I think we complement each other," Cassie said.

"You do, but some others don't think so," Daniel said.

"Daniel, we're not worried about others," Cassie answered.

"Not normally, but there is a recent 'other' that needs some worrying about."

"What recent other?" Scott asked, coming out with an arm around Ness.

"Who do you think?" Devin asked, his face grim as he followed Monica onto the porch.

"Please. Please, please, please. We did *not* come here to talk about Travis Labranch Jr.," Monica said between clenched teeth.

Teresa's heart jumped. She hadn't wanted to initiate this conversation. She had decided that it wasn't appropriate. Having confirmation that he had turned himself in was enough. She didn't want to know anything that Trey couldn't tell her himself, but now the matter had been taken out of her hands.

"She said please four times," Daniel warned.

"It doesn't mean a thing unless it's six," Devin announced, adding, "right, Brown Eyes?" before leaning into her to give her a lingering kiss.

"Don't Brown Eyes me when we're talking about T. J."

"T. J.'s a sore subject?" Teresa asked the obvious question, knowing the answer but asking just the same.

"Yes," they all answered.

"I understand that he's caused you some trouble," Teresa forced herself to say, wanting to know and not wanting to know at the same time.

"T's caused quite a bit of trouble in this family." Cassie paused before adding, "He's my cousin."

"You can't help who your relatives are," Daniel said behind Cassie's head.

"Yeah, but this is one relative that I still have feelings for."

"You have feelings for a memory, Cass."

"Maybe," was all Cassie said.

The silence on the porch was broken by the door opening. Teresa's cousins Warren and Randy and their wives came out.

"It feels like a funeral out here," Warren commented.

"We were discussing T. J.," someone said.

"That explains it," Randy muttered, sitting on the steps, pulling his wife to sit beside him. "I thought we came here to forget T. J."

"Yeah, didn't he turn himself in? He'll get what he deserves," Warren said.

"I don't know about that. The station hasn't heard a word from the Feds since they took him away. I've got Frank keeping an ear out, but we haven't gotten any news yet," Randy said. "Something's up."

"Something's up all right," Devin said. "What I don't get is why he turned himself in. I spent thousands of dollars looking for him, and out of nowhere he shows up and confesses. Why?"

"Because it was the right thing to do," Teresa whispered.

Teresa could feel all eyes on her. They all held disbelief, all except Cassie. Cassie looked at her with—hope? Maybe.

"T. J. doesn't know the difference between right and wrong," Scott answered for everyone else. "He started by trying to break up my engagement because he didn't like the color of my wife, then he tried to ruin Devin's career and our business, and finally sank as low as to kidnap and—"

"Please, please, please, please, please, PLEASE! Refrain from talking about T. J. We all know what he did."

"That was six," someone said unnecessarily.

No one else interrupted the quiet with tales of T. J. Long minutes passed. Slowly they said their good nights some leaving hand in hand, others arm and arm, but each couple together.

Teresa yearned for Trey even more, wanting to comfort him as the memories of what he used to be came back. There was such a thick wall of justified loathing for him Teresa didn't think that any of her family would ever be able to see the new person he had become.

CHAPTER 16

Sunday was a flurry of activity. They caravanned to church and spent the morning cooking, talking, and finally enjoying the meal. Babies were passed from arm to arm. Brown-skinned babies, caramel-colored babies—contented, well-loved babies.

Surrounded by constant activity, Teresa had had only tiny, sporadic moments to dwell on the future and her impossible relationship with Trey. Most of them occurred when she found herself alone with or near Cassie. Teresa didn't know if it was because she was Trey's cousin or the probing looks Cassie had thrown her way a number of times today. Or maybe she was imagining it all in some weird need to have some connection with Trey.

Nightfall found all of the adults on the porch again. Jealously, both foreign and unwanted, twisted in her heart as she watched the couples holding hands, whispering to each other or just plain sitting together. Her aunt and uncle and even her mom and dad were out tonight, just as intent on each other as the younger couples. Not caring to feel jealousy, she stood, the rocker moving wildly at her abrupt movement.

"Something wrong, baby?" her mom asked.

"I'm just tired. Good night, everyone."

A chorus of good nights followed her inside. Turning to torture herself one last time, Teresa made eye contact with Cassie. She looked as if she wanted to say something. But not wanting to hang around, Teresa went into the quiet cabin in search of her corner of the den which was set up with an air mattress, pillows and covers.

She closed her eyes, hoping sleep would come but it evaded her. She was awake when she heard the couples come in. Hours later, awake when a baby's cry sounded upstairs and awake much later when a trio of cries came from the master bedroom.

Many sleepless hours went by before streams of sunlight filtered into the room, ending her quest for sleep. Teresa quietly made her way to the bathroom, pulled on her jacket and left the cabin, deciding that an early morning walk up the mountain before everyone awoke was a good idea.

Teresa had been walking for a good ten minutes when she heard a noise behind her. Assuming that it was some small animal scurrying across the path, Teresa ignored it until she heard her name. Stopping, she turned to find Cassie coming up the path.

"Thanks for stopping. I've been trying to get a minute to speak to you. I had just finished feeding Jax and was putting her down when I saw you from the window. I hope you don't mind me following you."

"Jax?" Teresa asked, latching onto the only thing that didn't have implications for Cassie's motive for needing to talk to her.

"The baby. Her name's Jessica Ann Xena. A little joke between me and Daniel since we decided not to name her after a brewery."

"Oh, yeah, I remember that."

"Do you mind if I walk with you?"

"No, not at all," Teresa told her, leery of the converstion they were bound to have.

For awhile there was no conversation at all as they trudged higher and higher. Cassie finally stopped and put a hand on Teresa's shoulder. "I give. I thought that going to the gym three times a week to get rid of the baby fat had put me in some kind of shape. I was obviously wrong," she said between labored breaths.

"I've been climbing every day. It took awhile for me to get used to it, too."

"How long did it take for you to fall in love with T?"

Unable to say a word, Teresa looked down at Cassie who was just as short as her mom.

"Look in your jacket pocket. The left one," Cassie got out, finding a flat rock to sit on. "I found them the other night and almost died of shock, but then everything started to make sense."

Teresa dug into her pocket and pulled out the 5x7 photos they had taken at the Ole Tyme Shop.

"Please," she said. "Come sit next to me. Tell me about T. Tell me about the two of you. You love him, don't you? I can see it in your eyes. I can see it in his."

Teresa couldn't answer at first. All she could do was stare at the pictures she and Trey had taken. There was love there, just as blatant as it had been on the porch these last two nights between her cousins and their spouses, her mom and dad, her aunt and uncle. It was there in the picture.

"Do you know what else I see?"

"What do you see?" Teresa sat on the rock next to Trey's cousin.

"I see my cousin T. Not the monster he had become."

"Tell me about who he was before he became the man that my family hates."

"We're in the same place, aren't we? Loving the person everyone else in our family loathes. It's a hard place to be."

"An impossible place."

"Maybe not. Let me tell you about T. He was my playmate, my hero, my everything. I looked up to him as a kid. He's five years older than me, and I loved him to death. I don't think I remember exactly when or how he began to change. It was a gradual thing, I guess. I've thought back on it and have to say that I didn't notice it at all. Not until I discovered what he had become. We'd lost contact. I was based in Houston working as a flight attendant and hadn't been home in years. When I came home pregnant with Daniel chasing behind me, that's when I discovered T's other life."

"I've heard a lot about what he was like before the accident that brought him to me. Tell me more about what *you* remember."

Teresa listened as Cassie revealed to her the man she had come to know. The sweetness, the humor, the determination. It was as if Cassie were reading her mind.

"Thank you," Teresa laid a hand on Cassie's shoulder to say.

Cassie turned the tables, "Your turn. Tell me all about him. Tell me how he changed. I know he's changed. I saw him the day he came to the station to turn himself in. He looked at me with steady eyes and told me he was sorry. Then my dad found a letter on the floor in the station. It explained it all. He talked about falling in love. He talked about you. I wanted to meet you, and I'm still shocked to have found you so easily."

"Where should I begin?"

"The plane crash. Start with the crash. T believes it was the beginning of his salvation. You were the rest."

That sounded exactly like Trey. As Teresa began her story, having never told it to anyone else, all the emotions she'd been feeling began to unleash. Cassie was her one woman rapt audience asking questions, making comments, as she spoke. It felt so good to openly talk about Trey, to share her feelings without feeling guilty. She hadn't even told her parents yet because then she'd have to tell them who Trey was.

"How do you feel?" Cassie asked.

"Relieved. Unsure of where to go next."

"Me too. We have to decide what to do about the family and their view of Trey. Trey, the name fits."

Teresa smiled.

"Time's up," a voice said behind them. Monica with Vanessa stood behind them. "We saw you heading up here about an hour ago. Everybody's wondering where the two of you are."

"Daniel's gonna to start a search party if you're not back in ten minutes," Ness told Cassie.

"Oh, we got carried away," Cassie explained.

"I'm sure, considering the subject you were discussing."

"You know?" Teresa asked her cousins.

"Last night, when the whole world was sleeping and we were up feeding babies, Cassie showed us the pictures," Monica said.

"And let us read the note T. J. had written to her," Ness added.

"So we've come to a few conclusions," Monica said. "We already know from experience that love finds you, not the other way around."

"And that maybe this accident and your love *have* turned T. J. around. The very fact that the two of you are in love is a convincing piece of evidence," Ness added.

"Talk about ironic, the interracial relationship T was trying to destroy was the exact thing that saved him," Cassie said.

"I'm not sure that our husbands will be so easy to convince, but it's enough for us, Teresa." Ness was at her side, wrapping an arm around her.

"We want to see T. J. for ourselves, in person, Cuz," Monica was on her other side.

"It's Trey," she told them, feeling a unity, a sisterhood with these women who had every reason to hate her future husband, but understood the power of love.

"Let's head back down before Daniel loses his mind, then together, we'll find a way out of this mess."

As they came down the mountain, a dozen things seemed to happen simultaneously. Scott, Devin, Josh, and John were carrying boxes out of the vehicles. Daniel, keeping watch on the porch, came running up the path when he spotted his wife. A dark four-door car pulled up to the cabin and Angelfruit came racing up the path in an excited frenzy.

"Where have you been?" Daniel was asking his wife as he pounded up the path.

Teresa stood where she was, suspecting, almost certain, that Trey was inside the car. The back door opened. His long, muscular frame appeared. Angelfruit went wild, jumping all over him, making everyone outside the cabin stop and look.

He glanced at the cabin, then at the path. Finding her, he slammed the door and started running toward her. Teresa found her feet running down to meet him, not knowing or caring how he was able to come her, just relieved that he was here.

The slamming of the door drew Daniel's attention away from his wife and to the new arrivals. Giving him a brief glance, Teresa saw him do a double take. "T. J.!" he yelled, pulling Cassie behind him.

Echoes of "T. J.!" resounded in the air until the trees themselves whispered it in the wind.

Trey sat on the hospital bed, his arm freshly bandaged from the bullet that had grazed him. He had done what was asked of him. He'd risked his life and endured the company of people he hated to set things right. The risks he took credited him with time served but still, he had a debt to pay, owing a non-negotiable number of hours of community service, specifically in the black community.

When he had first told his story to the FBI agents, he could tell that it was viewed with a high level of disdain. But no matter how many ways or how many hours spent in interrogation, his story never changed. The FBI had even corroborated his version with what Resa had said to them. He felt terrible that they'd involved her. Just one more thing for him to ask her to forgive him for. They spoke to the Grays and the doctor he had visited before even considering that he might be telling the truth. After that, he spent days being examined by their doctors and psychologists.

"Job well done, Labranch. You'll even have a scar to remember the day you played your part in disbanding a group of hate mongers," Agent Adams came into the room to say.

Trey nodded. "I've only done what I thought I should. Think of it as my way of cleansing myself of their hold on me."

"I think you've done that," Agent Matthews, the only woman in the group, added. "Your old ties got you back in, and your explanation for your disappearance was tight."

"Almost. The amount of money I plugged into the organization was enough to forgive me of anything. Crashing the plane was nothing, leaving without permission to stop my cousin from marrying a black man was admired. Disappearing because I had amnesia was partially true and understandable. Everything fell into place. At least until someone showed up with that picture of Resa and me in Chattanooga. I told that woman not to post it." Trey shook his head.

"Some people don't listen. Unfortunately, her stubbornness was the cause of all hell breaking loose," Adams interjected.

"Thanks for saving my life, Adams."

"Had to. It's my job, but by then we had enough tape to lock the general up for life. Let's say we get out of here. We're taking you back to New Orleans. You've got a judge to see there."

"I know." One arm in a sling, he stood awkwardly, holding his hands out, waiting for the cuffs to be slapped onto his wrists.

"That won't be necessary, Labranch. We're your escorts, not your guards."

"Escorts?"

"Your cooperation and that bond you paid has released you on your own recognizance, making you a free man," Matthews explained.

"Oh, thank you."

"Don't thank us. It's all your doing. Frankly, I didn't believe your story when I first heard it. I thought it was a bunch of crap. I guess seeing is believing. You've made me a believer. Some people can change."

"If I'm free, can I ask you a favor?"

"You can try," Adams answered.

"On the way to see this judge in New Orleans, can we make a stop? I have someone I need to see."

"A certain lady who lives in a cabin in the middle of the Smoky Mountains," Matthews guessed.

"Exactly."

"We met her. Nice lady."

"Thank you."

"I love a happy ending. What do you say we oblige the man, Adams?"

"I'm a sucker once in awhile myself."

The time it took to drive to Del Rio seemed like hours. It had killed him earlier knowing he had been so close to Resa and unable to see her. Driving past the

Grays' and full of nervous energy, he hung his head out the window to yell at the dogs, who promptly followed along.

"Looks like your girl's got company," Adams commented as they stopped.

Trey froze for a second. Resa had company, all right. Her family was here. He hadn't expected this. A second later he opened the door, realizing it didn't matter. If he was going to be a part of Resa's life, if they were going to get married, he'd have to face her family sometime. Angelfruit was all over him as he searched for Teresa. He absently rubbed the dog behind her ears with his one good hand. She wasn't on the porch or anywhere around the cabin. Seeing someone dash off the porch and up the path where Resa took her walks changed his focus. She was there. She smiled at him. She was far away, but he could tell she was smiling at him because his face was spilt in half with a wide grin of his own.

"Labranch, you might want to wait," he heard Matthews say just before he took off up the path, not stopping even after he heard the surprise and the angry utterance of the name he dreaded.

"T. J.!" rolled past his eardrums without his acknowledgement. Resa was here, and he needed to put his arms around her. Before he could make it to her, he was yanked back, spun around and his breath knocked out of him with one solid punch in the gut. It didn't stop there. He took one in the chin and got socked in the eye before he fell, not once thinking of defending himself.

Dazed and disoriented, Trey opened his eyes to discover that the ground was his bed and Resa's lap was his pillow. He was in heaven. Full of pain, but in heaven. Not remembering how or why he was on the ground, he searched Resa's face, held her eyes with his own and peered into them, looking for something important. What was it?

"You get out of my sight, hurt yourself again, and if that's not enough, you run into other people's fists. What am I going to do with you, Trey?" she leaned down to ask.

He found it. It was there. Love. She didn't hate him. He reached up to pull her down for a kiss, freezing at the sound of a loud, angry voice.

"Get your hands off my cousin!" Daniel yelled, moving toward them.

Adams and Matthews were at Daniel's side, gently restraining him. Cassie was there trying to reason with her husband, it seemed. But there was no sense in trying to reason with a man defending the people he loved.

"I got it now. I was beat up by Cassie's husband."

"Yeah."

"I deserved that," Trey said to Resa, who was running her fingers through his hair.

"I can understand why you'd think so, but nobody else is going to be beating on you today."

"Are you going to try to stop them?" he asked, raising his head to see Devin, Scott, Randy, and a couple of older gentlemen coming up the path. "Are you going to attempt a gumbo feat?"

"Neither one of us will," she told him.

"Josh! John! Keep those kids inside the cabin!" someone yelled.

"How many job titles do you think we've got now, John?" echoed up to them. "Custodian, babysitter…" Josh's voice trailed away as he went to do as his father asked.

"Get up, you coward!" Daniel was saying. "Do you ever get your hands dirty or do you just give the orders?"

"Calm down, Daniel," Cassie was saying. "It's okay."

"Sir, we are going to have to ask you to contain yourself," Adams was saying.

"What is T. J. doing here?" Randy threw at the agents.

"What's going on?" Devin asked.

"Why are you holding that man's head on your lap?" Clarence Lewis boomed at his daughter.

"Baby girl, answer your father," her mom insisted before Resa had the chance to even open her mouth.

"Want me to tell 'em?" Trey asked. "I'm already down, I can't go any farther."

"We're already down. They're my family, I'll tell them. Can you get up?"

"Sure," he said. Trey glanced Daniel's way, and saw that Cassie had been able to calm him maybe a couple degrees, not enough to matter. But he really couldn't blame the guy. Trey took a quick glance at the faces surrounding him, identifying almost everyone, feeling the understandable loathing on some faces, and the confusion on others.

The suspended tension hung as thick as the smoke that covered the mountains as everyone waited for Teresa to answer. "Mom, Dad, everybody, this is Trey, my fiancé."

"That's a lie!" Daniel shouted.

"Your what?" Teresa's mom exclaimed, ending with a, "Oh, my Lord!"

"He won't marry you; he hates black people. He threatened my unborn child. He kidnapped my wife!" Daniel exploded all over again.

"Trey didn't do those things," Resa told everyone. "Travis did," she declared, her arms folded, her stance defiant.

"And who is that standing next to you?" Devin calmly asked.

"I'll answer that, Resa," Trey told her, stepping away, a hand briefly caressing her shoulder. "I am Travis Labranch Jr. I have the same features, and the same face, but I am not the same man."

"What is he talking about? Some kind of conversion?" one of the older men bellowed.

"You could call it that. I'm not the same man you used to know."

"And we're suppose to believe that?" Scott asked.

"I do," Vanessa said.

"Me too," Monica agreed.

"And I've always believed that something happened to change you to begin with," Cassie said, her eyes moving from her husband to Trey and back again.

The husbands looked at their wives in disbelief. Trey was sure he wore a similar expression, not expecting support from the people he had tried to hurt. "I know that it's almost impossible to believe, but I *have* changed. My opinions, my view of people, my whole outlook on life is completely different. Not so much different, more or less that my true nature has made a comeback."

"He's up to something," Daniel muttered, breaking away from Cassie to confront Trey again.

In the next instant Trey found Resa in front of him, her hands gripping her folded arms. Trey gently tugged each arm down. "I don't want you to protect me, baby, it should be the other way around." Pulling her behind him, Trey turned to face Daniel. "You can beat me up again, if it'll make you feel better. I won't fight back."

"What kind of game are you playing?" Daniel asked.

"No game," Cassie said at his side. "T's telling the truth."

"I'm thinking, it's about time we intervene," Matthews interjected. "Travis, T, Trey, whatever you want to call him, is telling the truth. He aided in the capture of a group of racists bent on attacking institutions predominately owned by African-American, Hispanic and Jewish communities throughout the country. Ladies and gentlemen, I'm talking about churches and schools, women and children. This man was instrumental in the capture of the ring leader of this organization."

"We were able to detain nearly a thousand men and women involved and capture over half a millions dollars' worth of anmuniton and weapons," Adams added.

All was silent. Not a sound dared to disturb the stunned atmosphere surrounding them.

"You did that?" Resa asked him.

"Yes, but not alone." Trey cocked his head toward the agents. "Adams, Matthews, and dozens of their friends did the bulk of the work. I did my small share."

"Putting yourself in their company and placing your life on the line got us in the front door and gave us enough evidence for justice to be served."

"What about the justice he's required to serve?" Randy asked. "Does this wipe his slate clean?"

"Not completely," Trey answered. "I still have a debt to serve. I'm willing and ready to pay for the crimes I committed before the bang on the head and the love of a good woman changed me." Trey stopped, his eyes on Resa so that everyone knew exactly who he was referring to. "All I'm asking is that you give me a chance. Forgive me. Let me prove myself."

"That's asking a lot," Devin said.

"Is it asking the impossible?" Teresa asked her family, looking at each one in question.

"Explain again why you put your life on the line," Daniel demanded, visibly calmer than he had been before.

"I had to set things right. I had to right a wrong."

"For?"

"For every one of you, for me and Resa, for my sanity. I had no other option. There was nothing else I could have done."

"There's something else you could do right now," a deep voice declared.

Everyone turned to Resa's dad. "Come into the cabin, sit down, and work your way into explaining how you got involved with my daughter."

"I would be pleased to, Mr. Lewis," Trey told the man he hoped he could soon call father-in-law.

"That would be a very good idea," Resa's mom muttered.

"All right everybody, let's go down to the cabin and get some things straightened out," the other older man yelled.

"That's my Uncle Cal," Resa whispered, leaning into him. He wrapped his arms around her, not caring if anyone approved.

As they made their way down the path, a young man came through the door, followed by a cute, blond-headed little girl. Trey recognized her as one of the little girls he had attempted to kidnap months ago.

"Will you marry me, Uncle John?" she asked the young man who stood on the porch unaware of their approach.

"Sure thing, Vicki," he answered. She jumped into his arms with a childish giggle that died in her throat when she spotted Trey.

"Why are you holding me so tight? What's wrong, Vicki?"

Trey felt every eye on him.

"Let's go inside, sweetie," Scott was saying to his daughter with Ness right beside him. She went into her father's arms, visibly shaken.

Trey replayed the image of himself scooping the girls up and running across a field with them kicking and screaming and felt his whole world shatter. How could he ask? How could he expect this family to tolerate him, let alone welcome him into the family? Daggers bore into his skin. Trey was ready to give it all up, his life, his love. It wasn't fair to put Resa through this.

The door swung open again. Two little girls came out, one brown as molasses the other pale as snow. They were holding hands and laughing.

"What's wrong with Vicki?" asked one of the girls, the one he'd pushed during the attempted kidnapping.

"She's afraid—," Scott began.

"Of him!" Vicki pointed.

Trey stepped back, unable to endure the pain in the little girl's eyes.

"Why? Because he looks like the bad man? He's not the bad man," the little girl who was obviously her sister said.

"How do you know it's not him? He looks like him," Vicki insisted.

"He's not," Megan said, as if it was plain for all to see.

"Yeah, he's not the bad one," the other girl answered. They called her Jazz, Trey remembered. She was standing on the balls of her feet, her brown eyes peering into his soul. "I think the bad one's gone. Come see."

"Can I see, Daddy? MaNessa, can I?" Vicki asked her parents.

Scott and Vanessa looked at each other. "If you want to," Scott agreed as the little girl slid out of his arms.

Trey wanted to pull Scott and Vanessa into his arms to hug and kiss them both, but instead he stood quietly as the three girls came over. Trey felt Daniel and Devin's presence as they inched closer to him.

"Mister," the littlest one said, "come here."

Trey stooped down, and her little face peered into his. "See," was all she said. Her sister nodded. The other little girl nodded.

"Can we play outside now?" Vicki asked her parents, giving a hoop when they nodded.

The ton of guilt that had weighted him down lifted away. Tears filled his eyes, but through them he reached for and found his love. For long moments they stood hugging until Resa's uncle said, "From the mouths of babes. Are we going inside or what?"

As everyone filed into the cabin, a loud voice called out, "Josh! John!"

"We know, watch the kids!" they answered together.

Trey sat on the sofa. Resa sat next to him. He felt a tentative melting, a possibility of forgiveness. His new beginning was becoming a reality.

EPILOGUE

Teresa parked in front of a building she hadn't entered in almost six months. Its familiar red bricks sent a wave of anticipation through her. The actual building had nothing to do with it. The people inside had everything to do with it.

Stepping inside, she surprised Darryl, the orderly, who greeted her with a huge smile and hug. Motioning for him to keep quiet, she crept into the community room, taking a seat in the back where she could observe each and every person. Lady D sat right up front, completely enamored with the reader, with Mama Lee coming in second. Miss Mary and Miss Marie sighed every few paragraphs, and even Mr. Stevens' face held an expression of deep concentration she had never seen him wear before.

The reader ended the story, his voice holding the audience until the last word.

"I told you ladies that a decent mystery with a tiny bit of that romance mess you all like so much would make a halfway decent story." Mr. Stevens tapped his cane to emphasize his point.

"There was more romance than mystery," Lady D told him.

"Whatever! Anything's better than a romantic romance!"

"Nothing's better," Miss Mary and Miss Marie said together.

"It was an excellent choice that satisfied everybody," the reader announced, expertly smoothing any ruffled feathers with ease. Spotting Teresa in the back of the room he gave her a wink. "I've got a surprise for all of you."

"We love surprises," the sisters said.

"I hate surprises," Mr. Stevens grumped.

"This is one you'll all love."

"I'll be the judge," Mr. Stevens insisted.

"If you remember, last week I told you all that I was getting married."

"That's right!"

"Of course we remember, we're old, not fools!"

"You promised us pictures."

"Where are they?"

The various exclamations put a grin on her face but Teresa remained quiet, waiting for Trey to continue.

"I have pictures. But I can do better than pictures. Everyone, meet my wife."

"It's Teresa!"

"Our sweetheart!"

"Oh, we've missed you!"

All the ladies had something to say as she hugged each and every one of them. Mr. Stevens remained quiet until she stood before him.

"So you're back."

"I'm back."

"You left to write books about black people and came back married to a white man."

"That's about right."

"Well, ain't that something?"

Trey stood beside her and wrapped an arm around her. "Think she made a good choice?"

The ladies instantly agreed, Mama Lee clapping her consent.

"Since I've gotten used to you these last two months and sort of, kind of, like you just a little bit, I guess I can say she could've done worse."

"That might be true, Mr. Stevens, but I couldn't have done better," Trey said.

"A real live romance!" Miss Mary exclaimed.

"Tell us about it!" Miss Marie insisted.

"I'm not sitting through any romance stories unless I hear a few about those Tuskegee Airmen," Mr. Stevens demanded.

"No problem. I've got a preliminary copy of both books with me. I'll read them to you if you like."

"We like," he answered for everyone, rolling his chair closer to the sofa where Teresa and Trey had settled.

Her friends gathered close to hear about the gift the mountain had given to both of them.

"Try not to be so nervous; it's just a fishing trip," Resa told Trey later that night. She was fresh out of the shower, the wire engagement ring he had originally given her strung on a gold chain, the only thing she wore, the outer foil having long ago worn away. Beads of water glistening on her brown skin begged him to lick them off. Anxiety about the trip he would be taking tomorrow pushed the idea to the back of his head to use for future enjoyment.

"It's more than a fishing trip. This will be the first time I'm going to be alone with almost every male member of your family, and we'll be in the middle of Lake Pontchartrain. I think I have a right to be nervous."

"Are you afraid they'll throw you in?"

"Exactly."

"My dad won't let it happen. He likes you."

"True."

"And once everyone knows you as I do, they'll forgive you and realize what a wonderful person you are." She kissed him as she pulled on one of those small spaghetti-strapped tops that she liked to sleep in.

"That's going to take more. than a fishing trip, Resa."

"True, but it's a beginning and it shows that at least they're willing. Consider it a gumbo feat."

"More like a jumbo gumbo feat. Daniel can barely say two words to me. Devin and Scott watch me like a hawk if I so much as say hello to their kids. Did you know that Randy showed up in his uniform at the Outreach Center where I do my community service. I was coaching the basketball team. He stayed for the entire practice."

"Why?"

"To see if I was doing the required community service, I suppose. He hung around long enough after to give the boys a few tips before he left."

"That's progress, Trey." She wrapped her arms around his neck. "You have to remember that it's only been three months since you've turned yourself in. By our first anniversary, this won't even be a major issue."

"Which is why I should wait until then to be taken out in the middle of the lake with people who hate me for very good reasons."

"Trey, I love you because you are you. That's what's most important. My family will all discover the real you," she told him, pulling on a pair of panties that Trey knew he would be pulling off in a few moments.

"In the meantime, legally changing my name seems to have helped."

"At least no one calls you Travis anymore," she said, going into the bedroom they shared.

"No one even calls my dad Travis anymore," he said looking for the toothpaste, deciding that no matter how nervous he was of being in the company of Teresa's family he would have to trust them to mean no ill to him if he wanted them to trust him. He had just recently begun to build a real measure of trust with his dad.

"Resa!" he called a second later from the bathroom door. "Where's the toothpaste?"

"In the garbage can."

"Why? There was at least two good brushes left in that tube."

"It was empty. Here's a new one, deal with it." She grinned, her arms folded as she stood in the doorway.

Trey looked down at the new tube, at his toothbrush, and then at Resa's arms folded across her full breasts as she stood in that cami thing and her panties and laughed. Resa joined him. "We sound like an old married couple already. A whole week and look what marriage has done to us."

"It's done quite a bit," Resa agreed, leaning against the door jam as he proceeded to brush his teeth. Of its own accord, her hand reached out to graze his neck, her fingers moving down to lightly scratch his back. Once. Then once more before he gave her a look that sent a few surges straight through her.

A quick rinse later, and swift maneuvering had her on the bed and under his hard, wanting body. "Marriage has done quite a bit all right. It's given me the freedom to do this," he growled, his hands going to her waist and inching higher until his fingers rested below her breasts. His thumbs teased the sides of her breasts, moving toward her nipples, then away, only to come back again, barely touching her there, barely satisfying the need he was building.

"Trey! Are you trying to make me crazy?"

"Yes." He smiled down at her, and lifted the camisole she wore to expose the brown hardened tips begging for his attention. Trey used his lips and tongue to give Resa what she wanted. The sighs and moans she was making seemed to come from somewhere deep inside her, making him want her more. How could he want her more when he'd had her to himself almost nonstop since the day they had gotten married?

Moving down, his hands taking over where his lips had loved, he kissed his way to her stomach, to her navel, taking a second to lay his head on her belly. His hardness was fast becoming a painful need at the sounds she made. Moving down to hook her panties with his thumbs, he pulled at them, kissing his way around the heart of her. Slowly, he inched up her inner thighs, her legs opening for him, her fingers running through his hair, urging him on. Trey lay between her thighs, his warm breath caressing her there, lips persistently teasing her sensitive skin, building the anticipation. She shifted with a restlessness he would soon appease. Inching closer, he pressed his lips against her warm heat only to pull away a long second later to enter her, moving inside of her with an urgency he felt deep in his bones, exploding inside of her and she, around him, sharing without words the love they had found.

Hours later, Trey awakened to find Resa staring at him, her eyes telling him how much she loved him. His responded in kind before closing. Applying the technique he had used when he was blind, his lips landed somewhere on her chin, traveling up until he found his prize. He lingered there, pulling her close when their lips parted.

"There's something we have to do," he told her, breathing in her scent.

"And what might that be?" Resa asked, imagining another round of lovemaking.

"After I survive the fishing trip and finish my community service, we have to take a honeymoon."

"To where?"

"To the mountains, of course. I have to thank them for helping me find the love of my life."

"Yes, we have to thank the mountains," Resa agreed, snuggling into her husband's arms. She had always thought of Trey as her gift from the mountains and she'd worried for a time that the mountains would take him back. But they hadn't. Instead, they'd made them both into better, stronger persons whose love had brought peace and joy to both their families.

Yes, indeed, they had to thank the mountains.

2009 Reprint Mass Market Titles

January

I'm Gonna Make You Love Me
Gwyneth Bolton
ISBN-13: 978-1-58571-291-5
ISBN-10: 1-58571-291-4
$6.99

Shades of Desire
Monica White
ISBN-13: 978-1-58571-292-2
ISBN-10: 1-58571-292-2
$6.99

February

A Love of Her Own
Cheris Hodges
ISBN-13: 978-1-58571-293-9
ISBN-10: 1-58571-293-0
$6.99

Color of Trouble
Dyanne Davis
ISBN-13: 978-1-58571-294-6
ISBN-10: 1-58571-9
$6.99

March

Twist of Fate
Beverly Clark
ISBN-13: 978-1-58571-295-3
ISBN-10: 1-58571-295-7
$6.99

Chances
Pamela Leigh Starr
ISBN-13: 978-1-58571-296-0
ISBN-10: 1-58571-296-5
$6.99

April

Sinful Intentions
Crystal Rhodes
ISBN-13: 978-1-585712-297-7
ISBN-10: 1-58571-297-3
$6.99

Rock Star
Roslyn Hardy Holcomb
ISBN-13: 978-1-58571-298-4
$6.99

May

Paths of Fire
T.T. Henderson
ISBN-13: 978-1-58571-343-1
ISBN-10: 1-58571-343-0
$6.99

Caught Up in the Rapture
Lisa Riley
ISBN-13: 978-1-58571-344-8
ISBN-10: 1-58571-344-9
$6.99

June

Reckless Surrender
Rochelle Alers
ISBN-13: 978-1-58571-345-5
ISBN-10: 1-58571-345-7
$6.99

No Ordinary Love
Angela Weaver
ISBN-13: 978-1-58571-346-2
ISBN-10: 1-58571-346-5
$6.99

2009 Reprint Mass Market Titles (continued)

July

Intentional Mistakes
Michele Sudler
ISBN-13: 978-1-58571-347-9
ISBN-10: 1-58571-347-3
$6.99

It's In His Kiss
Reon Carter
ISBN-13: 978-1-58571-348-6
ISBN-10: 1-58571-348-1
$6.99

August

Unfinished Love Affair
Barbara Keaton
ISBN-13: 978-1-58571-349-3
ISBN-10: 1-58571-349-X
$6.99

A Perfect Place to Pray
I.L Goodwin
ISBN-13: 978-1-58571-299-1
ISBN-10: 1-58571-299-X
$6.99

September

Love in High Gear
Charlotte Roy
ISBN-13: 978-1-58571-355-4
ISBN-10: 1-58571-355-4
$6.99

Ebony Eyes
Kei Swanson
ISBN-13: 978-1-58571-356-1
ISBN-10: 1-58571-356-2
$6.99

October

Midnight Clear, Part I
Leslie Esdale/Carmen Green
ISBN-13: 978-1-58571-357-8
ISBN-10: 1-58571-357-0
$6.99

Midnight Clear, Part II
Gwynne Forster/Monica
  Jackson
ISBN-13: 978-1-58571-358-5
ISBN-10: 1-58571-358-9
$6.99

November

Midnight Peril
Vicki Andrews
ISBN-13: 978-1-58571-359-2
ISBN-10: 1-58571-359-7
$6.99

One Day At A Time
Bella McFarland
ISBN-13: 978-1-58571-360-8
ISBN-10: 1-58571-360-0
$6.99

December

Just An Affair
Eugenia O'Neal
ISBN-13: 978-1-58571-361-5
ISBN-10: 1-58571-361-9
$6.99

Shades of Brown
Denise Becker
ISBN-13: 978-1-58571-362-2
ISBN-10: 1-58571-362-7
$6.99

2009 New Mass Market Titles

January

Singing A Song...
Crystal Rhodes
ISBN-13: 978-1-58571-283-0
$6.99

Look Both Ways
Joan Early
ISBN-13: 978-1-58571-284-7
$6.99

February

Six O'Clock
Katrina Spencer
ISBN-13: 978-1-58571-285-4
$6.99

Red Sky
Renee Alexis
ISBN-13: 978-1-58571-286-1
$6.99

March

Anything But Love
Celya Bowers
ISBN-13: 978-1-58571-287-8
$6.99

Tempting Faith
Crystal Hubbard
ISBN-13: 978-1-58571-288-5
$6.99

April

If I Were Your Woman
La Connie Taylor-Jones
ISBN-13: 978-1-58571-289-2
$6.99

Best Of Luck Elsewhere
Trisha Haddad
ISBN-13: 978-1-58571-290-8
$6.99

May

All I'll Ever Need
Mildred Riley
ISBN-13: 978-1-58571-335-6
$6.99

A Place Like Home
Alicia Wiggins
ISBN-13: 978-1-58571-336-3
$6.99

June

Best Foot Forward
Michele Sudler
ISBN-13: 978-1-58571-337-0
$6.99

It's In the Rhythm
Sammie Ward
ISBN-13: 978-1-58571-338-7
$6.99

2009 New Mass Market Titles (continued)

July

Checks and Balances
Elaine Sims
ISBN-13: 978-1-58571-339-4
$6.99

Save Me
Africa Fine
ISBN-13: 978-1-58571-340-0
$6.99

August

When Lightening Strikes
Michele Cameron
ISBN-13: 978-1-58571-369-1
$6.99

Blindsided
Tammy Williams
ISBN-13: 978-1-58571-342-4
$6.99

September

2 Good
Celya Bowers
ISBN-13: 978-1-58571-350-9
$6.99

Waiting for Mr. Darcy
Chamein Canton
ISBN-13: 978-1-58571-351-6
$6.99

October

Fireflies
Joan Early
ISBN-13: 978-1-58571-352-3
$6.99

Frost On My Window
Angela Weaver
ISBN-13: 978-1-58571-353-0
$6.99

November

Waiting in the Shadows
Michele Sudler
ISBN-13: 978-1-58571-364-6
$6.99

Fixin' Tyrone
Keith Walker
ISBN-13: 978-1-58571-365-3
$6.99

December

Dream Keeper
Gail McFarland
ISBN-13: 978-1-58571-366-0
$6.99

Another Memory
Pamela Ridley
ISBN-13: 978-1-58571-367-7
$6.99

Other Genesis Press, Inc. Titles

A Dangerous Deception	J.M. Jeffries	$8.95
A Dangerous Love	J.M. Jeffries	$8.95
A Dangerous Obsession	J.M. Jeffries	$8.95
A Drummer's Beat to Mend	Kei Swanson	$9.95
A Happy Life	Charlotte Harris	$9.95
A Heart's Awakening	Veronica Parker	$9.95
A Lark on the Wing	Phyliss Hamilton	$9.95
A Love of Her Own	Cheris F. Hodges	$9.95
A Love to Cherish	Beverly Clark	$8.95
A Risk of Rain	Dar Tomlinson	$8.95
A Taste of Temptation	Reneé Alexis	$9.95
A Twist of Fate	Beverly Clark	$8.95
A Voice Behind Thunder	Carrie Elizabeth Greene	$6.99
A Will to Love	Angie Daniels	$9.95
Acquisitions	Kimberley White	$8.95
Across	Carol Payne	$12.95
After the Vows	Leslie Esdaile	$10.95
(Summer Anthology)	T.T. Henderson	
	Jacqueline Thomas	
Again My Love	Kayla Perrin	$10.95
Against the Wind	Gwynne Forster	$8.95
All I Ask	Barbara Keaton	$8.95
Always You	Crystal Hubbard	$6.99
Ambrosia	T.T. Henderson	$8.95
An Unfinished Love Affair	Barbara Keaton	$8.95
And Then Came You	Dorothy Elizabeth Love	$8.95
Angel's Paradise	Janice Angelique	$9.95
At Last	Lisa G. Riley	$8.95
Best of Friends	Natalie Dunbar	$8.95
Beyond the Rapture	Beverly Clark	$9.95
Blame It On Paradise	Crystal Hubbard	$6.99
Blaze	Barbara Keaton	$9.95
Bliss, Inc.	Chamein Canton	$6.99
Blood Lust	J. M. Jeffries	$9.95
Blood Seduction	J.M. Jeffries	$9.95
Bodyguard	Andrea Jackson	$9.95
Boss of Me	Diana Nyad	$8.95
Bound by Love	Beverly Clark	$8.95
Breeze	Robin Hampton Allen	$10.95

Other Genesis Press, Inc. Titles (continued)

Broken	Dar Tomlinson	$24.95
By Design	Barbara Keaton	$8.95
Cajun Heat	Charlene Berry	$8.95
Careless Whispers	Rochelle Alers	$8.95
Cats & Other Tales	Marilyn Wagner	$8.95
Caught in a Trap	Andre Michelle	$8.95
Caught Up In the Rapture	Lisa G. Riley	$9.95
Cautious Heart	Cheris F Hodges	$8.95
Chances	Pamela Leigh Starr	$8.95
Cherish the Flame	Beverly Clark	$8.95
Choices	Tammy Williams	$6.99
Class Reunion	Irma Jenkins/	$12.95
	John Brown	
Code Name: Diva	J.M. Jeffries	$9.95
Conquering Dr. Wexler's	Kimberley White	$9.95
Heart		
Corporate Seduction	A.C. Arthur	$9.95
Crossing Paths,	Dorothy Elizabeth Love	$9.95
Tempting Memories		
Crush	Crystal Hubbard	$9.95
Cypress Whisperings	Phyllis Hamilton	$8.95
Dark Embrace	Crystal Wilson Harris	$8.95
Dark Storm Rising	Chinelu Moore	$10.95
Daughter of the Wind	Joan Xian	$8.95
Dawn's Harbor	Kymberly Hunt	$6.99
Deadly Sacrifice	Jack Kean	$22.95
Designer Passion	Dar Tomlinson	$8.95
	Diana Richeaux	
Do Over	Celya Bowers	$9.95
Dream Runner	Gail McFarland	$6.99
Dreamtective	Liz Swados	$5.95
Ebony Angel	Deatri King-Bey	$9.95
Ebony Butterfly II	Delilah Dawson	$14.95
Echoes of Yesterday	Beverly Clark	$9.95
Eden's Garden	Elizabeth Rose	$8.95
Eve's Prescription	Edwina Martin Arnold	$8.95
Everlastin' Love	Gay G. Gunn	$8.95
Everlasting Moments	Dorothy Elizabeth Love	$8.95
Everything and More	Sinclair Lebeau	$8.95

Other Genesis Press, Inc. Titles (continued)

Everything but Love	Natalie Dunbar	$8.95
Falling	Natalie Dunbar	$9.95
Fate	Pamela Leigh Starr	$8.95
Finding Isabella	A.J. Garrotto	$8.95
Forbidden Quest	Dar Tomlinson	$10.95
Forever Love	Wanda Y. Thomas	$8.95
From the Ashes	Kathleen Suzanne Jeanne Sumerix	$8.95
Gentle Yearning	Rochelle Alers	$10.95
Glory of Love	Sinclair LeBeau	$10.95
Go Gentle into that Good Night	Malcom Boyd	$12.95
Goldengroove	Mary Beth Craft	$16.95
Groove, Bang, and Jive	Steve Cannon	$8.99
Hand in Glove	Andrea Jackson	$9.95
Hard to Love	Kimberley White	$9.95
Hart & Soul	Angie Daniels	$8.95
Heart of the Phoenix	A.C. Arthur	$9.95
Heartbeat	Stephanie Bedwell-Grime	$8.95
Hearts Remember	M. Loui Quezada	$8.95
Hidden Memories	Robin Allen	$10.95
Higher Ground	Leah Latimer	$19.95
Hitler, the War, and the Pope	Ronald Rychiak	$26.95
How to Write a Romance	Kathryn Falk	$18.95
I Married a Reclining Chair	Lisa M. Fuhs	$8.95
I'll Be Your Shelter	Giselle Carmichael	$8.95
I'll Paint a Sun	A.J. Garrotto	$9.95
Icie	Pamela Leigh Starr	$8.95
Illusions	Pamela Leigh Starr	$8.95
Indigo After Dark Vol. I	Nia Dixon/Angelique	$10.95
Indigo After Dark Vol. II	Dolores Bundy/ Cole Riley	$10.95
Indigo After Dark Vol. III	Montana Blue/ Coco Morena	$10.95
Indigo After Dark Vol. IV	Cassandra Colt/	$14.95
Indigo After Dark Vol. V	Delilah Dawson	$14.95
Indiscretions	Donna Hill	$8.95
Intentional Mistakes	Michele Sudler	$9.95
Interlude	Donna Hill	$8.95

Other Genesis Press, Inc. Titles (continued)

Intimate Intentions	Angie Daniels	$8.95
It's Not Over Yet	J.J. Michael	$9.95
Jolie's Surrender	Edwina Martin-Arnold	$8.95
Kiss or Keep	Debra Phillips	$8.95
Lace	Giselle Carmichael	$9.95
Lady Preacher	K.T. Richey	$6.99
Last Train to Memphis	Elsa Cook	$12.95
Lasting Valor	Ken Olsen	$24.95
Let Us Prey	Hunter Lundy	$25.95
Lies Too Long	Pamela Ridley	$13.95
Life Is Never As It Seems	J.J. Michael	$12.95
Lighter Shade of Brown	Vicki Andrews	$8.95
Looking for Lily	Africa Fine	$6.99
Love Always	Mildred E. Riley	$10.95
Love Doesn't Come Easy	Charlyne Dickerson	$8.95
Love Unveiled	Gloria Greene	$10.95
Love's Deception	Charlene Berry	$10.95
Love's Destiny	M. Loui Quezada	$8.95
Love's Secrets	Yolanda McVey	$6.99
Mae's Promise	Melody Walcott	$8.95
Magnolia Sunset	Giselle Carmichael	$8.95
Many Shades of Gray	Dyanne Davis	$6.99
Matters of Life and Death	Lesego Malepe, Ph.D.	$15.95
Meant to Be	Jeanne Sumerix	$8.95
Midnight Clear	Leslie Esdaile	$10.95
(Anthology)	Gwynne Forster	
	Carmen Green	
	Monica Jackson	
Midnight Magic	Gwynne Forster	$8.95
Midnight Peril	Vicki Andrews	$10.95
Misconceptions	Pamela Leigh Starr	$9.95
Moments of Clarity	Michele Cameron	$6.99
Montgomery's Children	Richard Perry	$14.95
Mr Fix-It	Crystal Hubbard	$6.99
My Buffalo Soldier	Barbara B. K. Reeves	$8.95
Naked Soul	Gwynne Forster	$8.95
Never Say Never	Michele Cameron	$6.99
Next to Last Chance	Louisa Dixon	$24.95
No Apologies	Seressia Glass	$8.95

Other Genesis Press, Inc. Titles (continued)

No Commitment Required	Seressia Glass	$8.95
No Regrets	Mildred E. Riley	$8.95
Not His Type	Chamein Canton	$6.99
Nowhere to Run	Gay G. Gunn	$10.95
O Bed! O Breakfast!	Rob Kuehnle	$14.95
Object of His Desire	A. C. Arthur	$8.95
Office Policy	A. C. Arthur	$9.95
Once in a Blue Moon	Dorianne Cole	$9.95
One Day at a Time	Bella McFarland	$8.95
One of These Days	Michele Sudler	$9.95
Outside Chance	Louisa Dixon	$24.95
Passion	T.T. Henderson	$10.95
Passion's Blood	Cherif Fortin	$22.95
Passion's Furies	AlTonya Washington	$6.99
Passion's Journey	Wanda Y. Thomas	$8.95
Past Promises	Jahmel West	$8.95
Path of Fire	T.T. Henderson	$8.95
Path of Thorns	Annetta P. Lee	$9.95
Peace Be Still	Colette Haywood	$12.95
Picture Perfect	Reon Carter	$8.95
Playing for Keeps	Stephanie Salinas	$8.95
Pride & Joi	Gay G. Gunn	$8.95
Promises Made	Bernice Layton	$6.99
Promises to Keep	Alicia Wiggins	$8.95
Quiet Storm	Donna Hill	$10.95
Reckless Surrender	Rochelle Alers	$6.95
Red Polka Dot in a World of Plaid	Varian Johnson	$12.95
Reluctant Captive	Joyce Jackson	$8.95
Rendezvous with Fate	Jeanne Sumerix	$8.95
Revelations	Cheris F. Hodges	$8.95
Rivers of the Soul	Leslie Esdaile	$8.95
Rocky Mountain Romance	Kathleen Suzanne	$8.95
Rooms of the Heart	Donna Hill	$8.95
Rough on Rats and Tough on Cats	Chris Parker	$12.95
Secret Library Vol. 1	Nina Sheridan	$18.95
Secret Library Vol. 2	Cassandra Colt	$8.95
Secret Thunder	Annetta P. Lee	$9.95

Other Genesis Press, Inc. Titles (continued)

Shades of Brown	Denise Becker	$8.95
Shades of Desire	Monica White	$8.95
Shadows in the Moonlight	Jeanne Sumerix	$8.95
Sin	Crystal Rhodes	$8.95
Small Whispers	Annetta P. Lee	$6.99
So Amazing	Sinclair LeBeau	$8.95
Somebody's Someone	Sinclair LeBeau	$8.95
Someone to Love	Alicia Wiggins	$8.95
Song in the Park	Martin Brant	$15.95
Soul Eyes	Wayne L. Wilson	$12.95
Soul to Soul	Donna Hill	$8.95
Southern Comfort	J.M. Jeffries	$8.95
Southern Fried Standards	S.R. Maddox	$6.99
Still the Storm	Sharon Robinson	$8.95
Still Waters Run Deep	Leslie Esdaile	$8.95
Stolen Memories	Michele Sudler	$6.99
Stories to Excite You	Anna Forrest/Divine	$14.95
Storm	Pamela Leigh Starr	$6.99
Subtle Secrets	Wanda Y. Thomas	$8.95
Suddenly You	Crystal Hubbard	$9.95
Sweet Repercussions	Kimberley White	$9.95
Sweet Sensations	Gwyneth Bolton	$9.95
Sweet Tomorrows	Kimberly White	$8.95
Taken by You	Dorothy Elizabeth Love	$9.95
Tattooed Tears	T. T. Henderson	$8.95
The Color Line	Lizzette Grayson Carter	$9.95
The Color of Trouble	Dyanne Davis	$8.95
The Disappearance of Allison Jones	Kayla Perrin	$5.95
The Fires Within	Beverly Clark	$9.95
The Foursome	Celya Bowers	$6.99
The Honey Dipper's Legacy	Pannell-Allen	$14.95
The Joker's Love Tune	Sidney Rickman	$15.95
The Little Pretender	Barbara Cartland	$10.95
The Love We Had	Natalie Dunbar	$8.95
The Man Who Could Fly	Bob & Milana Beamon	$18.95
The Missing Link	Charlyne Dickerson	$8.95
The Mission	Pamela Leigh Starr	$6.99
The More Things Change	Chamein Canton	$6.99

Other Genesis Press, Inc. Titles (continued)

The Perfect Frame	Beverly Clark	$9.95
The Price of Love	Sinclair LeBeau	$8.95
The Smoking Life	Ilene Barth	$29.95
The Words of the Pitcher	Kei Swanson	$8.95
Things Forbidden	Maryam Diaab	$6.99
This Life Isn't Perfect Holla	Sandra Foy	$6.99
Three Doors Down	Michele Sudler	$6.99
Three Wishes	Seressia Glass	$8.95
Ties That Bind	Kathleen Suzanne	$8.95
Tiger Woods	Libby Hughes	$5.95
Time is of the Essence	Angie Daniels	$9.95
Timeless Devotion	Bella McFarland	$9.95
Tomorrow's Promise	Leslie Esdaile	$8.95
Truly Inseparable	Wanda Y. Thomas	$8.95
Two Sides to Every Story	Dyanne Davis	$9.95
Unbreak My Heart	Dar Tomlinson	$8.95
Uncommon Prayer	Kenneth Swanson	$9.95
Unconditional Love	Alicia Wiggins	$8.95
Unconditional	A.C. Arthur	$9.95
Undying Love	Renee Alexis	$6.99
Until Death Do Us Part	Susan Paul	$8.95
Vows of Passion	Bella McFarland	$9.95
Wedding Gown	Dyanne Davis	$8.95
What's Under Benjamin's Bed	Sandra Schaffer	$8.95
When A Man Loves A Woman	La Connie Taylor-Jones	$6.99
When Dreams Float	Dorothy Elizabeth Love	$8.95
When I'm With You	LaConnie Taylor-Jones	$6.99
Where I Want To Be	Maryam Diaab	$6.99
Whispers in the Night	Dorothy Elizabeth Love	$8.95
Whispers in the Sand	LaFlorya Gauthier	$10.95
Who's That Lady?	Andrea Jackson	$9.95
Wild Ravens	Altonya Washington	$9.95
Yesterday Is Gone	Beverly Clark	$10.95
Yesterday's Dreams, Tomorrow's Promises	Reon Laudat	$8.95
Your Precious Love	Sinclair LeBeau	$8.95

4 239-3510 Party Saturday.

Order Form

Brianna

Mail to: Genesis Press, Inc.
P.O. Box 101
Columbus, MS 39703

Name _____
Address _____
City/State _____ Zip _____
Telephone _____

Ship to (if different from above)
Name _____
Address _____
City/State _____ Zip _____
Telephone _____

Credit Card Information
Credit Card # _____ ☐ Visa ☐ Mastercard
Expiration Date (mm/yy) _____ ☐ AmEx ☐ Discover

Qty.	Author	Title	Price	Total

Use this order form, or call **1-888-INDIGO-1**	**Total for books** _____ **Shipping and handling:** $5 first two books, $1 each additional book _____ **Total S & H** _____ **Total amount enclosed** _____ *Mississippi residents add 7% sales tax*